Vicky Winchester was born in France in 1949. She grew up in Guyana, Iraq, India and England. She qualified as a State Registered Nurse in 1971. She has since travelled extensively but now lives with her husband in Devon. She is a keen gardener and enjoys Italian opera.

To the memory of Jenny, a much-loved friend who died in 2020.

Vicky Winchester

A Correct Way to Behave

Austin Macauley Publishers
London * Cambridge * New York * Sharjah

Copyright © Vicky Winchester 2025

The right of Vicky Winchester to be identified as author of this work has been asserted by the author in accordance with sections 77 and 78 of the Copyright, Designs and Patents Act 1988.

All rights reserved. No part of this publication may be reproduced, stored in a retrieval system, or transmitted in any form or by any means, electronic, mechanical, photocopying, recording, or otherwise, without the prior permission of the publishers.

Any person who commits any unauthorised act in relation to this publication may be liable to criminal prosecution and civil claims for damages.

This is a work of fiction. Names, characters, businesses, places, events, locales, and incidents are either the products of the author's imagination or used in a fictitious manner. Any resemblance to actual persons, living or dead, or actual events is purely coincidental.

A CIP catalogue record for this title is available from the British Library.

ISBN 9781037104350 (Paperback)
ISBN 9781037104367 (ePub e-book)

www.austinmacauley.com

First Published 2025
Austin Macauley Publishers Ltd®
1 Canada Square
Canary Wharf
London
E14 5AA

I am grateful to my husband, John, for providing the geological information.

One
2019

Looking back at their Caribbean holiday, apart from the heartbreaking news which came through at the end, it had been the small things which made the deepest impression.

Connie and Matthew Shaw had booked up on impulse, having seen what appeared to be a good value offer in a newspaper. It had proved useful in deflecting enquiries about what they were planning for Matthew, who was about to turn seventy. Neither of them had ever liked to make a fuss about birthdays, even ones with noughts on them. A quiet dinner somewhere was how they usually liked to mark these events. However, being able to cite a February cruise starting from Barbados and ending with three days in a good hotel there helped satisfy society's expectations.

It wasn't their first cruise, but it was the first on an American liner with two thousand six hundred passengers and nine hundred crew. It was a culture shock, especially for Connie.

"I don't think I can stand this for a whole week," she said, looking around in dismay while queuing for the registration procedure.

"Well, you'll have to," replied Matthew. "We've paid out a lot of money for this and, anyway, we have nowhere else to go."

Eleven decks rose up around an enormous atrium. The walls were painted a shiny, metallic bronze with black stripes and festooned with strings of orange light bulbs. The carpets were purple and gold; pop music dribbled from every direction; it was a combination of Las Vegas and Hades.

Their cabin was a pleasant surprise, more spacious than anticipated, light and airy with a large window and comfortable bed. Relief changed to outraged exasperation when Connie opened her suitcase and discovered that her travelling kettle had been removed. Remonstrating at Passenger Information availed her nothing. With scrupulous courtesy, she was told her kettle was a potential fire risk and banned on security grounds. All the careful arrangements with teabags, Coffee Mate and mugs were wasted.

There was a mandatory security briefing before setting sail. All passengers were herded into a massive auditorium but instead of straightforward, professional instruction on how to behave in the event of an emergency, the tour rep behaved like a second-rate comedian, wowing his audience. Sheep-like responses were expected to his idiotic questions and generally complied with. There was much clapping and 'woo-hooing'. Connie felt herself become increasingly stony-faced; she hated being patronised.

Matthew maintained an air of equable good humour. He was working out a ruse to bribe their steward to lend him a thermos flask. Armed with this, he could then walk the half mile to the Coconut Grove dining room at six o'clock each morning, fill it up with boiling water and return to make the tea before Connie woke up.

They quickly adapted to life on board. The inevitable jet lag following the flight from Gatwick evaporated; the balmy tropical air permeated everything, causing them to feel languorous, tolerant and healthy. The food was delicious. A special effort was made at dinner, served graciously at tables laid with damask cloths and napkins. Waiters wearing frilly shirts would weave around, occasionally launching into a dance routine to catchy music.

Each evening, the ship would set sail across the sea, a shimmering mix of sapphire, indigo, turquoise and aquamarine. The following morning, they would wake up to the next palm-fringed exotic venue. One afternoon, Matthew and Connie were having tea on the deck while still in port when they heard the sounds of a military brass band. They looked down at the harbour and saw soldiers marching. They were escorting a hearse draped in a flag. It was dignified and very moving, a wonderful antidote to the slight tackiness and terrible music on board.

The small things were what Connie would remember. To reach the Coconut Grove dining room from their cabin, it was necessary to negotiate the pool area. Walking past the supine bodies and jacuzzis, which brought to mind childish images of cannibals with cauldrons and missionaries, she passed a sunbed bearing a vast West Indian woman in a bikini. Nestling amid the folds of adipose was the sweetest, tiniest baby girl wearing a leopard skin bathing suit. She was dozing contentedly, her rosebud mouth and plump limbs moving gently. Connie, overwhelmed by the beauty, longed to stand and stare but didn't. It simply wasn't allowed.

On St Kitt's, it wasn't the Batik Fabric outlet in the garden of what had been a plantation belonging to Thomas Jefferson's great-great-grandfather or the Brimstone Hill Fortress built on top of a cinder cone and lovingly restored for tourists that Connie would recall. It was the American family of five sharing the minibus. She wondered if they were 'born again' Christians because they were so insanely nice to each other, despite them all having to sleep packed together in a standard cabin with a small shower room. Apparently, berths would concertina out of the wall at a higher level above the main bed. Connie had noticed the potential for this arrangement in her own cabin.

This family passed around a bottle of water, all taking turns at having a salivary swig. The youthfully slender mother called everyone 'Sweetie' and every so often would embrace her well-nourished adolescent son, murmuring, "Big boy, Momma's big boy, give your momma a hug." The boy was unfazed.

When visiting Nelson's Dockyard on Antigua, a place of astonishing beauty and historical significance, Connie was awestruck by the huge expanse of artificial grass and by the excessively long queues outside the restrooms, especially the Ladies. She decided to join the queue outside the Gents, jokingly explaining to the fellow behind that she was exercising her human right to change gender. She thought she was being funny but he hadn't looked amused.

In St Lucia, she and Matthew took a private taxi to see the volcano at Soufrière. It was the only place Matthew insisted on visiting. They drove up through wonderfully lush scenery, the famous twin pitons dominating the skyline, and directly into the crater. Steam poured out through the fumaroles and little ponds of mud and water were bubbling and splashing. There was an overpowering smell of sulphur and an apocalyptic atmosphere.

In the American Virgin Islands, it was a large torpid iguana draped over a tree branch and watching them out of lidded eyes, which made an impression.

St Maarten was memorable because of the shops. They were taken by an immaculate water taxi across the sparkling sea from the ship to a modish promenade full of boutiques and beauty parlours. To her lasting shame, Connie was seduced into paying two hundred dollars for a cosmetic which erased wrinkles. The pretty and very persuasive beautician demonstrated on one side of her face. It worked; the lines around her eyes were expunged. What remained unexplained was the temporary nature of the wonder substance. It wore off after a couple of hours. Another purchase was an emerald green linen dress, bias-cut and stunning. Connie didn't like trying on clothes if she felt even mildly hot and damp, so she just bought them and hoped for the best.

There were no cultural talks or classical concerts on the ship, no gentle dancing to steel bands. There were bars, films, discos and various shows. One room had been decorated in the style of a library in a British stately home. Connie and Matthew retreated there with books after dinner and almost always had it to themselves.

In the Coconut Grove dining room, which was only one of several eating places, there was a self-service ice cream machine. Connie virtuously ignored it for the first three days but, having once given in to temptation, she became addicted. Holding a cornet in the left hand, depressing a lever with the right hand and watching a stream of creamy confection swirl its way down, forming a little point on the top, filled her with childish pleasure.

On their first evening in the Barbados hotel, Connie was sitting on the edge of the sunken bath and massaging cream into her feet. By some strange twist of gravity, she found herself sliding inexorably backwards and landing with a bump in a U-shaped position. It had been surprisingly difficult to extricate herself. It was the second undignified episode of the day.

Earlier, she had slipped her new green dress over her head and tried to pull it into position. It stuck fast; she couldn't get it down or up. "Matthew," she called. "Please, can you help me?"

He came, assessed the situation and eased the dress up and off. "Why are you wearing a pair of pants over your face?" he asked.

"I should have thought that was obvious to the meanest intelligence." She felt annoyed.

"Mine is not of the meanest."

"It's to stop make-up from rubbing off onto the fabric."

"Oh, I see," replied Matthew, examining the dress. "Did you not realise that there is a zip in the side seam?" He undid the zip and handed back the dress, which went on easily.

Connie tried to avoid being seen in a state of undress these days. She wasn't fat and looked perfectly respectable with her clothes on. Nonetheless, the smooth contours of her midriff had disappeared and when she drew her arms together, the once velvety cleavage looked like an aerial view of the Nile Delta. To Matthew, she looked much the same as she always had. Deep brown eyes in a face that was expressive rather than beautiful and rich chestnut hair framing her face like a smooth helmet. Its colour and healthy gloss now required expensive maintenance but the rest of her was untouched by artifice.

They sat down for dinner. The hotel on the south coast was pleasant, not one of the ultra-luxurious on the west coast but with its full share of comfort in the form of a large, cool bedroom containing two double beds. The French windows opened onto a veranda, complete with a comfortably cushioned sofa. The beds had heavy, carved mahogany, colonial-style headboards, crisp white sheets and soft pillows. The gardens had been laid out with flair and imagination. A set of pools connected at different levels; interspersed with ornamental bridges and balustrades and beautiful planting. Lit up in the evening, it was magical.

"You see the beady-eyed pair of elderly sisters at the table near the door?" Matthew asked.

"They probably refer to us as that dried-up pair of old trouts by the window," replied Connie. "And how do you know they're sisters?"

"They look very alike. They might call me a dried-up old trout but certainly not you."

Matthew's gallantry had always been a bit clunky but Connie appreciated it nonetheless.

"Anyway, the hotel receptionist asked me on their behalf if they could share our taxi to Hunte's Garden tomorrow. I said we'd be delighted."

"Yes, of course," said Connie, wondering if she would have to chat pleasantly all the way. Sharing transport with two other people brought with it certain social obligations. In a large group, people could safely ignore each other. Being generally knowledgeable and interesting, Matthew was good at talking to drivers and guides, while she liked to daydream and enjoy the scenery. He was less good at small talk with women.

Connie had a friendly nature. When with other people, she had a compulsion to ensure their ease and inclusion. She hated cliques. She knew that this tendency reflected her own lack of social confidence and that many people neither needed nor appreciated her concern for their emotional welfare. However, the habit was so ingrained that only when on her own or with her husband could she properly relax.

In the event, she needn't have worried and was free to stare at the sugarcane fields and tropical landscape. The ladies proved to be a receptive and gratifyingly appreciative audience as Matthew explained that a feature of limestone was its porosity. Rainfall would pass through it and form underground caves and rivers. Rainwater also dissolved the rock, accelerating the process. Hunte's Garden was planted in a sinkhole which had been formed by the collapse of the roof over a large cavern.

Matthew enjoyed holding forth about matters that interested him. Encouraged by the response, he went on to explain that most of the Caribbean Islands are part of an island arc made up of a line of volcanoes caused by subduction of the Earth's crust, the American plate being dragged under the Caribbean plate. However, Barbados, Trinidad and Tobago are situated east of the island arc and are not volcanic but largely made of limestone.

He went on to talk about an ocean trench and explain that island arc volcanoes produce much more ash than lava. Their sort of magma is 'sticky' and more resistant to pressure, so a huge amount of trapped gas can build up to form an explosive eruption. Connie noticed a slight 'glazing over' in the eyes of their companions and signalled to Matthew that it was time to stop. He couldn't stop until he'd explained that the pressure sending the column of ash high into the stratosphere would eventually ease. The column would then collapse, producing a nuée ardente, or burning cloud, which would flow down valleys leading away from the volcano and have an internal temperature of 750°C. Anything in its path would be incinerated.

Although calmer and quieter now, Connie had always been sociable, making enduring friendships wherever she went. As Matthew liked to remind her occasionally, this had once almost landed them both in a prison cell. In 1978, after their wedding, she went with him to Israel for work purposes. At the time, there was still heightened tension between Arabs and Israelis after the 1974 war. Once the business side of things was complete, they hired a driver, called Samira, to take them around, seeing as many interesting places and sights as could be fitted into the time available. It had been a good experience. Samira was well-informed, helpful and flexible.

At the end of the week, Matthew and Connie arrived at Tel Aviv Airport rather late, having been held up by a bomb alert on a Palestinian bus. They hastened through the booking process and arrived at Immigration, the last port of call, where they were questioned by an official. All went smoothly until they were asked if they had made any friends during their visit. Matthew replied 'No' but Connie replied 'Yes'. This sparked another prolonged and more aggressive interrogation, mercifully resolved by an impatient pilot who came to find out what was holding up his plane.

Once safely airborne, it took Matthew a little time and a couple of stiff drinks to regain some equanimity, whereupon he asked Connie why on earth she had been so stupid. She replied that if you weren't allowed to use the term 'friend' for a kind taxi driver who had looked after you for four days, then who else could possibly qualify as such a person? He had no answer to that.

Hunte's Garden was a place of total enchantment and beauty; two acres of concentrated tropical colour and loveliness enhanced by a gentle tape recording of Beethoven and Chopin piano concertos emanating from discreetly placed speakers. The soft music floated like a breeze, inducing feelings of dreamy contentment and pure well-being. Paths weaved up and down, in and out; there were many places to sit, little terraces and pretty, ornamental structures for shade. Anthony Hunte's house, converted from the original stables, had a huge veranda where refreshments were served and the rooms behind were full of paintings and artistry. There wasn't much conversation in the taxi on the way back to the hotel. It just wasn't required.

The second day was spent walking around the local area, first along the beach, admiring the frontages and gardens of neighbouring hotels. There was a lovely array of tropical trees; frangipani, jacaranda, casuarinas, flame and cashew nut. There were a great many trees with bean pods looking like shimmering gold in the sunlight. Connie asked several people for the name of these but none of them knew it. After lunch by the hotel swimming pool, they set off again, passing some barracks and walking around the white-fenced racecourse. Following a signpost, they came to George Washington's House.

He came here in 1751 when he was nineteen, with his older brother, Lawrence, who had tuberculosis. It was hoped that the warm climate would cure him. It didn't. George caught smallpox there but he did recover, acquiring lifelong immunity in the process. The house was lovely; light, airy and gracious without being pretentious. To one side, a path led up to the original privy. It was a small outbuilding containing a broad wooden seat with two holes for companionship. As Connie and Matthew approached, an American visitor emerged, quite overcome with emotion and excitement from seeing where the first American President had performed his natural functions.

It was the last day of the holiday and a taxi driver took them to St Nicholas Abbey, a Jacobean plantation house now maintained as a museum with a working rum distillery. The front of the house had three Dutch gables and a grand portico with arched openings. Inside, it was comfortable, almost homely; the polished mahogany dining table laid with Wedgwood pottery and a vase of flowers. It had an English country house feel to it with Chippendale furniture, cedar panelling and even an original Thomas Crapper loo off the back corridor.

Matthew and Connie sat on the terrace behind the house, listening to the birdsong coming from the exotic garden. They had the place to themselves as the house seemed not to be one of the more popular tourist venues.

"It's easy to forget the dark side of places like this," remarked Matthew.

Connie didn't want to dwell on the horrors of slavery any more than she could bear to think about the Holocaust, the millions who died under Chairman Mao and Stalin, the unspeakable cruelty of the Spanish Conquistadores, the thousands of innocent women burnt alive as witches, the piteous tumbrils of aristocrats wheeled to the guillotine amidst a jeering hate-filled mob, the small children being made to work in coalmines in the pitch dark during the Industrial Revolution. She had come to accept that buried deep in human DNA was a savagery unsurpassed anywhere in the animal kingdom. It was an unpleasant fact.

That evening, their packing mostly done and ready for the journey home, they were enjoying their last dinner when Matthew looked at his smartphone. A message had just come in.

"It's from Bella," he said. "Tim is dead."

"Oh no." Connie was aghast. "In their Christmas card, they said he was doing well. The specialist had said that the treatment had worked and that he was going to be fine. He would die one day like everybody else but it wouldn't be of prostate cancer."

Matthew's expression was grim but he showed no emotion. Men were often like this. Connie wondered if it was some evolutionary quirk that enabled warriors to cope with the battlefield. It was different with her. She felt deep distress and a pressure rising up inside. She didn't want to overreact in front of Matthew; he would think it disproportionate. She stood. "I'm going to our room to get one of my antacid pills. The sauce with the fish was very rich. I'll pass on pudding but you go ahead and have yours. I'll miss out on coffee as well."

She walked calmly out of the dining room, down some steps, across the paved, bougainvillea-strewn courtyard, up some more steps and along a covered walkway to their room. She went into the bathroom and locked the door. She heard a strange keening noise and realised it was her. Then came gulping sobs as tears streamed down her face.

Tim had been a friend of long standing but, for Connie, he had been much more than that. They'd had an unspoken emotional intimacy, a spiritually nourishing relationship, which only the two of them understood and enjoyed. And now he was gone, never to return. Her sense of loss was crushing.

Two
1977

Connie was laying the tables for lunch on a bright Saturday morning in November when the telephone rang. She left the dining room and picked up the receiver at the reception desk.

"The Royal Oak Hotel. Good morning."

"Connie, it's Bella. I need to talk to you."

"I can't talk at the moment. I'm on duty and I'm not supposed to take private calls on the work phone. I have a couple of hours off this afternoon and I'll ring you back at about three. Is that okay?"

"I suppose it will have to be. Bye for now." Bella put her receiver down forcefully.

The Royal Oak was a beautiful Devonshire eighteenth-century coaching inn, which had been taken over by a benign ex-army officer, George Miles, and his wife, Helen, as a retirement project. It had a thatched roof, a great archway through to the car park and an interior which smelled of log fires and beeswax. It was staffed by a cohort of friendly village women. Connie had been in a state of limbo because her ten-pound passage to Australia had been postponed until the following summer due to some bureaucratic hitch. She had replied to an advertisement in *The Lady* magazine and been taken on as a sort of general factotum.

Her day started with delivering trays of early morning tea. She had waitressing duties for breakfast, lunch and dinner, she acted as receptionist, checked up on the cleaning, did the odd bit of painting and decorating and occasionally walked the labrador, Sheba. These walks were a delight; the countryside was beautiful even in winter, snowy white sheep contrasting with emerald fields, the crystalline gurgling brook, evergreen foliage, birds and rabbits. For all this, she received a salary of twelve pounds a week, plus board and lodging. She was extremely happy. She had a lovely bedroom with its own fashionably decorated bathroom and a private telephone. Also, the food was delicious. These were unaccustomed luxuries for Connie.

George and Helen treated her like a daughter. She'd been mortified late one evening to be caught raiding the fridge, which always contained a bowl of fresh fruit salad and a huge pot of clotted cream. She'd been in her dressing gown and had a frilly mob cap over her rollers. George pretended that this was perfectly normal behaviour for his employees. He had also been magnanimous when a client berated him for 'boiling' his Beaujolais, although the fault had been entirely hers. He had shown her how to bring red wine, stored in the cellar, up to room temperature by briefly plunging it into hot water. On this occasion, she had left the bottle stewing for far too long with unfortunate results.

Connie and Bella had met in Oxford the previous year while on a business course for graduates. It was really just high-powered secretarial training but, in the years to come, Connie found it more generally useful than her geography degree from Exeter University. Bella had a psychology degree from Bangor and the two girls shared a room in the residential wing of the business college. Oxford was full of eligible men. Most of the colleges were exclusively male and the girls soon found boyfriends.

Bella met Tim, whose friend and colleague, Matthew, felt an instant affinity with Connie. They made a dynamic foursome, taking full advantage of the concerts, talks and general culture on offer. The two men were geologists, both in the process of completing doctorates. They were also both members of the Oxford University Mountaineering Club. Matthew invited Connie to go with him to North Wales one weekend in early May.

"I'll organise everything," he said. "Just make sure you have some sturdy boots and rainwear. You won't need a rucksack; I'll carry all our clobber in mine."

It took nearly five hours in an old Ford Anglia to reach the campsite. Matthew had decided on luxury accommodation in the barn rather than a tent. He laid out two sleeping bags on dusty planks on the upper level accessed by a ladder. He had borrowed one for her and she didn't like to query its level of hygiene, although she did wonder about the previous occupant. It didn't smell too bad. He then set about making them a meal on a little camping stove. This was particularly disgusting, comprising a concoction of tinned meat of unrecognisable provenance stirred up with a bag of soggy sprouts which had been frozen on purchase. It was followed by a tin of pineapple chunks and a tin of rice pudding.

Matthew noted her hesitancy with some amusement. "If you'd suffered the privations of boarding school like I did and been made to eat the sort of pigswill served up there, you would regard this modest repast as food fit for the gods."

"I am finding it all extraordinarily delicious and am most appreciative of your efforts," replied Connie. He'd laughed then. There were pre-buttered rolls to go with the stew, more of them with marmalade added for breakfast and still more with slices of cheese inside for lunch the next day. He'd thought of everything. He brewed up mugs of strong tea with sugar and evaporated milk and then they turned in for the night.

They both slept well but what upset Connie's composure quite badly was her experience the next morning. She took daily ablutions very seriously and was unprepared for the heckling of a queue of angry campers outside the primitive stone hut containing the only facility for the whole site. She was, after all, being as quick as possible.

The climb up Tryfan was exhilarating. Connie thought of herself as a keen walker but her only experience of high-level activity was a cable car ride up and a gentle walk down a mountain in Austria. "It's not difficult, just a bit steep," said Matthew as she trudged up the two thousand feet from the road to the top and then down to the Bwlch Tryfan Pass, followed by a vertigo-inducing scramble across Bristly Ridge to Glyder Fach. "Not difficult," repeated Matthew, "just awkward and a bit exposed." They sat at the top, eating their dried-up cheese rolls and Mars Bars, looking down at Llyn Ogwen with its myriad steely glints in the sunshine.

Feeling hot, tired and rather grubby, Connie drank from her tin of Coca-Cola and tried to work out why she felt so safe and happy with the shy, erudite man sitting beside her.

The descent down the Gribin Ridge was almost worse than the climb up had been. Connie was exhausted, her knees were wobbling and she began to suspect that Matthew was trying to impress her unnecessarily with his physical prowess. Apparently not, because as soon as they arrived back in Oxford, he suggested a more challenging expedition. This would be around the Snowdon Horseshoe and they would do it with Tim and Bella.

~

It was obvious that Bella came from a moneyed background. She arrived in Oxford with her own car, a top-quality record player with stereophonic speakers and some lovely clothes. She had a clipped and authoritative manner of speaking and was extremely attractive with a Nordic blonde and blue-eyed look. She was generous and funny and Connie found her to be a good friend.

When Tim and Matthew announced that they'd managed to get last minute tickets for the May Ball at Exeter College, Bella went straight out to buy a new dress; a sophisticated black gown with a daring slit from ankle to thigh up one side. Connie's parents were comfortable enough financially, with her father paying all her fees and ensuring that she had more than enough to live on. However, she'd been reared by a mother of legendary frugality, whose sole purpose in life was to accumulate money.

The advantage of this was that Connie had learned how to sew; all her skirts, dresses and blouses were homemade. The residence, which was off the Banbury Road, had two sitting rooms; one with a television and this was filled with people and cigarette smoke each evening. The other was rather gracious, with French windows opening onto a garden and, in one corner, a table with a sewing machine. This room was always empty. Connie caught the bus into the city centre and went to Elliston's, the main department store, where she bought several yards of a silky fabric; cherry red with black velvet polka dots.

Also, some black satin lining and netting to make a petticoat and then some fine white satin-striped cotton and a length of three-inch-wide lace. She found a wide elasticised black belt and some cheap fake pearl earrings in the shape of bunches of grapes. She already had a real pearl choker given to her for her twenty-first birthday.

She spent many happy hours cutting out, pinning, tacking, stitching and hemming. Bella looked on in bemusement. "Why all this bother?" she asked. "Let's just go and buy a dress; I'll lend you the money." The result was a triumph. The gypsy blouse, with softly gathered lace encircling the neckline and draping becomingly over her breasts and shoulders, had wide sleeves, gathered in a band below the elbows and falling in graceful lace-edged folds to her wrists. The skirt was made of eight panels, each small at the top and very wide at the hem. It was supported by two layers of netting attached halfway down the satin petticoat and swirled glamorously, just skimming the floor.

The wide belt accentuated her tiny waist. Somewhere at the back of her mind, she could hear her mother's voice, *Your hair looks a mess. If you could just see yourself from behind in that miniskirt.* Connie laughed at the memory. She was leaving the gaucherie of her girlhood behind. She was seized with optimism; life was proving richer than she'd anticipated.

The specially cleaned Ford Anglia pulled up outside the residence. Matthew and Tim emerged looking handsome in dinner jackets and bow ties. Bella and Connie wafted down the path in clouds of expensive perfume and they drove off in high spirits.

The four of them walked through the entrance from Turl Street into the magical atmosphere of Exeter College. So much beauty. The golden stone of the ancient buildings, the tall gothic chapel between two quads, the emerald lawns, all beautifully decorated and redolent of history, sophistication and romanticism. There was a lavish abundance of fine food and drink. Tables and chairs were set out invitingly. There was a choice of music, the most popular being the steel band but there was a string quartet for ballroom dancing and disco music for modern dancing. Matthew was entranced by Connie, while she was enthralled by everything.

~

"Connie and I have discussed the matter at some length," said Bella, as the four of them were having supper in The Mitre on the High Street. It was a Berni Inn and did wonderful steak and chips. "Much as we are both good sports and enjoy roughing it, and much as we strongly disapprove of wasting money, we both feel it to be imperative that a proper establishment, either a guesthouse or a bed and breakfast, is booked before we can tackle Snowdon."

"That's the wrong attitude altogether," replied Tim.

Matthew nodded gravely. "It would certainly compromise the principles of the mountaineering club."

"Well, I'm sorry," said Bella, "but unless Connie and I can have a decent night's sleep, the use of a bathroom, a good breakfast and a decent packed lunch, it wouldn't be safe for us to undertake a perilous expedition of the sort you are proposing."

Matthew and Tim glanced at each other with a questioning air and gracefully conceded defeat.

There were two rooms left in the guesthouse, one with a double bed and the other with twin beds. "You girls can have the double," said Matthew. "I had to share a double bed once with my supervisor in the Highlands and I don't intend to repeat the experience with Tim."

Neither couple had progressed to the stage of being lovers, although Bella had hinted to Connie that Tim was 'hot stuff'. Also, the house was filled with crucifixes and religious texts, implying that the landlady might have a keen eye for wedding rings.

The next morning, they arrived early at the car park at Pen-y-Pass at the top of the Llanberis Pass before it filled up with the cars of other walkers. The first bit of the walk was easy, along a path and around craggy hills to the base of Crib Goch. Tim and Matthew walked ahead while Connie and Bella followed behind, giggling. Despite the godly ambience in the guesthouse, the landlady sported what looked like a recently inflicted black eye. They knew this wasn't remotely funny but still, they giggled.

Also, the four of them had politely refused the offer of an in-house dinner the evening before, preferring to go to the pub. On their way out, they'd seen the other guests being wonderfully animated and sociable around a large dining table. At breakfast, however, the friendliness had evaporated and been replaced by a distinct froideur. This was also a cause of mirth. Everything was.

Observing the men from behind, Connie was reminded of a silhouette of Christopher Robin with Pooh Bear. Neither man had a particularly good physique. Matthew was tall and willowy; Tim was stocky with powerful shoulders and rather bandy legs. Their shared passion for rocks meant that they never ran out of things to discuss; both were full of ideas for possible future research projects. They were both in possession of a huge bank of general knowledge; boredom and ignorance played no part in their existence and this might have accounted for their generally good-natured and humorous temperaments.

The next stage of the walk was a steep scramble up Crib Goch. Matthew led the way and Tim brought up the rear. At the top, Bella was looking pink and a bit cross. "Time for a rest," she said, plonking her rucksack down and getting out a tin of lemonade. The next part of the walk was the ridge linking Crib Goch with Crib y Ddysgl, Snowdon's second highest peak. This involved a knife-edge ridge scramble with terrifyingly steep drops on either side, especially on the north side.

"You'll be fine," said Tim to Bella. "I'll catch you if you fall. Just don't look down; it is a little daunting."

"I call that remark an understatement bordering on the insane," she replied through clenched teeth but managed the crossing without incident. They eventually reached the line of the Snowdon Mountain Railway and carried on up the path until they reached the top with its café. Having made use of the facilities, they sat down away from the crowds and admired the magnificent panorama. They could see Anglesey beyond the Menai Straits, the Llyn Peninsula and the coast of Cardigan Bay, as well as several other mountains, including Cnicht and Cader Idris.

It was awe-inspiring and Connie would always remember this day because it was the last time the four of them were together before they split up and went their separate ways.

~

Bella and Tim were married. It was a low-key affair in a register office. Apparently, Bella's parents didn't approve of the match but it was a while before Connie found out why. Tim had been offered a post-doctoral fellowship at Reading University and Bella did a counselling course. Counselling was becoming fashionable and her psychology degree made her a good candidate.

Matthew had accepted a highly paid job offer with a mining company in Australia and was due to fly out to Sydney in August. Connie had decided to do a teacher training course in Cheltenham before joining Matthew at the end of the following year. She was determined to be independent, self-sufficient and employable. Matthew proposed, terrified that he'd lose her, and Connie joyously accepted.

Full of tenderness and sadness at their impending separation, also awash with those sweet sensations of a less spiritual nature, they made love. However, it wasn't quite the rapturous event that Connie had anticipated. "Sorry," said Matthew. "I know that wasn't very good for you. I haven't had much practice; in fact, I haven't had any; it was the first time for me."

"It was the first time for me, too," replied Connie, "but at least we've worked out what we're supposed to do and we'll have plenty of time to refine our technique."

Matthew laughed. "One of the many things I really love about you, darling Connie, is the way you can turn any disappointment, any failure, any disaster into a joke or a challenge."

"I get that from my father, who is the antithesis of my mother." When she'd told her parents, Graham and Deirdre Langford, about her engagement and plans for Australia, her mother had been negative. "We'll never see any grandchildren. Dad is most upset."

Once out of earshot, her father said, "I'm not upset at all. I'm very glad for you both. Seize every opportunity and never do anything to hold Matthew back."

Three

It was unusual for Connie and Bella to telephone each other, although they regularly exchanged letters; chatty, funny, light-hearted accounts of whatever they were doing at the time.

"Hello, Bella, it's Connie. Sorry, I wasn't free to talk this morning."

"That's okay. How are you?"

"I'm fine, thanks. How are you?"

"Fine, absolutely fine. I want to ask you to do something. In your last letter, you said you were due some time off and were thinking of going to Ireland to visit a friend living in County Kerry but that nothing definite was actually planned."

"That's right. The hotel is quiet at the moment and, as long as I'm back for the run-up to Christmas, I can have two or three weeks off whenever I like."

"Well, I'm wondering if you would consider giving your friend a miss and driving up to Belmullet instead?"

"Where's Belmullet? I've never heard of it."

"It's in County Mayo."

"But that's in the opposite direction."

"I know it is."

"Why are you asking me to go there?"

"Because Tim is there and I'm worried about him."

"Why is he there and why are you worried?"

"He's doing fieldwork for his research project but something is wrong. He should have been home by the end of October but he won't come and I can't contact him. He was staying in a guesthouse and I used to ring him there in the evenings. He left about a month ago. Mrs O'Reilly, the landlady, says he's living in a caravan somewhere now. I think she's a bit fed up with him. He probably offended her by moving out. I think he must be having some sort of breakdown."

"Why don't you go and find him?"

"I can't get away at the moment because of my job, which, from the sound of it, is a little more arduous than yours. You are the only person I can think of who might help."

Connie did some rapid thinking. She wasn't entirely sure that it was a good time to land on her university friend, Annette, who was in the middle of house renovations in Killarney. She wanted to spend a few days with her parents, who lived in Dorset. She had a strong emotional bond with her father. They were physically similar, with deep brown eyes, strong chins and slender bodies. His qualities of humour, integrity and generosity were not shared by her mother but, for his sake, Connie tried hard to maintain the illusion of harmonious family life so craved by society. She also wished to visit her brother in Somerset, whose wife had just given birth to a little boy. He was so overcome with joy and pride at having sired a child that it was almost comical.

Thanks to a small legacy from a much-loved, childless great aunt, she'd been able to buy a car and have enough left over to pay for whatever the trip might cost. As well as all this, she liked Tim and hated the thought of him being unhappy.

She couldn't help wondering if Bella was keeping something back. Once friends married, a sort of veil came down. There was an unspoken barrier and you barged through this at your peril. The chemistry of the friendship changed in a very subtle way.

In a jocular tone, Connie said, "So, you don't mind setting me loose with your husband, then?"

"Don't be ridiculous," replied Bella. Her voice was tight with suppressed irritation. "I know for a fact that you are not his type. Tim and I are extremely happy. If you and Matthew are half as happy as we are, you'll be incredibly happy."

It was that remark which made Connie realise that things might be serious. She would go and find out for herself. "Do you know what the work problem might be?"

"Haven't a clue," replied Bella. "He did try to explain but I'm not a geologist and I didn't understand. He's working on what are called 'basement' rocks and I think there has been a difference of opinion with someone."

Connie agreed to go to County Mayo and immediately felt a surge of excitement. The girls chatted on for a bit, with Bella handing over what limited information she had, including Mrs O'Reilly's address and telephone number.

Connie promised to ring Bella as soon as she'd found Tim and do her best to persuade him to come home.

Two days later, Connie went to the travel agency in Okehampton to book a ferry crossing from Pembroke to Rosslare. She acquired an AA Handbook for Ireland, which gave details of places to stay and bought a road atlas. She set about plotting her route.

~

It was still dark when Connie set off from Beaminster in her green Mini. The day before, her father had checked the car's tyre pressures and oil and filled up the windscreen washer bottle and petrol tank. It was a long drive to Pembroke Dock but she arrived in good time for the afternoon ferry. The crossing was smooth, even after leaving the shelter of Milford Haven, and it was dark once again when the ferry docked in Rosslare four hours later. She drove straight to the hotel for supper and a deep sleep.

Refreshed and replete with bacon, sausage and egg the next morning, Connie consulted her road atlas and drove off through Wexford and across some fairly flat farmland towards the hillier countryside surrounding Waterford, famed for crystal glass-making. She had planned her route to include a visit to the Rock of Cashel in County Tipperary, a place that had intrigued her ever since she had seen it pictured in a National Geographic magazine. From Waterford, she headed west to Clonmel, following the broad valley of the River Suir, and then took a small road to Cashel, where the extraordinary ancient citadel rose up from the top of a limestone outcrop.

She parked outside a hotel and, after a sandwich and some coffee, she walked up the hill to look around. There was nobody else there and it felt peaceful but a bit spooky. She walked through the ruined cathedral and the chapel and stared up at the round tower, almost a hundred feet high. There was a graveyard with several high crosses and stunning views from every angle. The magazine article had stated that this had been home to the kings of Munster for several hundred years before the Norman invasion but that most of the current buildings dated from the twelfth and thirteenth centuries.

However, Connie liked the legend of how it originated in a mountain called the Devil's Bit twenty miles to the north. Apparently, St Patrick banished Satan from a cave there, thus causing the rock to fly out and land in Cashel.

She sat on the pediment of an intricately carved sarcophagus and rummaged in her bag for a bar of chocolate and Matthew's latest letter. It wasn't only Tim who was a cause of concern; Matthew sounded miserable as well. The blue aerogramme was covered in red dust fingerprints.

Wiluna 18th November 1977
Darling Connie
I can't wait to get out of this place. It really is a sordid dump and I can't pretend any longer that I enjoy charging around the bush in a rattly old Landrover, getting punctures when it is one hundred degrees in the shade. I usually opt for the night shift, when it's cooler, but can't sleep during the day because of the heat and there are always trillions of filthy flies buzzing around. I do try to keep a sense of humour about the awfulness of everything but it isn't easy.
It's my job to tell the men where to drill. At each drill site, they have to bore down about three hundred feet because we need to have a core of fresh rock brought up. When the rig has to move, a quaint little procession starts up. The rig leaves its position somewhere in the middle of the bush and is driven to the next site, which is another equally anonymous place. At night, everything looks the same and it is quite difficult to find the peg marking the next site, especially as it will be some distance away and the scrub is so thick you can't see very far ahead.
Also, cattle come and scratch on the pegs, knocking them over. So, the geologist (me, wondering where the hell he is) weaves slowly through the mulga scrub in a Landrover, followed by the truck carrying the drilling rig, the water truck towing the generator van and, finally, the driller's Landrover. At night, it's often the case of the blind leading the blind and you can imagine the language when the geologist has to confess to having overshot and would they mind, please, all turning around.
Last night, I had a dream. I remember you saying that you thought people who recounted their dreams were the ultimate bores, but this dream was special. I was lying on a white sheet placed in the middle of a stack of fragrant hay. I was making love to a naked goddess of incomparable beauty. A full moon lit up the surrounding silver birches and owls hooted. I was bathed in the most exquisite rapture and happiness and, because it was a dream, there wasn't a single midge.
Thank you for your letters, dearest Connie. They are the only things which make life worth living.
All my love
Matthew

Walking down the hill, Connie reflected that the postponement of her departure for Australia was a good thing. The tone of Matthew's letters had changed since being sent to Wiluna on his return to work after he'd flown home for their summer holiday in the Scottish Highlands. They'd camped in a barn on a farm some miles inland from Ullapool. They'd slept on a haystack which was shared with chickens. Each morning, they woke to find clusters of eggs laid neatly within the nests. There was a nearby brook with a small waterfall, which served as their shower. The weather had been wonderful. They were based quite close to the Corrieshalloch Gorge with the Falls of Measach, above which a delicate Victorian bridge was gracefully suspended.

Stac Polly and other mountains towered majestically in the near distance; there was purity and peace and beauty all around. Connie and Matthew walked in the Fannich Forest and visited the subtropical Inverewe Gardens. They cooked fresh trout on their camping stove for dinner and fried the freshest of eggs for breakfast. The contrast with Wiluna had been stark.

Wiluna had flourished once with a gold mine but that had closed down in 1947, leaving a ghost town of about one hundred and fifty people. Matthew was under orders to drill for nickel but wasn't having much luck finding any. His office, also his home, was half a mile from the town and comprised the old clubhouse for a golf course which had been laid out with black clinker in the absence of any grass. It was now covered in mulga scrub, a form of vegetation in which it was all too easy to get lost because it grew just high enough to be impossible to see over the top, even when standing on the bonnet of a jeep. Conditions were rough.

The drilling was carried out at regular intervals along the lines of a grid which had been plotted on the basis of an aerial survey. A plane would fly backwards and forwards, about two hundred feet above the ground, picking up signals on a magnetometer and scintillometer. Matthew told her much later that he'd asked his American bosses to carry out a ground survey as well as the aerial survey. This had yielded results, on the strength of which he'd managed to get a job in Britain on his return with a Mineral Exploration Consultancy Company based in London.

Matthew's earlier letters had been happier. He'd spent a few months at the University of New South Wales in Sydney, doing a sort of mining induction course, and there had been rave reviews about the beauty of the harbour, the Opera House and the excellence of the geology department. He had then been sent to Mount Isa in Queensland; an enormous mine producing lead, silver, zinc and copper. He'd sent Connie a photograph taken from a plane and she didn't find it uplifting. The foreground was occupied with well-spaced bungalows set in scrubby, dusty squares intersected by roads. A watercourse flowed through the middle and beyond were more housing and ugly industrial buildings with chimneys belching smoke. A hellish, brutal prospect.

It probably looked better from the ground. His letters tried to make his bungalow sound attractive, describing the garden with its fruit trees; peach, grapefruit, lemon and mango.

Then, he moved to Orange in New South Wales, three thousand feet up and west of the Blue Mountains. It was cooler here and he lived in a flat. He wrote about the eucalyptus trees and weeping willows which grew along the watercourses. He sent photographs showing flowers and there were friendly colleagues who invited him for barbecues and drinks. He tried hard to be positive and cheerful but Connie could feel the aching loneliness and depression amid his determination to make a success of the new life he was planning for them both.

It was another thirty-two miles to Limerick, where Connie had booked into a small hotel on the Ennis Road on the far side of the bridge crossing the River Shannon. Until planning her route to Belmullet, Connie had thought of Limerick as a small county town famous only for its funny rhymes. She had childhood memories of sitting in the back of the car with her brother, both helpless with laughter as their father bellowed out his own musical rendition of these verses in a melodious voice embellished with snorts and other rude noises.

In fact, after Dublin and Cork, it was the largest city in the Irish Republic. It had been founded by the Vikings at the beginning of the tenth century but was later fortified by the Anglo-Normans after their conquest of Ireland. Driving over the bridge, Connie glanced to her right and saw King John's Castle, which had been built at that time.

The kindly landlady took her suitcase and led her through to a pretty sitting room where Connie sat in an armchair in front of a cheerful fire. A tray with a large pot of tea and a plate of hot buttered toast was placed on a side table. After months of waiting on the patrons of the Royal Oak, Connie relished being on the receiving end of warm hospitality. For supper, there was buttery colcannon with crispy lamb chops. This was followed by a steaming soak in an old-fashioned bathtub and a blissful sleep in a soft double bed.

Connie arrived in Belmullet two days later, having driven from Limerick, through Galway to Westport, where she spent the night and enjoyed her first view of Croagh Patrick with a cloud sitting on the top like a soft hat. She could have opted for a much shorter journey cross-country from Rosslare but had chosen this route because she'd long wanted to see something of Connemara with its beautiful lakes and mountains. She wished Matthew was with her. She was a competent map reader but always had to stop the car to look at the atlas; whereas, if Matthew were driving and the atlas was open on her lap, he would cast his eye in its direction and absorb the information so quickly that even slowing down was unnecessary.

Northwest from Oughterard to Teernakill, along the northern shore of Lough Corrib, back along Lough Nafooey went the little green Mini and then up to Leenane near the head of Killary Harbour, where Connie found a bar which served tea. The scenery was richly coloured, even in winter; the voluptuous curves of the mountains aflame with a coppery glow, lustrous evergreens undimmed by the chill, rich grass and the calm, pellucid blue of the lakes reflecting the sky.

The last stretch of the drive, the following day, involved following the road around Clew Bay with its mass of drumlins and then north through the peat bogs of Mayo towards Belmullet. The landscape was magnificent with islands, inlets and a view of the Mullet Peninsula on the far side of the bay.

It was a long journey. On reaching the guesthouse, Connie felt extremely tired and completely deserted by her capacity for positive thought. Everything felt wrong and she began to wish fervently that she hadn't come. She couldn't blame Bella, who hadn't actually physically been there but who had implied that it would all be something of a treat. People who asked for a favour and then made out that it was they who were conferring it were annoying. Connie found herself muttering ripe imprecations under her breath as she unpacked her case. She failed to find the slightest charm in her immediate surroundings. The one redeeming feature was the magnificent view from the bedroom window looking straight down Blacksod Bay.

The room was large, damp and unheated. The only vestige of warmth came from the electric blanket on the bed. There was a huge washbasin with tarnished taps and a plastic beaker encrusted with the toothpaste deposits of previous users. On opening the drawers of the chest, she found fungus growing inside them. On locating the bathroom, she was shocked to find the bath so blackened with filth, it couldn't be used. There was a just-about-tolerable lavatory but no shower.

Mrs O'Reilly was a statuesque and generously proportioned woman who had reared eight children, the youngest of whom still lived at home. He was a handsome, inarticulate youth, so tall that he had to duck under the door frames and who operated the doors not by using the handles for the purpose but by grasping the tops and swinging them back and forth. Very engagingly, he served Connie with dinner as she sat at a small table by the meanly draped window. It was a pork chop with four potatoes and four carrots, followed by a sponge pudding with custard. She was hungry and ate everything.

She then sat on a moquette sofa in front of sullenly smouldering peat briquettes; a low-wattage bulb glowered down from its cheap shade, casting shadows on the damp patches alternating with faded prints around the walls. A pot of tea was brought in. She craved coffee but it wasn't on offer. Connie tried to look and sound appreciative but she was lonely, cold, miserable and homesick. She was also profoundly relieved that she had arranged to stay for only two nights.

Four

The following morning brought with it a return of optimism. Connie had made an exciting discovery the night before in the shape of a rusting electric fire set into the bedroom wall. It had been concealed, perhaps deliberately, behind an easy chair but it worked and the improvement to her spirits was dramatic. She slept well. On awaking, she slipped out of bed to switch on the fire and then snuggled back under the blankets.

She draped towels in front of the fire while she had a strip wash at the basin. She shampooed her hair and the soft water made it feel silken and lustrous. She rinsed out some undies, hoping they would dry, and then dressed in a favourite red and blue tartan midi-skirt and an arran jumper. Fortified with a huge breakfast, she set off to find the post office in Belmullet. She took her place in the queue, conscious of being stared at as her gaze roamed the shop and alighted on the notice board. This had a photograph of a white bungalow with the words 'HOLIDAY LET' written beneath it. It belonged to the postmistress and, within minutes, a happy arrangement had been agreed; it would be warm and ready to receive her the following day.

The same lady was able to give her precise instructions on how to find a Dr Tim Melrose. She knew him well as he called in regularly, once or twice a week, to collect any mail directed there for him.

"You're not his wife, then?" Connie shook her head and had a feeling that many more questions would have been asked if it hadn't been for the pressure of other customers. Connie drove back past Mrs O'Reilly's and on towards Binghamstown, where there was a scattering of small houses. Between two of them, she saw a caravan which had been weighted down with cables and rocks. She turned into a farm track and drove along until it became impassable. She parked beside a grubby van and saw a small building with a corrugated iron roof about two hundred yards off. It had a blackened, derelict air and was surrounded by flat, yellowish grassland.

There was a cold wind getting up and the sky was filling with ragged, grey clouds. She pulled on a cagoule and walked briskly over. There was no answer to her first, tentative knock, so she banged loudly on the half-rotten door. It flew open.

"What in the name of God are you doing here?"

There was no hint of pleasure or warmth in his voice or eyes. Connie felt insulted.

"What in the name of God are you doing in this sordid hovel? You're supposed to be in a caravan."

"I was in a caravan but it's not safe at this time of the year because of the Atlantic gales. The farmer insisted on moving it between two bungalows for shelter."

"You could still live in it, though?"

"At the moment, I can't bear to be too close to my fellow man."

"Why?"

"Because I hate the whole of humanity and the effort of pretending otherwise is just too much."

"Can I come in?"

"No, you can't."

"Why not?"

"I'm busy. Go away."

"Please let me come in. It's starting to rain."

"It's not far to your car. I can see it next to mine."

"Be reasonable, Tim."

"I was once a reasonable man but I'm not any longer. I suppose Bella sent you."

Connie was wondering what to do. Having come all this way, she couldn't just turn around and go all the way back. Tim looked awful, haggard and unkempt, with dull, weary eyes.

"I need to talk to you about Matthew. I think he's even more miserable than you are. And I have a proposition."

Tim hesitated, then stepped back and gestured for her to enter. Determined to be uncritical, she went in and sat on one of the two upright chairs, looking straight ahead.

"Tim," she said, "there is a truly terrible smell in here."

"It's probably me. I'm sorry."

"No, it's far worse than that and it's something I recognise." She thought hard. "Do you have any potatoes in here?"

"Well, yes, actually I do. The farmer gave me a sackful, but I never eat them because they need peeling and I can't be bothered."

"I think one of them has gone mouldy. Bella and I shared a flat briefly when we'd finished our business course. We had a horrible landlord who chucked us out without any warning because he couldn't pay the mortgage. Anyway, we left it in a totally immaculate condition but put a rotting potato where he'd have trouble finding it, just to teach him a lesson."

Against his will, Tim laughed. "That would have been your idea. Bella would never have thought of that. I'm feeling better already. Let's go and look in the sack." Sure enough, there was the oozing and offensive article sitting on the top. Tim picked it up with a piece of newspaper and hurled it out of the door.

"Do you have a bathroom?" Connie asked, very politely.

"Of course, I have a bathroom. There is a spring fed water supply coming into the sink over there in the corner and a latrine outside. The door was lost in a gale but it has three walls, an excellent piece of mahogany to sit on and a wonderful view of Inishglora. Or, there's a handy clump of gorse not far off."

"Now, Tim," said Connie, "it's time to get down to business. You'll be dismayed to hear that I'm booked into a holiday cottage for up to a week, starting from tomorrow morning, and I should like to invite you for dinner tomorrow evening. What would you like to eat? Shall I do roast beef?"

"Can you make Yorkshire pudding?"

"Yes, of course." Connie had noticed some tins of unappetising food stacked up beside a camping stove. "I could also use up some of those potatoes. A shame to waste them. Also, you'd be very welcome to have a hot bath and please bring over any clothes, sheets and towels you have because the cottage has a washing machine and we might as well make use of all the facilities."

Tim looked uncertain.

"I told Bella I'd ring her when I found you but she'll be at work now, so I'll ring this evening from Mrs O'Reilly's. She is very worried about you; thinks you're having a nervous breakdown. With your permission, I'll tell her that you're in good shape, physically and mentally. I'll say nothing about your living conditions but, perhaps, I could reassure her that you will be coming home soon and that you will be in touch?"

"Bella loves diagnosing mental instability. She's full of mumbo-jumbo from her psychology degree. She's decorative and well-intentioned but a bit short on emotional intelligence."

"You're basically happy, though?"

"She's my wife. I married her and I love her. Just remember, when you wed that ruffian of yours in Australia, that signing a marriage certificate is the equivalent of signing a 'non-disclosure agreement'."

"I'll bear that in mind. Bella thinks you have a work problem."

"She's right about that but it's a long story. Is Matthew enjoying life?"

"No, he isn't. I think he's desperate to come home. He envies your job in academia."

"It's not all that enviable. Competition is fierce and the pay is poor. There's nothing on offer in Oxford. At the moment, someone is trying to ruin my reputation before I've even managed to acquire one. I am suffering from a blackness of soul and have a great many negative and antisocial thoughts. Eighty per cent of the human race are venomous hypocrites, as far as I'm concerned. No doubt, you'll be appalled."

"On the contrary, I think you are being too generous. I would put the figure at nearer ninety per cent."

Tim stared at her. She took a notebook and pen out of her bag and wrote down the address of the holiday cottage. "I'll go now," she said. "I'll see you tomorrow."

Tim stood up. "What are you going to do today?" he asked.

"I haven't a clue. I'll probably drive around and explore, find somewhere for lunch, locate the cottage, write to Matthew. The cottage is quite close to here but I need to find it. Things will be much better tomorrow because I'll have my own little home."

"Would you like a trip down to Achill Island? I feel like a day off."

~

Connie drove back to the guesthouse and changed into jeans and walking boots. Tim followed and they set off in the van along the direct road to Bangor. A few miles past Bunnahowen, they were flagged down by a woman in a headscarf and heavy tweed coat. She was carrying a large, square wicker basket with a lid. Tim stopped the van, Connie wound down her window and they readily agreed to give the lady a lift to Bangor. This involved Connie climbing into the back of the van and sitting on a crate of rocks while the new arrival took over the front seat next to Tim.

The lady proceeded to give a loud and voluble explanation of her predicament. The musical cadence of the Irish brogue was delightful to Connie and she could listen to it endlessly, whatever the subject matter and even when it was punctuated by squawks from the two chickens inside the basket. Their passenger had intended to take a pony and trap to her sister, who lived in Bangor and wanted the chickens, which were exceptionally good layers. However, the pony was lame and her husband had passed out from having too much to drink the night before. Apparently, the husband was a 'useless article' at the best of times. She could have walked the five miles but her bunions were playing up and she was very, very glad of a lift.

The stream of chatter was unremitting and Connie found herself smiling when she noticed Tim looking at her in his rear-view mirror. The complicit humour and restored warmth in his deep blue eyes invoked a pleasurable and rather stirring feeling of intimacy. Having discharged their passenger, they drove south through wonderful scenery to Mulrany.

Tim was an entertaining companion. He told her of the occasion when he'd passed an Irish flag being flown at half-mast outside a small village. On entering the bar, he expressed his regret that someone had died but was told that there had been no death and the reason for the flag being at half-mast was because the owner couldn't get it to go up any higher. Then, another client in the bar said in a mournful voice that there had, in fact, been two recent deaths in the village. One was a woman who had put both feet in the same hole of her knickers and had fallen down the stairs as a consequence.

The other was the local judge who suffered a stroke while standing at his bedroom window, admiring the view, and then fell forward straight out of the window onto the concrete paving below. Tim had tried to look suitably saddened until the barman said, "He always tells new customers that story because it never fails to cheer them up."

From Mulrany, they drove around Corraun, stopping at a hotel for refreshment before crossing the bridge to Achill Island and exploring the majestic scenery. The rugged mountains in the north rose directly from the sea and there were beautiful white crescents of sand in the south. Tim pointed out Slievemore, a mountain rising to two thousand two hundred feet, which he had climbed.

"From my hotel in Westport, there was a wonderful view of Croagh Patrick," said Connie. "Have you climbed that?"

"Not yet," replied Tim, "but I'd like to someday. It's a holy mountain, named after Saint Patrick who was thought to have cast all the snakes out of Ireland. It's two and a half thousand feet high and, every year in July, thousands of pilgrims climb to the top, where there is a chapel celebrating Mass throughout the day. The truly devout go barefoot and some even on their knees. Pilgrimages have, in fact, been a regular feature of Croagh Patrick for five thousand years, starting well before the Christian era. It's thought that the Stone Age pagans might have been celebrating their harvest."

There was a short silence as they drove down a long steep road to Keem Strand. The sunshine was punctuated by occasional sharp downpours of rain; the intensity of the sapphire blues and emerald greens was intoxicating. "Why do you have an old typewriter in the back of your van?" Connie asked. "I noticed it when I was sitting on the crate."

"It comes in useful every so often because there are a few awkward people around who won't let me onto their land. I type out an official-looking document, purporting to come from the Irish Government, requesting that permission be granted for entry to the estate in the interest of scientific progress. It has always worked."

"That sounds highly illegal."

Tim laughed. "Of course, it is but it's better than being shot at, and, on the scale of general wickedness, I consider it a much less heinous crime than leaving a mouldy potato in an innocent landlord's flat." He parked. "Some of the rocks here are marble. Shall we walk to the top of the cliff? It's a bit of a pull up but the view is fantastic." At the top, they gazed out over the immensity of the Atlantic Ocean. "There's nothing between us and America apart from this sea, which looks calm today but can be savage. Many of the ships in the Spanish Armada came to grief along this coast when they were trying to sail home after their failed invasion."

Connie felt awed and thought of Matthew; his soul withering in dun-coloured, fly-ridden, scrubby surroundings. She knew she had to persuade him to come home.

~

Belmullet
Monday 29th November 1977
Darling Matthew,

I finally reached Belmullet yesterday afternoon. The day before, I drove through Connemara, which was especially lovely, although it would have been a thousand times more enjoyable if you had been with me. I only saw a small part of it.

I've brought a stack of your recent letters with me, so that I can re-read them. What comes through, more and more with each one, is that this job doesn't suit you and it is futile to pretend otherwise. I think you should work out a good time to tell the company you are leaving. Having done that, you'll probably find the remaining months more bearable.

Don't waste time worrying about being a 'failure' or fretting about future employment prospects. My feeling is that you won't regret your experience in Australia and that it will stand you in good stead in some capacity or another when you come home.

As you know, Bella asked me to come here to check up on Tim because she thinks he might have gone round the bend. He certainly looked like a madman when I found him this morning. He has a great bushy beard and wild hair and wasn't at all pleased to see me. He's working on 'basement' rocks in the Mullet Peninsula but his findings don't accord with those of a fairly senior academic in a different university who has an established reputation. This man was one of the referees for Tim's latest paper, which was rejected. Tim is certain that his own theory is correct but, in order to demonstrate this, he needs to have his rock samples dated.

This is very expensive and, because his own credentials have been called into question, he can't get funding. He is a mass of seething rage, frustration and resentment and I don't blame him.

I'm wondering if there is a remote possibility that someone in the lab in Sydney, where you did your mining course, might agree to do some 'dating' on the side as a favour. Probably not but I have the impression that there is more money available for these things in Australia than there is in the United Kingdom.

I'm longing for us to be together again. My passage out to you is still booked for the summer but I'm beginning to hope that you will come home to me instead. I'm quite sure that everything would work out well.

It's pouring with rain at the moment and everything is fresh and cool but I don't want to make you jealous!
All my love
Connie

~

The butcher was wrapping a sumptuous piece of best rump beef. "Could you tell me, please, how to make Yorkshire pudding?"

He gave Connie a quizzical look and called out, "Siobhan, I have a young lady here who wants to know how to make Yorkshire pudding."

A disembodied voice came from somewhere behind the shop. "Tell her it's easy."

Connie laughed. "That's nice to know but what do I have to do?"

A smiling woman in a white apron appeared in the doorway. "Four tablespoons of plain flour, a bit of salt, half a pint of milk and one egg. Whisk it all up together. Heat up some fat in a baking dish or patty tin, pour in the mixture and bake in a hot oven for twenty minutes to half an hour."

"Thank you very much," replied Connie. "Also, is there anywhere that sells logs as well as briquettes, please?"

"You'll find some at the garage but they're expensive. There aren't many trees in these parts."

Connie had moved into the cottage, not far from Binghamstown, and was well pleased with everything. It was warm with electric radiators in all the rooms. There was a bright sitting room with a huge soft sofa, two bedrooms, a bathroom and a modern kitchen, which was well-equipped with everything she needed. The postmistress had left her a bottle of milk and some teabags but, apart from some salt and pepper, there was nothing edible.

To one side of the cottage was a shed. She peered inside and found garden furniture and two bicycles as well as gardening tools.

She'd written out a long list of basics and set off for the shops. She'd found everything she needed for the next few days and, crucially, for the main course that evening. However, she had the greatest difficulty thinking up what to make for a pudding. She'd grown accustomed to the array of delicacies at the Royal Oak; pavlova, cheesecake, grape galette, chocolate mousse, lemon soufflé, sherry trifle, pastries and many more. There was no time to make any of these and she decided on a simple nursery mix of sliced bananas with custard and cream. Chopped nuts and drizzled melted chocolate could be optional extras.

Connie had telephoned Bella the evening before. The line wasn't very good and she'd been aware of Mrs O'Reilly timing the call from the kitchen.

"Hello, Bella, it's Connie."

"Oh, hello." Bella's voice sounded surprised as if she hadn't expected a call and didn't particularly welcome it.

"I'm just ringing to say that I've found Tim and, apart from needing a haircut, he's in good shape. He's planning to drive home next week and he'll ring you from the post office when he has accumulated the right number of coins."

"Well, that's good news. Thank you. I suppose you'll be coming home now."

"Not for a few days. I feel like a break from travelling. It's rather lovely here and I'm hoping to come back with Matthew someday. Tim is going to show me around."

"He won't have time for that, surely."

"Maybe not, in which case, I'll show myself around. I have a map. Anyway, you don't have to worry any more. All is under control."

~

"I can honestly say that I have never before tasted such ambrosial beef." Tim sat on the sofa, mesmerised by the crackling logs and with the remains of a bottle of red wine in front of him.

"I'm glad you've brought that," Connie said when he'd arrived. "I'll put some in the gravy." The meal had been a triumph; even the flat and slightly soggy Yorkshire puddings had been delicious. She made a pot of coffee and joined him on the sofa.

"I've written to Matthew and told him that you need some rock dating done."

"What I really need is someone in the Sydney department to be persuaded that what I'm doing is worthwhile and to be prepared to collaborate. We could write a joint paper. I'd have to send him some rock samples for zircon dating. The zircon makes up a tiny proportion of the rock but contains the uranium necessary to get the dates. If Matthew could make some enquiries, I'd be eternally grateful. You've given me a small glimmer of hope."

He was relaxed and comfortable and Connie didn't like to think of him going back to the gloom of his dank and derelict hut. "You can move in here if you like," she said. "There are two bedrooms."

"I'd love to," Tim replied, "but apart from ruining your reputation, Bella wouldn't like it."

"No, she wouldn't," agreed Connie, pouring some more coffee.

"You're quite intrepid, driving all this way in the middle of winter," remarked Tim.

"Bella asked me to come and I could hardly refuse. Besides which, I pride myself on independence of spirit. I've done a car maintenance course. I was the only female in the group and the only one properly dressed in a very clean boiler suit. It caused a few laughs. Also, I've been to judo lessons. So, I can change a wheel and anyone thinking of attacking me does so at their peril."

"What did you learn in your judo class?"

"To begin with it was learning how to fall without getting hurt. There was a lot of hurling ourselves around and somersaulting onto mats. I ended up with a lot of bruises."

Tim laughed.

"Then, I learned something useful which involved tripping up an opponent so that they landed on the floor. It was called a 'salter garry', or something like that."

"I've heard of an 'O soto gari'," said Tim. "You were quite good at that, I suppose?"

"Well, I never got to the black belt stage but, with all due modesty, I might have been moderately competent."

"Would you care to demonstrate?"

"Are you sure you're ready to be slammed on the floor after that huge meal?"

Tim nodded.

"Okay then. We'll move the coffee table and you stand over there and don't move."

"Why can't I move? I should approach you with a menacing air."

"Because I can't do it if you're capering around. Please stand still, I'm supposed to take you by surprise."

Tim stood motionless with his arms by his side and adopted a gormless expression. Connie chuckled and then sprang forward, held his arms, hooked her right foot around his right leg and pulled. She then found herself literally airborne, moving upside down in a graceful arc before being deposited gently back on her feet.

Connie was speechless for a few moments. "That wasn't meant to happen and I'm not sure it was quite fair. Perhaps, we could try again?"

"Certainly not," said Tim. "At any rate, not until you've had a few more lessons."

~

Before leaving the evening before, Tim asked Connie if she would like to see some of the rocks he was working on. They were on the shore of a beach at Cross Point, a few miles away and at the end of a track. Tim talked about schists and gneisses, sedimentary rocks and basement rocks, amphibolites, metamorphism, deformation and the Dalradian Supergroup.

Reluctant to appear unintelligent, she tried to follow what he was talking about and was full of enthusiasm for the expedition. She suggested they use the bicycles in the shed and planned a picnic of beef sandwiches, apples, chocolate and a flask of tea. The next morning, having packed the food and spare clothing into rucksacks, they discovered that the smaller bike wasn't all that small. Tim adjusted the saddle but Connie's feet only just reached the pedals.

They set off regardless and bowled along happily, enjoying the crisp, pure air and the empty peacefulness. The road was quiet and they soon turned off onto a farm track which led around some fields, skirting the top of Cross Lough. The track became sandier and harder to negotiate, so they stopped next to an ancient chapel, opposite a graveyard full of Celtic crosses, and walked the short distance to the beach. The pale gold sand was soft, fringed behind with long grass and caressed in front by a calm, lapis-tinted sea.

Tim led the way down some steps, to the right of which was what looked like a nest of gigantic birds' eggs; great, smooth, oval boulders of varying colours. There were creams and pale rose pink shades with green stripes. "These are banded gneisses," said Tim. "Those little speckles are garnets. The dark green boulders are amphibolites and they were basalts before being metamorphosed. They have all been eroded out of the cliff and the action of the sea has smoothed and rounded them."

"They are very beautiful," said Connie, her hand passing over the tactile surface of the nearest one.

"The geologist responsible for the rejection of my paper worked on these rocks for his doctoral thesis ten years ago. His research was very good but, in science, nothing stands still and I have noticed various features that he missed and which call into question the basis of his findings. This sort of thing happens all the time but trying to shut someone down because they don't agree with you is unprofessional and very unpleasant.

"I find geology fascinating and the last few years have been very exciting indeed. Because of new technology to map the ocean floor and a mechanism to monitor the changing of magnetic poles in the basalts, which make up the ocean floor, and the introduction of isotope dating, what was an idea based on simple observation of the shapes of the continents is now a fully accepted Plate Tectonic Theory. About sixty million years ago, give or take a few million, all the continents were bunched together in a great mass called Pangaea.

"Very slowly, they split apart to be where they are now. The Mid-Atlantic Ridge is pushing us away from North America at the rate of about two centimetres a year. Australia is moving northwards at the rate of five or six centimetres a year. India split off from Africa and bumped into Asia, forming the Himalayas. This bit of County Mayo was once attached to northwestern Newfoundland. The rocks correspond."

"What actually causes the movement?" Connie asked.

"It's heat from the Earth's core, presumably caused by radioactivity, rising up in convection currents and escaping through the Earth's crust. The force causes tectonic plates to move and, where they are crushed together, the resulting pressure causes rocks to be folded, deformed and metamorphosed."

"Well, I think it's time for our sandwiches," said Connie. "I'm hungry. Let's find a sheltered spot; not that we need shelter because the weather is perfect."

They walked along the beach until they came to a hollow that had been scooped out of the sand. It was aerodynamically perfect for their picnic, with leg room, a backrest and shelter from the breeze. Gulls were wheeling around on the air currents. They settled themselves in and Connie passed Tim a sandwich.

"My rage and hatred seem to have evaporated," said Tim, munching the food with great relish. "I've been feeding off negativity for weeks and shan't know how to manage without it. It has kept me going. Apparently, there are two families on the Mullet Peninsula who have been sworn enemies for generations because of an ancestral squabble over a lobster. My quarrel with this other geologist is about my belief that these gneisses are basement rock whereas he thinks they are just a distinctive part of the Dalradian. Does it really matter? Well, of course, it does but I am seeing things more in perspective now."

"That's good," replied Connie. Her eyes were closed as she enjoyed the winter sunshine on her face. It was very peaceful.

"If Matthew decides to come home, you'll be getting married in Dorset, I suppose?"

"Haven't a clue. I don't want a lot of fuss; I'd like to do things quietly, like you and Bella. The thought of speeches, bridesmaids and my mother in a silly hat fills me with gloom."

"Bella would have loved the full, glamorous works but her parents felt she was making a terrible mistake. They thought that if they refused to acknowledge our engagement, it would somehow go away."

"What was their objection?"

"They thought I was an 'oik' because I come from Durham and my father is a miner. You have to admit, I do look like an 'oik'."

Connie turned to appraise him for a few moments. "I'm sorry to disappoint you but physical manifestations of 'oikdom' are a bit sparse. As the classical poets would have put it, you have a noble brow indicative of high intelligence. You have strikingly beautiful eyes, a finely-chiselled nose and, under that beard, I know you have a strong chin and a sensual mouth. For a man, you have delicate ears. Even Lord Byron would have envied them. Did you know that Byron regarded his ears as his best feature?"

"No, I didn't know that."

"On top of all that, you have fine hands with long, sensitive fingers; unlike the bunches of sausages some people have; usually the people with aristocratic pretensions. Bella's parents must be the most shameless snobs."

"They are but, underneath the tribalism, they are kind and gentle people. I like them and, because of the upsets caused by the other in-laws, I am now viewed with less disfavour than before."

"What upsets?"

"Well, Bella is the youngest of three children. She has two brothers who are quite a bit older than she is. The family is stiff with money but, I'm glad to say, Bella is not materialistic. She has a social conscience and tries very hard to be good. The trouble is, goodness doesn't come all that naturally, so the effort drains her. She said once after a day of counselling that she wished people would stop bothering her with their wretched problems and what on earth did they think she could do about them. She wasn't over sympathetic with my problem either. She would say that it wasn't exactly the end of the world and not really all that serious and would I, please, stop moaning." Tim laughed. "I can see her point now. Self-obsession and self-pity are not attractive qualities. I shall make amends.

"Anyway, there was much delight and triumph a few years ago when the first-born married a woman with a title. I don't know why she has a title but she is 'Lady Charlotte'. Bella's parents very generously handed over their manor house and moved into the Dower House. Lady Charlotte has now made it clear to Bella's mum that she is only allowed to visit what was her own house and garden on receipt of a prior invitation. Mum has been 'outsnooted' and is very unhappy about it.

"Things get worse. The younger brother, not to be outdone, also married a woman out of the 'top drawer', as they like to put it. They now have two small children and plenty of money but, on the pretext of temporary homelessness, moved into the Dower House with Bella's parents. It's a lovely house with several bedrooms and a pretty garden but the young family have been there for six months now and have made it clear that they have no intention of moving out. Bella is wondering if it is an early attempt to secure their own inheritance. She thinks it is the respective wives who are the chief trouble-makers, not her brothers.

"Her parents don't know what to do. Every room in the house is strewn with toys and general paraphernalia. It is assumed that they are permanently available for childcare duties. Their own social life has imploded and, much as they love their grandchildren, they are exhausted. Daughter-in-law has a strong personality and has taken over the kitchen, imposing a vegetarian regime on the whole family. Bella's mum loves cooking and is distraught but feels helpless. There has even been a jocular hint about moving the parents into the gardener's cottage. It is beyond belief but what is to be done?"

"Easy," said Connie. "Wait until the four of them are out for the day. Change the locks and dump their stuff on the driveway. Then, put a big notice on the front door saying 'GO AWAY'."

"Funny thing is," said Tim, "I suggested exactly that but Bella said that there is a correct way to behave and that it is socially unacceptable to chuck out your own kith and kin."

Five

It would have been a straightforward ride home if it hadn't been for the pony and trap driven by a maniac. The route was slightly uphill but perfectly manageable. Connie was in front setting the pace and, when she saw the pony charging towards her on the narrow track, she thought it would be safer to stop; she applied her brakes accordingly just before the cart swept past her. She'd been startled and because her feet were further from the ground than they ideally should have been, she wobbled and then crashed to the ground with the bike on top of her.

Tim was there in a flash, his face full of concern. He lifted the bike out of the way and his gentle hands helped her up.

"That stupid oaf was going much too fast," he muttered. "Are you alright, Connie?"

"Absolutely fine, I think," she replied, wincing. "I hope I haven't damaged the bike."

"Bugger the bloody bike. You came down with the hell of a thump."

"I'm rather worried about all this shocking language being thrown around. What I'd like to know is why life is always so bloody embarrassing?"

"It just is and probably gets worse. You have to accept it. Shall I go and get the van? It's not all that far off."

"No, thank you. Honestly, I'm fine. Let's get home; it will start getting dark soon."

Once back at the bungalow, Connie ran a deep bath and checked herself over for abrasions. Thanks to her thick anorak and jeans, the only sign of injury was a monumental bruise on her left thigh. She had a long, soothing soak and then got dressed in her homemade, bias-cut, fully lined, red and blue skirt with its perfectly matched side seams. She slipped her cream jumper over her head and decided on a few enhancements in the form of lipstick, mascara, dangly earrings and a few sprays of Chanel No. 5, bought by Matthew from the airport duty free shop on his summer visit from Australia.

She went through to the sitting room where Tim had a bright fire going, a tray of tea on the table and some slices of bread with a toasting fork on the hearth. He noticed the refinements but didn't remark on them. They made him feel strangely happy. He knew she wasn't trying to be enticing but simply enjoying the good things in life. He passed her some hot toast, smothered in butter.

"I had an idea when I was in the bath," she said.

"And what was that?" he replied, holding the next piece of bread in front of the flame.

"It was about the situation in the Dower House. I thought of a plan which would involve getting hold of a humane mousetrap; you could probably borrow one from the biology department at the university. Bella's father could catch some mice from around the stable area and surreptitiously release them into daughter-in-law's bedroom. She would be horrified and leave on the instant. It would be best not to consult Bella's mother. She must be an innocent party."

Tim looked thoughtful. "It might be worth a try. I'll see what Bella says or, perhaps, we should leave her out of it, too. I've been wondering what to do tomorrow. I'd like to go north, towards Erris Head, because the cliffs and scenery there are magnificent."

"What about the work you're supposed to be doing?"

"It's finished for the time being. There's nothing more to do except pack up, go home and get on with things there. I know Bella's fed up with me."

"I think she'll forgive you."

They sat in companionable silence for a while, drinking their tea. Eventually, Tim looked at his watch and said, "Would you like me to go into town later on and get some fish and chips for supper?"

"I was going to make a tuna fish pie. We still have loads of potatoes."

"Tell me what to do and I'll make it. You've suffered a terrible trauma and must take things easy."

"Okay. First of all, you have to peel some potatoes."

"How many?"

"It depends on how big they are. You must use your judgement."

"I haven't got any."

"I thought you were supposed to be clever."

"Don't know what gave you that idea."

"I'll put out the requisite number. Anyway, having peeled them, you cut them up and boil them until they're soft. It takes twenty to twenty-five minutes. Then you mash them with lots of butter, salt, pepper and some milk. Then, you open two tins of tuna fish and mix it all together. Pile the mixture into a baking dish and put it in the oven for half an hour. We can slice up some tomatoes to have with it. There are some tins of raspberries for pudding and a tin of tomato soup for starters. Sorry about all these tins."

They listened to the news on television and Tim started preparations in the kitchen. Connie lay on the sofa, reading *Silas Marner* and listening to Beethoven's *Eroica* on the radio. It was nearly half past eight when she was summoned to the kitchen. The blue formica-topped table had been laid. Tim served the soup and then, with a flourish, poured in a generous swirl of double cream. It made a beautiful pattern.

"That's how a gneiss rock would form," he said, "with lighter and darker elements mingling when they were partly molten and then it would be folded again and again."

~

Tim arrived the next morning with a couple of packets which he put in the fridge. "Sausages, tomatoes and onions for our supper," he said, "and I suppose we'll be eating more of those blessed potatoes."

They set off in the van towards Erris Head. "I have a slightly doomed feeling about today," said Tim. "The weather forecast isn't good. Things are looking perfect at the moment but it's going to change. I had been planning to do the three-mile walk around the headland but, in winter, it can be a bit unpleasant. I don't want to have to explain to Matthew how it came to pass that a freak gust of wind took you over the cliff, never to be seen again. So, I think we'll do a shorter walk over the fields to Ooghwee. There's a sheltered inlet there and the scenery is just as dramatic." He paused and squinted at the road. "I think there is trouble ahead."

There was indeed. Just short of Clooneen, a hearse had veered off the road and was sticking out of the ditch. A group of black-clad mourners stood around; helpless and tragic. Tim pulled up and got out of the van but assistance wasn't needed. The local farmer and his tractor had been summoned and it was just a question of waiting for them.

Tim and Connie continued on their way. "Usually," remarked Connie, "when faced with great indignity, the best thing to do is laugh. The exception to this rule is, of course, if you've fallen off your bicycle. However, I can't imagine what etiquette might require in a situation like this one."

"This is definitely not an occasion for laughter," replied Tim in a grave voice. Then, he glanced across at Connie. "But, perhaps, we could allow ourselves a modest chortle. Incidentally, when I was in the bakery, getting our picnic lunch, I was persuaded to buy tickets for the Céili tomorrow evening. It'll be in the village hall. Hope that's okay with you?"

It sounded good to Connie. She liked dancing, especially the structured sort with lively music. This didn't include disco dancing. She'd once observed her parents at a party, stepping from side to side in front of each other like a pair of demented crabs, waving their arms and grinning wolfishly to demonstrate what a good time they were having. It had been painful.

They arrived at the end of the road and Tim pulled off onto a grassy verge. In front of them was a great gash in the cliff with the sea a long way down but their path veered off to the left. It was chilly; they both wore anoraks and hats and had rainproof cagoules in their rucksacks. They soon left the path and walked over rough pastureland towards the west. It felt empty and wild. Connie was very conscious of the fact that she wouldn't want to be doing this walk on her own but felt completely safe with Tim.

She had the same feeling when out in the wilderness with Matthew. These men had an affinity with natural surroundings; obsessed by rocks but knowledgeable about trees, plants, animals and birds. They listened to weather forecasts but could judge what would happen by observing the wind direction and shape of the clouds. They usually carried a compass but could steer and tell the time by the position of the sun. They knew about latitude and longitude and how these affected the length of the days. They were self-sufficient and interesting to be with.

"Ooghwee is a poetic sort of name," remarked Connie. "Does it have a meaning?"

"Not that I know of," replied Tim. "There's a place called Spinkadoon south-west of us. That has even more of a ring to it."

"What is there to see at Ooghwee?"

"Absolutely nothing. It's an inlet and we can scramble down the rocks to get to the sea. The rock there is metamorphosed sandstone. It's called 'psammite' and is a pale grey colour. Compared to the beautiful banded gneisses at Cross Point, it is rather dull but Ooghwee is a magical place. There are a great many birds around this bit of coast, although they're not so much in evidence at this time of year. There are dippers, wagtails, kingfishers, curlews, oystercatchers and many more. In spring, you can see choughs nesting on the cliffs. If you're lucky, you sometimes get a glimpse of seals, dolphins and porpoises in the sea. What you don't get much of around here is other people."

"What happens if you fall over and break your ankle?"

"That would be most unfortunate."

"But what would you do? There would be nobody to help."

"I always carry spare clothing, a bivvy bag, a few iron rations and a basic first aid kit. Also, I have, not an arrangement exactly, but an unspoken understanding with the farmer. He would notice if my van went missing for a prolonged period and would send out a search party."

"They wouldn't know where to start looking."

"That's true but there's a sort of 'bush telegraph' in these parts. There would be sightings; people would somehow know."

"If you couldn't move and weren't found, especially at this time of year, you could die."

"Until a couple of days ago, that prospect wouldn't have worried me at all."

Connie was silent. She let Tim lead the way and followed behind. She was aware of a strange exhilaration and a feeling of pure happiness. She depended on Tim's manly strength for physical protection while knowing, at the same time, that his spiritual strength derived in part from her. It was a state of exquisite balance and harmony. She also knew that she wasn't entitled to enjoy it. There was a disconnect between natural law and social law and she was encroaching upon another's territory.

They found a flat rock to sit on and ate their pasties, doughnuts and apples. Connie poured out steaming coffee from a thermos flask. She planned to start her journey home on Saturday and was going to spend the next day, Friday, cleaning the cottage, packing her things, writing to Matthew and working out a faster route cross-country back to Rosslare. Tim was also planning his departure in a few days' time. Their respective missions had been accomplished.

On the way back, there was a torrential downpour. The sky turned from blue to black and, in an instant, they were drenched with rain of a biblical ferocity. There was nowhere to shelter. They trudged on with their heads down and, by the time they reached the van, the sun had come out again and was shining with a mocking brilliance. They removed their cagoules and spread them in the back of the van. It was so warm that they both discarded their anoraks and got into their seats. Tim started the engine and pressed the accelerator. The wheels spun and the van didn't move.

"Hell and damnation!" he muttered. "The grass has turned into a bog. Connie, would you please get into the driving seat and steer while I get out and push?"

Connie did as she was asked. The wheels spun and the van was immobile. She got out and saw Tim standing behind the van. He was plastered from head to foot in thick mud. She started laughing and couldn't stop; peal after peal after peal of hilarity. Tim knew that as long as he stood there looking unamused, she would carry on. It was a sound so musical and beautiful to him that he remained stock still with a grim expression.

Eventually, he said, "That's quite enough disrespectful mirth. I'd forgotten that the van is back-wheel drive. We have to devise a plan of action." Connie stopped, with difficulty. "At the risk of causing grave offence," continued Tim, "I am going to have to drive home in my underpants." Connie started laughing again, rocking backwards and forwards, helplessly, while Tim stripped off his jumper and trousers, bundling them up and stuffing them into the crate of rocks. "These will go straight into your rubbish bin when we get back. I will avail myself of your bathtub and I promise to clean it afterwards. I seem to remember seeing a pile of things in the cottage that you've been kind enough to wash for me. Meanwhile, I'll see if I can reverse the van off the verge."

This manoeuvre worked and they were on their way.

~

Her feet started hopping and skipping as soon as she heard the music coming from the village hall. Connie had always been fascinated by the way music could affect her state of mind.

Anything by Elvis Presley would induce a sentimental romanticism; a military march would invigorate flagging energy levels; there was a solo from Rossini's Stabat Mater, *Cuius animam*, which would invoke an extraordinary sensation of heroism, a feeling that she could tackle any dangerous challenge with unflinching courage, while knowing full well that as soon as the music stopped, she would revert to cowardly inertia. The number of tragic operatic arias which could reduce her to tears was beyond counting but Céili music induced a feeling of irresistible joyousness and an urge to gallop and whirl.

She and Tim went through the double doors to be enveloped in a cloud of affability. Bunches of balloons festooned the walls. At one end of the hall was as a stage with at least half a dozen musicians in white shirts, red braces and black trousers. They were all ages, ranging from a plump youth with a snare drum to a sinewy man, who could have been in his eighties, playing a flute. Connie also noticed a violin, an accordion, a concertina and a banjo. Everyone was smiling.

Tim had undergone a complete metamorphosis. Gone were the wild hair and beard. After his trip to the barber, he'd found a clothes shop and was looking very smart. He'd even bought some new, polished shoes. Connie was in a scoop-neck, ribbed, white top and a pretty, tiered, gypsy-like skirt made of green needlecord. She'd found it in Dorothy Perkins and knew it suited her, especially when worn with her wide, black elasticated belt.

There were tables and chairs arranged around the room. At one of them, they saw Patrick and Siobhan from the butcher's and Sean and Bridget from the bakery, all waving and gesticulating for Tim and Connie to join them. On one side of the hall were two trestle tables, draped in white cloths and laden with food. On the other side was the barman with another trestle table, heaped with glasses and great barrels of beer and cider. Included in the cost of the ticket was as much food and drink as everyone could manage until it ran out.

"Take your partners and form groups of eight." The caller's stentorian voice rose above the general clamour. There was a stampede; the band played the opening chord; women curtsied and men bowed. There followed a thunderous galloping to the right and then to the left, setting to one's partner and twirling around, forward and back, the forming of archways and ducking through them, taking turns at promenading down and back between rows of dancers while they all clapped, forming star shapes and rotating back and forth. The caller told them what to do and the steps were easy. It was exhilarating and there was much old-fashioned charm and chivalry amid the loud whoops of excitement.

In between dances, they would return to their table for a brief respite and drink. As the evening wore on, the chatter became more hilarious and the laughter louder. There was a St Bernard's Waltz and a Military Two-Step, both of which Connie remembered from her school days. Halfway through, the music stopped and everyone queued up for plates of sandwiches, pies and cakes. There was a delightful sense of good fellowship.

The band returned to the stage. A deep voice rang out. "Take your partners for the Rosa Waltz." Connie looked enquiringly at Siobhan, who said, "This is a lovely dance but there won't be a caller. If you watch Patrick and me through the first set of steps, you'll get the hang of it and then it just repeats over and over again."

The slow, hauntingly beautiful music started. Tim and Connie watched and then took up a place among the other people. She was a natural dancer and he was remarkably nimble. Connie drew herself up: head high and shoulders back. She looked graceful and regal. Facing each other with palms together, their arms swayed from side to side and then they twirled so that Tim was behind her holding her hands, which were crossed over her chest. Then came four steps to the left, not short military steps but deep, gracious movements involving the whole body. Four steps back, another step from side to side and then a twirl so that they faced each other once again.

With Connie's right hand in Tim's, they moved forwards and back, twirled in a courtly manner and repeated this once more. Tim's arm went around Connie's waist in a standard dance hold; there were two deep steps to one side, two to the other side and then a waltz until the music indicated that the sequence should start again from the beginning. It was a rich and sensuous dance. At the end of it, Tim bowed and released her with some reluctance.

Another rest to catch their breath was followed by more of the simpler dances, ending with a riotous and rather wild Strip the Willow, the music becoming ever faster. Connie's feet seemed to fly through the air as she was spun by one man after another alternating with Tim, who finally lifted her completely off her feet and whirled her around.

The cold air sobered them both up as they returned to the van.

"Are you safe to drive after all that beer?"

"Not in the least. Would you prefer to walk?"

"No." She giggled.

Connie had a bit of trouble inserting her key in the keyhole of her front door and promptly tripped over as she stepped inside. Tim picked her up and plonked her on the sofa.

"I'll make some coffee," he said. When he returned with two mugs, she had dozed off. He put the mugs on a sideboard and lay down beside her, slipping his arm under her neck. She nestled into him, feeling warm and comfortable, like a child.

Then, he kissed her. Connie had had many boyfriends and they had all kissed her. She regarded kissing as a normal courtship rite of passage and had done her best to enjoy it, while simultaneously thinking it a bit of a waste of time. This, however, was completely different, a new experience altogether. She was overwhelmed by the soft, languorous beauty of it and the extraordinary level of sensuality that it invoked. She responded; she couldn't help herself; it would be madness to reject such natural, heavenly pleasure.

A vision clawed its way up from her subconscious; a not altogether welcome vision. It was a classroom with rows of schoolgirls, all in white shirts, blue ties adorned with badges and pleated skirts. They were sixth-formers and they were listening with rapt attention to a young and rather handsome vicar.

"Once past a certain point," he was saying, "a man can't contain himself. It is up to the woman to exert control over the situation."

Connie's 'all girls' school had been quite enlightened. The biology mistress had given them a solid grounding in human reproduction but the reverend had been recruited to provide sensitive relationship training. He had put a box with a slot in the top on his desk. He invited the girls to write down any questions they liked on anonymous slips of paper and put them into the box. The questions could be about anything at all and he would answer them all with openness and honesty the following week. They had found it quite thrilling.

Connie couldn't remember what any of the questions might have been but what she did recall, rather strangely, was the way he had insisted that a register office was the place for marriages; emphatically not a registry office. The latter was where people used to go to find jobs.

The vicar would have been gratified to learn that his wise advice had subsequently triggered a warning light in one of his pupils; a warning light that was sufficiently powerful for Connie to give Tim an almighty shove and say, "Get off me, you great idiot."

He rolled off the sofa and landed on the carpet with a thud. He lay there with his eyes closed, absolutely still. Connie got off the sofa and knelt beside him. "I hope I haven't hurt you," she said. "Why don't you open your eyes?" He remained completely motionless.

"It will be very awkward explaining to Bella that I've killed you." She softly probed his neck, looking for a pulse but couldn't find one. She then felt his wrist and did find one, a perfectly strong one.

Tim opened one eye and she laughed with relief.

"Connie," he said, "I am deeply and sincerely sorry. My behaviour was unforgiveable."

"Please don't apologise, Tim. It was my fault as much as yours. Let's not worry about it."

He gave a sort of grunt.

"About a week after I bought my new car," said Connie, "well, it wasn't actually new, it was second-hand but it was new to me. Anyway, I was in a car park about to reverse into a space when a car reversed into me. An elderly fellow got out and was terribly distressed and apologetic; not belligerent like some people can be. I reckoned it was partly my fault because I'd seen what was about to happen but didn't toot my horn because I couldn't remember where it was. The damage was extremely trivial and I suggested that we should both forget about it. He looked so relieved. We shook hands and parted company feeling very happy. It would be embarrassing for us to shake hands but could we, please, just agree to forget about it?"

"That might be difficult," replied Tim, "but I'll do my best."

Six
1988

The white farmhouse looked idyllic with its wisteria and apple trees, surrounded by what had been farmland but which was filling up rapidly with smart, redbrick houses. Next to the farmhouse was a farmyard and on the far side of this was a modern bungalow built by the farmer and his wife, Mr and Mrs Spragg, for their old age. Behind the bungalow was a paddock, home to a herd of bullocks. Mr Spragg liked to hold on to something of his old life.

In the farmhouse lived Matthew and Connie Shaw. They had bought it at auction for eleven thousand pounds soon after Matthew, looking gaunt and unhealthy, came home from Australia nine years previously. Working in the outback hadn't suited him. England in May seemed like an earthly paradise and he was filled with renewed optimism. He found employment with a mining exploration consultancy based in London. The job involved commuting from their home outside High Wycombe into the office and there was also a lot of travelling abroad. He wasted no time marrying Connie and by the age of thirty, she had produced three little boys—Charlie, Jamie and Ned.

Inside, the house smelled of Fairy washing powder and was full of toys. Upstairs, the bedrooms were decorated with pretty wallpaper and matching curtains. Downstairs, the walls were white and Connie had made rich velvet curtains for the windows; deep red for the sitting room, Wedgewood blue for the dining room and soft gold for the study.

With Matthew's help, Tim had succeeded in getting his rock samples dated by a good-natured geologist with similar interests in the Sydney laboratory. Tim's theories were vindicated and his reputation was restored. He was offered a lectureship in his old department at Oxford and he and Bella bought a small house in Wheatley.

The four friends kept in touch. There had been a slight coolness from Bella after the Irish episode but Connie ignored it and it wore off. They would meet quite regularly, always with mutual pleasure. They would take turns at hosting occasional Sunday lunches at their respective homes. Bella and Tim had a daughter, a sweet and delicate child called Marina, who loved playing in the large garden of the farmhouse. As a toddler, from the moment she was lifted from the car, her arms would start flapping like the wings of a fledgling bird and she would race off with the rumbustious boys, all of whom adored her and took turns at pushing her on the swing.

Sometimes, the four of them would meet in London or Oxford for dinner followed by a cultural event; an opera, ballet or concert. These evenings were expensive and, therefore, rationed but Connie really enjoyed them. They would dress up and feel glamorous; there was an intimacy and ease between them and much laughter.

Bella and Connie used to frequently chat on the phone.

"Hello, Connie. How are you?"

"Hi, Bella. I'm exhausted. How are you?"

"I'm okay, I suppose, but a bit fed up with Tim. He's obsessed with work and never seems to stop even at weekends. Every evening, he comes home for a meal and then shuts himself away in his study. It's almost as if he isn't aware of my presence. The only thing that motivates him socially is the prospect of doing something that involves Matthew."

"At least, he's there if you need him. Matthew's in Alaska at the moment, being eaten alive by mosquitoes. I can cope with being alone for a week or so but, when it stretches to two or three weeks, I find it hard. He used to expect a hero's welcome on coming home but my pleasure at seeing him is mixed with resentment that he went in the first place. It's irrational but it takes a couple of days to feel normal. Added to which, after the journey, he's tired and jet-lagged and a bit grumpy but that wears off quite quickly. I'm pretty self-sufficient because I have to be but, when Matthew is around, I regress into a stereotypical wimp. If I find a spider in the bath, I ask him to remove it."

Bella laughed. "Your parents help out, don't they?"

"Yes, Mum and Dad love coming. They come separately so that they can get away from each other. My father is wonderful, a real help and comfort but my mother is a nightmare. After she's been, I feel utterly drained, every spark of joy expunged."

"Oh dear," said Bella. "What about Matthew's parents?"

"They come every summer to see us and seem to enjoy it. They live outside Nairobi in a lovely rambling old house with a huge garden. Paul inherited it from a relative who used to farm out there and, when he retired from the army, Laura suggested that they relocate. They have a pretty good life but have forgotten what things are like over here."

This was an understatement. They expected to be waited on hand and foot.

"You wouldn't last five minutes with my mother-in-law. She stays in bed until midday, gets up for lunch and then goes back to bed for an afternoon nap. She gets up for tea and fills in the time doing nothing until dinner.

"I take her breakfast in bed and it's not just a mug of tea and piece of toast. It's a tray with a starched cloth and linen napkin and best china; teapot, milk jug, cup and saucer, plates, little dishes for butter and marmalade, silver toast rack and prepared grapefruit or melon. Once, when I'd carried it all up and knocked on the door, she said, 'Please will you come back in ten minutes because I haven't yet finished my prayers.'"

Bella gasped in shock. "Why do you go to all that trouble?"

Connie paused and wondered how to answer that question. She couldn't admit to a pathetic desire to please. Self-professed virtue was always met with suppressed irritation from friends or sneering dislike from people who weren't your friends. There was more to it than that, anyway. What she liked about the breakfast tray was its aesthetic perfection. It was an art form. It was beyond criticism. "I suppose it must be the grovelling Uriah Heep side of me trying to escape."

Bella laughed. "Tim and I have been invited to a posh wedding next Saturday. My cousin is marrying some very rich guy who works in the city and everything will be done with no expense spared. Tim is full of dread and keeps trying to think up reasons for getting out of it. I sometimes despair, I really do."

Connie looked at her watch; it was nearly time to collect the boys from school. "Tim will enjoy it once he's there. I'm sure you'll both have an excellent time and, when Matthew comes home, we'll fix a date for our next get-together. I have to go. Bye for now."

Connie sometimes found that Bella lacked imagination. For someone who had a degree in psychology and counselled people as part of her job, she was strangely conventional in her attitudes towards human behaviour. She had her own ideas about how things should be and resented anything that deviated from the narrative. For Bella, it would be unthinkable not to adore one's parents; equally unthinkable that a wedding day might not invariably be a very happy occasion for all concerned. It would not occur to her that Tim's reluctance to attend the cousin's forthcoming nuptials might have something to do with the guest list including people sufficiently intellectually stunted to regard him as an inferior being and unsuitable husband.

Connie hadn't much enjoyed her own wedding. She disliked being the centre of attention and detested social stress. Matthew's mother had not approved of the engagement. "All a bit sudden, darling, don't you think?" had been Laura's response to the announcement.

The marriage took place in the church at Beaminster. Matthew and his parents stayed in a local hotel. Deirdre wondered if she should invite them to dinner but Connie couldn't face it and asked Matthew to arrange dinner for the six of them at his hotel. He agreed and then forgot; Connie collapsed in hysterical tears. Matthew hastily sorted things out but it hadn't been a comfortable evening. The mothers were competing. "But I'm actually older than you," said Deirdre with a fake smile, convinced she looked much younger.

"Oh, that's not possible," replied Laura with an even more artificial smile.

Matthew's father, Paul, was a genial man in possession of levels of frugality which matched Deirdre's. One bottle of red wine was to suffice for the whole meal and Connie marvelled at the skill with which the waiter eked it out. It was her own beloved father; a kind, intelligent, sensitive, generous man with a remarkable sense of humour, who managed to make them all laugh and feel that it had gone quite well.

The bridesmaid, Annette, her kind friend from university, came all the way from Killarney to lend support. Connie worried miserably about subjecting her to Deirdre's precarious housekeeping and nylon sheets. Then, there was the dress, another source of acute anxiety. She made it herself with white lace over taffeta. It was fiendishly difficult and not helped by a sewing machine, a gift from her mother, which was second-hand and defective. It was impossible to get the tension right and the side seams of the skirt were puckered. No amount of ironing with a damp cloth had any effect. Despite everything, family honour was maintained throughout the day, although Connie spent much of her wedding night weeping with relief that it was all over.

Connie had always loved St Mary's Church, set on a grassy hill not far from the town square. A wide path made of limestone blocks led up to the porch.

Inside, it was light and generously proportioned with graceful, stone arches, a delicate oak screen in front of the choir stalls and exceptionally beautiful stained-glass windows. There were elaborately carved white marble monuments that had been erected in remembrance of local gentry from earlier centuries; also, a fascinating architectural feature called a 'squint'. This was a tunnel through the stonework allowing people in the side aisle a view of the altar.

The path sparkled in the sunshine as Connie walked with her father and bridesmaid up to the church door. Alongside the path was a row of cottages and she saw that all the upstairs windows held people waving at her; smiling, admiring and wishing her well. She felt moved and grateful; her anxiety dissolved and, as the organ swelled into the traditional Mendelssohn, she glided towards Matthew, radiating happiness and regal poise.

~

When Graham came to stay, he blended in seamlessly; totally undemanding, unobtrusively helpful and always good-tempered. He would dig the garden, mow the lawn, wash up, mend things, take them out to lunch and never, ever criticise.

Like many men, Graham loved children and they loved him in return. His patience was endless, whether it was soothing a crying baby or playing games with children of whatever age. He loved their physical beauty and innocence and had a natural affinity with their little frustrations and problems. He enjoyed the small tactile bodies cuddling up to him on the sofa, while he read stories or watched cartoons on television. They would confide in him and show him their favourite toys, instinctively knowing that he would understand the importance of these things.

Graham had qualities of simplicity, protectiveness and fun. The boys would try and impress him; hanging upside down on the climbing frame, doing somersaults and cartwheels and trying to stand on their heads. They were always sure of approval and admiration.

Each morning, the boys would assemble in the bathroom to watch an old-fashioned shaving ritual. Their father used an electric shaver but Graham would lather on fresh-smelling shaving soap and then carefully cut little pathways through the white foam with his razor. In between each flourish, he would sing in his rich tenor voice,

There was an old man called Michael Finnegan,
He had whiskers on his chinnegan,
The wind came along and blew them in again,
Poor old Michael Finnegan begin again.

It was different when Deirdre came. She could not bring herself to acknowledge Connie as the lady of the house. Without any consultation, she would announce the day of her arrival and, in due course, she would announce the day of her departure. Having once been beautiful herself, she resented Connie's youthful charms and happiness. She was jealous of Connie's modern appliances but insisted she wouldn't have any of them herself, even if she was paid to. She loved the boys but wasn't naturally at ease with children. She was impatient and quickly roused to snappy irritability.

There were gratuitous 'put-downs'. On passing another mother with a smart pushchair, she would say, "There are such nice things around these days, so much better than yours were."

On one occasion, she wasn't feeling very well and remarked, "It's absolutely horrible being ill in someone else's house, quite unbearable."

Connie replied, "If you want to go home, please don't feel that you must stay."

"No, no, I must stay."

"Would you like a nice mug of hot chocolate? I have plenty of milk."

"Then order less."

"Oh dear, I have forgotten to collect the eggs."

"How careless of you."

"Mrs Spragg will keep them for me. She's very kind."

"In what way is she kind? Does she give you things?"

This last remark upset Connie. She and Matthew were on good terms with the Spraggs. There was mutual respect and affection. Mrs Spragg was not interested in glamour. A baggy tweed skirt sufficed for winter and summer and what looked like a rolled-up stocking fitted snugly on her head. She had periwinkle blue eyes and said to Connie, soon after they'd moved in, "I'm glad you got the house. I wanted you to have it."

Mr Spragg had banged on their door in the middle of a very wet night to enlist Matthew's help with rounding up his bullocks, escaped from their paddock and halfway down the lane. Matthew had some trouble understanding what was being said, because the elderly farmer was without his teeth, but hastily pulled wellingtons over his pyjama trousers and raced off to assist. A rapport had been established. Deirdre had sullied it.

~

It was on a cold, drizzling Friday morning in November, when Connie had a telephone call from her mother. "It's bad news; your father has died. It was a sudden heart attack last night. Your brother is with me. Now, don't go off in the deep end because I'm not feeling too good myself. There'll be arrangements to make and I'll be in touch but there's nothing more to say at the moment."

Connie put the receiver down in a state of deep shock. Her father was only sixty-five and had been perfectly fit. The pain and sense of loss were excruciating and she didn't know what to do. The telephone rang again; Connie picked up the receiver.

"Connie, it's Bella. Tim and I are about to set off for the Cotswolds for a weekend break but I have the date for next year's geology reunion and want to make sure that you and Matthew will be able to come. It's going to be held in Hertford College next May and should be lovely."

Connie tried to speak but nothing came out. She cleared her throat.

"Are you alright?" Bella asked.

Connie swallowed and, with an effort, said, "My father has died. I've only just heard."

"Oh, I'm so sorry. How awful. This certainly isn't a good moment to talk. I'll ring again next week."

"What's happened?" Connie heard Tim's voice in the background.

"Connie's father is dead."

Tim took the receiver. "Connie, is Matthew there?"

"No, he's in Zambia. The Copperbelt." She had to force the words out.

"Right, I'm coming over. I'll be there within the hour."

"Don't be ridiculous; you can't possibly go right now." Bella was furious. Connie heard no more.

Tim arrived; she opened the door and he saw the anguished devastation in her eyes. He put his arms around her and held her close. She dissolved.

It took a long time for the shuddering sobs to abate. He gently manoeuvred her into an armchair and went into the kitchen to put the kettle on. The room was large and welcoming with modern pine units and ivory worktops. It always looked light and airy, partly because there was a wide window overlooking the drive and partly because of the huge, cream tiles on the floor. The original farm table and pine dresser had been kept and they gave the room a homely feel. Tim made a mug of coffee and put it down in front of her. "Drink that. I'm going to make a couple of phone calls."

He disappeared into the study. After a few minutes, he came out and made himself some coffee. The phone rang and he answered it. Finally, he sat down opposite Connie. He smiled. "That's all fixed. Matthew's outfit will get him onto the first flight out of Ndola to Lusaka. From there, he'll be on the first flight out to Heathrow. With a bit of luck, he might be home by tomorrow evening. There's only a two-hour time difference between us."

Connie was feeling calmer. "Thank you, Tim."

"Presently, would you like me to ring your mother, to express my regrets, obviously, but also to let her know that Matthew is on his way and that you'll be in touch with her the day after tomorrow?"

"Yes, please. I'd be very grateful if you could do that. I can't bring myself to speak to her."

Tim looked a little surprised but said nothing.

"She killed him. I'm in absolutely no doubt about that. She has always been horrible to him. She has nagged, whined and sulked for as long as I can remember. He has never said a word against her and just put up with it. The constant stress would have damaged his heart. She's responsible and I'll never forgive her.

"Apart from Matthew, you're the only person I can say this to. What a fool she has been to have wasted all that potential for happiness. He was so good and so kind."

"There must have been some happiness along the way," ventured Tim, somewhat hesitantly.

"I hope there was but I can't imagine it. He was taken in by her prettiness and it was this that seemed to give her such an enormous sense of entitlement, which meant that she could take and take and take but never give anything back."

"Your father wasn't the first poor fellow to be beguiled by a woman's looks. Connie, I think you exaggerate her beauty. You are much lovelier than she could ever have been."

Connie ignored this. "She had her portrait done some years ago by an excellent artist who was also a family friend and who tried very hard to please. The oil painting was a perfect likeness but what it exposed, in a very embarrassing way, was the ugliness of the subject's character. The set of the mouth and expression in the eyes conveyed cruelty and discontent. My mother could see this and rejected the portrait. The artist tried again, straining every sinew to cast an air of benevolence on the features. She failed again. An artist can only paint what she sees even when trying to be flattering. The second attempt was also rejected and I suspect the poor woman wasn't even paid for her efforts."

"That's a tragic story, Connie, but it would be quite funny in different circumstances. Now, I'm going to make us a cheese sandwich for lunch."

Tim said he would collect the boys from school. "Would you like me to tell them about your father? In my experience, which I admit is very limited, children often react quite pragmatically to these things. If you tell them, you'll have another collapse and your distress will upset them. Being able to say that Matthew is coming home tomorrow will distract them and give them cause for cheer."

"Yes. Thank you, Tim. That's a good idea."

The school was within walking distance. Tim set off and soon Connie heard the four of them scrunching over the gravel of the drive. "What would you like for tea?" she heard Tim asking. "Cheese on toast, eggs on toast, beans on toast or sausages?"

"Can we have sausages on toast?" Ned asked.

"I don't see why not," replied Tim.

"That would be horrible," said Jamie.

"Might I make a suggestion?" Charlie asked. He was an intelligent child with a reading age far beyond his years. His current author of choice was Sir Arthur Conan Doyle and Dr Watson was his hero.

"Your suggestion will be welcomed and treated with the utmost respect," replied Tim.

"How about beans on toast with sausages thrown in?"

"An excellent proposition but we'll have to check with Mum first."

~

The rain eased off and the leafless apple trees stopped dripping. The sun shone briefly, causing the glossy leaves and buds of the rhododendron hedge surrounding the property to shimmer and sparkle before the winter darkness descended.

That night, Connie went to bed soon after the boys. She was heavy with sadness and a visceral longing for Matthew but her misery had been softened by Tim. Just as the human spirit instinctively responds to beauty, hers was consoled by his simple kindness and goodness.

Nothing was said but, one by one, the boys crept into Connie's bed. There were legs and arms everywhere but they all managed to sleep and took comfort from the closeness.

Seven

The next several months were hard for Connie. Matthew did everything in his power to comfort and support her but she was overwhelmed with sadness for the loss of her father. It was the first real hammer blow in her life which, for all its imperfections, had been comfortable and secure. She had many local friends who were kind and tried to help. She was grateful but had no time for psychobabble or the stages of grief. She knew that there were no shortcuts to recovery; the pain would have to be endured until it faded of its own accord.

Outwardly, Connie appeared to be her usual self, always saying she was fine when asked. Inwardly, there was a deadness; she had lost her capacity to find pleasure in things. She had to pretend. It was Mrs Spragg's no-nonsense approach which had the most positive effect. "He's gone," she said, "and there's absolutely nothing anyone can do about it."

Connie tried to be kind to her mother. Her initial anger had evaporated and been replaced by a wary compassion but this was often compromised. Her brother and sister-in-law, Ian and Louise, with their two children provided much practical support. They all agreed that Deirdre should move out of the large family home into something smaller and more manageable. An estate agent came around to value the property, which had developed a leak in the roof. Connie overheard her mother say, in a whining voice, "My husband would never agree to spend money on repairs."

Murderous rage was reactivated at this vile and dishonest slur. She was grievously upset on another occasion when she had been sorting through documents in her mother's desk and come across a couple of passport photos of Graham. They weren't good pictures but Deirdre glanced at them with cold eyes and downturned mouth and said, "Miserable looking sod." Connie wept for her father that night and knew, with absolute certainty, that she would never again willingly live under the same roof as her mother.

All this had a toughening-up effect and helped her resist maternal emotional blackmail. Deirdre was fond of pointing out how Asian families were much better than British ones at looking after elderly parents. Aged only sixty-four, she hardly qualified as elderly but often referred to a friend who lived with a daughter who was helped enormously as a result and extremely grateful for having the cooking and household management taken over. Deirdre would frequently point out that the additional advantage of this arrangement was the amount of money saved.

Ian and Louise took care of Christmas but the Shaws drove down at Easter to stay in the new house. They took their own bedding and towels because Deirdre still refused to have a washing machine. While Matthew and the boys went for long walks in the woods around Mapperton House, Connie spent hours adapting the sitting room curtains from the old house to fit the new. The fabric was gorgeous—pale gold floral chintz with flashes of olive green and white. Connie had bought it in a sale years before to use in her own house but Deirdre had expressed a liking for it, so Connie had handed it over.

She unpicked everything, washed the fabric at a local launderette, ironed it and, with new lining and rufflette tape, turned it into a set of new, beautiful, perfectly-fitting curtains. Matthew hung them up and the result was a triumph.

Instead of expressing appreciation, Deirdre pointed to another pile of old curtains on the floor in the corner of the room and said, in her mendicant's voice, "Well, now you've done those, perhaps you could find time to do something with all these?"

Despite everything, they got through the first six months. It took well over a year before Connie could think of her father without a painful sense of loss but by May, she was aware of a return of happiness and found herself looking forward to the Oxford reunion. She hadn't seen or spoken to Bella for ages. There had been a condolence card and a Christmas card; Matthew and Tim met up regularly for a drink. Matthew had returned to Zambia for a spell in February but a work promotion meant that, in future, he would be spending more time in the London office and less time as a field worker.

~

Matthew and Connie set off for Oxford on a fine Saturday evening, leaving the boys in the care of a member of their babysitting circle. Connie was looking very pretty in a white cotton skirt made up of panels, tiny at the top and fan-shaped at the bottom so that it swirled as she walked. Her top was a deep pink and dark blue tunic with cap sleeves and matching belt. Matthew looked smart in a dark suit and white shirt.

They parked in South Parks Road, near the science buildings, and then walked down Parks Road with the wall behind Trinity Gardens on their right and Wadham College on their left. Behind the wall, the trees rose up in their newly minted spring finery and the golden stone of the buildings was burnished to a rich lustre in the evening sunshine. Like the sap rising in the trees, Connie felt her own spirits lift with more than a hint of returning joy in the glory of being alive.

Connie held Matthew's hand or put her arm around his. Her elegant heels tap-tapped on the pavement as they crossed into Catte Street, passed the romantic Bridge of Sighs and walked through the gatehouse into the charming old quad of Hertford College. On the far side of the immaculate lawn were groups of people standing around, chatting. A table with a white cloth held glasses of wine and soft drinks. They spied Tim with a group of men and Bella was holding court with some women.

Matthew had long since given Connie a guided tour of the main old colleges. They were all beautiful, each with its own character, but Hertford was her favourite because of its cosy, homely quality. The buildings around the quad were of a classical design but the house opposite the entrance, illuminated by the evening sun, was built of rough stone with mullioned windows, although the third storey with dormer windows was rendered and painted cream. On the southern side were two fine curved archways, each with a pair of pillars, and these led into the chapel.

On the corner of the chapel was an exquisite octagonal tower, the top layered like a wedding cake. The uppermost tier was a lantern; a long, narrow window on each of the eight sides and topped with a green copper dome. The tier below was circled with pillars and had one window facing the quad. To the right of this structure could be seen the impressive dome of the Radcliffe Camera.

Matthew and Connie strolled around the velvety grass with its tulip tree at one end, stopping outside the chapel. "You carry on," she said. "I'm not quite ready yet to join the throng." She wanted to savour the surroundings, absorb the magic. Once in the crowd, you had to talk or listen and there was no time to look or feel. She gazed around. On the far side from the chapel were three-storey buildings, draped in Virginia creeper and an abundant wisteria, which was in full, scented bloom. Lovingly nurtured shrubs and spring flowers caressed the ancient walls and lapped the pathway around the lawn.

Rising above the roof of the entrance building could be seen the square tower of the Bodleian Library. To the right of the entrance was the exquisitely beautiful enclosed spiral staircase, topped with a structure shaped like a crown. Round-arched, diagonal-based, multi-paned windows appeared to be floating like clouds up a conveyor belt towards heaven.

Connie slipped through one of the arches behind her and went into the chapel. It was cool, peaceful, welcoming. The floor was marble, black and white, and laid out in the form of a maze. There were two rows of oak pews on either side of the central aisle. Above the ones at the back were ornamental oak pillars supporting a finely carved canopy which ran the full length of the pews. Beneath a high window which stretched the full width of the wall at the eastern end was the altar, behind which was a reredos of white Carrara marble carved into a depiction of the Crucifixion.

Her father had had an unostentatious and unquestioning faith. Connie felt close to him in here. She missed him badly and was still emotionally fragile. Her mother thought all religions were a load of old rubbish. Connie appreciated the cultural and philosophical aspects of Christianity but acknowledged that she was a taker of what the church offered but a poor contributor. Feeling calm and spiritually strengthened, she emerged into the quad and entered the fray.

Bella was wearing a smart navy blue and white polka dot dress and her hair looked magnificent. Connie took a drink from the table and approached Bella's group. She knew most of them rather vaguely from a previous occasion and they returned her smile.

"Hello, Bella," she said when there was a lull in the conversation.

Bella turned and gave her a cool, appraising stare. "Hi," she replied and turned away. A slight movement of her shoulder implied a metaphorical turning of the back. Connie was unprepared for the snub. She was taken aback but, whereas once she would have been cowed, she now just felt impatient. There was a side to human nature which revolted her; a tendency to ingratiate oneself into a clique and then use the power conferred by being part of a gang to exclude others. Her mother was good at this.

Her eyes roamed around the quad. Standing under a prunus tree and looking rather glum was an elderly couple. Connie wandered over. "I seem to find myself in the awkward position of having nobody to talk to. May I, please, avail myself of your company to salvage my pride?" They laughed and introduced themselves, explaining that the friends and contemporaries they'd planned to meet couldn't come because one of them was in hospital. Connie looked sympathetic. "But it's still worth coming, even so?"

"We're not sure that it is," was the morose reply.

At that point, they were joined by Matthew and Tim. "Good to see you, Harry," said Tim, shaking his hand. "I'm so sorry to hear about Angus. I hope it's nothing serious. He was a great help to me ten years ago when I was in a spot of difficulty." He turned to the others. "Angus is an expert on the Dalradian."

The conversation became quite animated; geologists usually have a lot in common. Matthew soon had them laughing uproariously with an anecdote concerning a drunken Australian cook in the outback camp. Bella materialised; smiling, glamorous and silken-voiced. She obviously thought that, by now, Connie had been punished enough and could once again be acknowledged as a friend. Bella was a shameless flirt, often targeting Matthew. Gallantry wasn't his strong point but he did his best to respond.

Connie didn't mind; she found chemistry between men and women to be generally enriching. She flirted herself with agreeable men but never with Tim, although she was very aware of his presence when in the same general area. Underneath Bella's charming surface lay a savage possessiveness, which Connie took care not to invoke.

They were summoned to dinner and Connie found Tim beside her as they walked up the spiral steps to the panelled refectory. "This staircase was designed by Sir Thomas Jackson at the beginning of the twentieth century," he said. "Apparently, he was inspired by the one on the chateau of Blois. I think he must have been a bit of a romantic, wandering around Europe and copying the best bits of their architecture. He designed the Bridge of Sighs, supposedly a copy of the Bridge of Sighs in Venice, although it looks much more like the Rialto Bridge to me. They obviously didn't worry too much about patents in those days. Jackson was also responsible for the chapel and the tower. A remarkable architect."

They found their places at polished refectory tables with candles flickering in the silver candelabra. A Grace was said, delightful in its brevity: *Benedictus benedicat, Benedicto benedicatur* May the Blessed One bless, May the Blessed One be Blessed. They sat down on the less than perfectly comfortable benches;

the sound of conversation and laughter filled the historic room and they were served with potted shrimps, roast lamb and sherry trifle. The wine and camaraderie flowed. Connie was conscious of huge privilege at being part of this. Her eyes roamed around. People looked so ordinary but there were many extraordinary intellects there. In her experience, the most sparkling of the intellects usually belonged to the most unassuming of the academics.

There was a speech and coffee. Eventually, they were told that time was running out for ordering drinks in the bar and most of them relocated.

"I think we should go now," Connie said to Matthew. "I don't want to be late for the babysitter."

"Yes, okay. I just want a quick word with someone I've just noticed. I'll be right back."

Connie saw Tim nearby, on his own. She went up to him. "I haven't thanked you properly for coming to my rescue last November. It would have been so terrible if you hadn't been there."

He gave her a look which was so full of warmth and kindness that emotion seized her. Tears filled her eyes. He put a hand on her shoulder. "It was nothing," he replied. "I was only too glad to return a favour."

Eight
1993

It was early October and four years had passed since the Oxford reunion. The four friends still met regularly; Connie and Bella would still have the occasional chat on the telephone. The Shaw family had moved to a bigger house. It had been a wrench leaving their farmhouse but the boys needed their own rooms. There had only been three bedrooms in the old house and so, if anyone came to stay, Charlie had to move out of his.

The new house had five bedrooms and a large garden. It was much closer to the centre of High Wycombe and had been built as part of a new estate among beech woods. Only ten years old and built of brick but the mock tudor front and leaded windows gave it a mellow and long-established air.

Charlie and Jamie had both been accepted by the nearby grammar school. Ned, who was ten and even brighter than his brothers, hoped to join them there the following year. For Connie, life was an unremitting routine of cooking, shopping, cleaning, washing, ironing, child supervision and gardening. Just at the moment, the garden was looking very lovely. When they moved in, it had been a rough lawn, surrounded by a few shrubs and pine trees; fine for football but aesthetically compromised. Connie had taken it in hand.

It was too soon to tackle a tidying-up operation for the coming winter. Vibrant, jewel-like colours still flashed from the dahlias. There were anemones, a second crop of alstroemerias, late roses and sprays of pure white tree poppies with their yellow stamens arching gracefully over neighbouring plants. These were still heavy with buds.

Connie was going to be forty in six months' time. It was a sort of turning point and she, increasingly, was taking stock of life. Matthew was forty-two and his career was going well. He still commuted to London and still travelled abroad, although less frequently and for shorter periods than before. He was well paid and very content with his stable family life. His weekends were taken up with cheering on his sons at their football matches, walking in the Chiltern Hills, mowing the lawn and, occasionally, taking charge of Sunday lunch.

Bella had become a fitness fanatic; jogging every day and swimming twice a week. She was strong and well-muscled. She had even taken up netball because Marina was so keen. Connie went to an aerobics class with a group of local women, all in body-hugging leotards and footless tights. They would bounce and twist and stretch and bend to catchy music, following the lead of a smiling instructress.

Tim's life was dominated by his research projects and students. He had an insatiable interest in his work and university matters but he and Matthew would still set aside time for climbing expeditions in Wales.

Connie invited a neighbour for coffee. She arrived with her baby, a sweet little girl dressed in the most exquisite clothes. Pat had been suffering badly with postnatal depression and liked to talk. Connie was a good listener. She had made things comfortable and welcoming; lighting the log stove, setting up the filter coffee machine, providing hot milk, cold milk and double cream. There were plates of cheese straws and chocolate brownies. Connie cuddled the baby while Pat described her glittering career and fascinating life. The baby was a temporary interruption and was soon going to be put into a very superior nursery.

Pat looked around the pretty sitting room and through the French windows to the garden. "This is all so pleasant," she said, "but surely it can't be enough for you."

Connie didn't know how to respond. The inference was clear. There was a deficiency of intellect in the Shaw household and someone was letting down the sisterhood. Inadequacy and a touch of envy crept into her normal composure. Connie didn't mention her recent attempt at a career because she instinctively felt that Pat wouldn't be interested.

She had applied for a job at the local school and, to her surprise and slight dismay, she'd been given it. Charlie and Jamie were both established in senior school but Ned was still at the primary stage and wasn't best pleased at the prospect of having his mother working alongside him. It was somehow damaging to his reputation.

Determined to be a success, Connie applied herself to the new life with great diligence but soon found it wasn't easy, especially when Matthew was away. Everyday life had to be planned with military precision. She got up an hour earlier and went to bed an hour later than usual. In the evening, after feeding everyone and supervising homework, she had lessons to plan and marking to do. The weekends were spent catching up on housework. There was no slack; no time for reading, gardening or leisurely shopping.

She enjoyed teaching and felt she had an aptitude for it. She didn't enjoy the mountains of paperwork or the staffroom politics. The other staff were not unfriendly but sensed that her motivation was a form of occupational therapy rather than financial necessity. Connie felt huge admiration and respect for them, especially as many had problems. There were marital difficulties and levels of depression. One of the teachers had been diagnosed with breast cancer. It was shocking.

Connie felt a creeping neurosis, often dreaming of having a mortal illness and leaving her boys motherless. One evening, while in the bath, she found a smooth, round lump in her left breast. These things always happened when Matthew was away and she felt distraught. The next day, she made an appointment to see her doctor and then rang Bella, who still had her job in a GP practice and had absorbed a fair bit of medical knowledge over the years. Bella was sympathetic and reassuring. However, when Connie rang Bella a fortnight later to say that the lump had been a harmless cyst, duly aspirated and forgotten about, she received the unsettling impression that Bella was more disappointed than relieved.

Anxiety took another turn and, again, it was when Matthew away. Connie developed an exaggerated protectiveness towards her children. She imagined intruders breaking into the house, kidnapping or hurting them. Obsessively, she checked and double-checked all the doors and windows each evening and devised plans for overcoming and disabling any dastardly felons who might even have cut her telephone wires. She slept with a hammer under her pillow. Bashing someone on the head with it would be easier than sticking a knife in them. The prospect of the resulting prison sentence didn't worry her at all.

In a joking sort of way, she explained all this to Matthew and he roared with laughter. He did, however, arrange for panic buttons to be installed by the front and back doors and on Connie's bedside. She found them a comfort.

What finally put an end to her career aspirations was a bout of 'flu. Charlie, Jamie and Ned were all struck down at the same time. Connie rang the school to say she wasn't coming in and was told that, although she herself was entitled to sick leave, she couldn't take it on behalf of her family. Other arrangements would have to be made. Very briefly, Connie considered ringing her mother but, instead, handed in her notice.

Pat left and Connie took the tray and coffee machine back to the kitchen. She'd loved her old kitchen but she loved this one, too. There were large, square, rosy terracotta tiles on the floor and the units were white. The sun broke through the clouds, flooding the garden with brilliance. Connie poured the rest of the coffee into a large mug, put a chunk of cheese, a tomato and an apple into the dish with the remaining cheese straws and took it all outside to the swing-seat on the terrace.

She rocked gently, pondering. A maple tree was changing colour; in a few weeks, it would be a brilliant, hectic red. The Virginia creeper draping the garage was ahead of it, already a deep, pinkish scarlet, almost the same colour as the kitchen floor. A robin hopped around her feet and she gave him a fragment of cheese. A woodpecker was looking for something in the lawn and a couple of squirrels chased each other around the apple tree. The air smelled sweet and it was very quiet.

How did one define and measure what was 'enough'? Sitting there in the sunshine, it was enough just to be alive. Being with people other than Matthew and her boys, who always made her feel that she was enough, often induced a feeling that she should be trying harder. The prevailing consensus was that 'people' were all-important but she had discovered that she could actually bear to live without most of them. They were often a source of pleasure and interest but they could also be a source of irritation, misery and destruction.

Having said that, she was naturally friendly and enjoyed being sociable. She remembered her mother's advice on how to behave. "You must cultivate people," Deirdre had said, making movements with her fingers as if she were mixing butter and flour to make a crumble. Well, Connie had no intention of trying to cultivate people or of being cultivated by them. She would just carry on as normal. It was enough.

That night, Matthew and Connie were in bed having swapped the light summer duvet for a middle weight one; it was very snug beneath the cloud of goose down. The window onto the garden was wide open; they could hear rain pattering on the canopy of the swing-seat below and the rustling noise of eddies of fallen leaves being blown around.

"I'm going to be too hot," said Matthew, stripping off his pyjamas and throwing them on the floor. "In the interests of health and safety, I think you should take off your nightgown." She slipped out of it and lay on her back. He languorously caressed her breasts.

"I wish we'd had more money to spend on nice clothes for the boys when they were little," she said. "They always looked like little ragamuffins."

"Rosy-cheeked ones, though," he replied. "They always looked fine to me. If we'd wasted a load of money on clothes then, we probably wouldn't be able to pay the mortgage on this place now."

"I'm going to ask you a simple question and I want an honest answer."

"Have I ever been less than honest?"

"I usually have complete faith in your integrity but you did tell my mother that you enjoyed her concoction of pasta shells with tuna; the dish that gave us all food poisoning."

"I admit to perjuring myself on that occasion."

"Well, what I want to know is, do you find me boring?"

"No."

"Should I get a job, not necessarily teaching?"

"You must do whatever you like but life is more fun for all of us when you're not working. I don't want anything to change."

The trajectory of his hand moved downwards. His lips brushed her shoulder and he moved closer. Connie asked no more questions.

Nine

The post dropped through the letter box just as Connie was about to open the door. She gathered it up and dumped it on the hall table. It was the usual load of junk except for a white envelope addressed in exquisite handwriting that she didn't recognise. It would have to wait. If she was late for her pottery class, all the best wheels would be taken. She drove to the local College of Further Education, parked her car and set off up a path carrying a bag containing a box of tools and one of Matthew's old shirts.

This class was the purest recreational delight for Connie. Enthusiasts of all ages gathered in the great room with its huge windows and furnished with tables and electric potter's wheels. It was run by a small, pretty, rounded woman who welcomed, demonstrated and encouraged with unfaltering generosity. She was a brilliant ceramicist and to watch her at work was awe-inspiringly thrilling. The skill and artistry of many of the outwardly modest people in the class were extraordinary.

Connie bagged her favourite wheel by a window, next to Nicholas, a quiet Yorkshire man. After several weeks of sitting next to him, she'd discovered that he was a mathematician, retired from a prestigious university. He didn't talk much but if Connie spoke to him, he always responded pleasantly in his gentle northern voice. He emanated an affable companionability and calm; there was no discomfort in their, sometimes, long silences. "Good morning, Nick."

"Morning, Connie."

Connie slipped Matthew's shirt over her head and rolled up the sleeves. She went over to a table which held a great slab of grey clay and cut off six chunks with a cheese wire. She proceeded to wedge and pummel them to remove any lumps or air bubbles. She carried the softened, creamy balls to her wheel and then collected a bowl with water and a sponge. She threw the first ball onto the wheel head, where it landed with a satisfying thud. She squeezed some water onto it and pressed the foot pedal. With fingers interlaced around the clay and thumbs on top, she massaged the spinning lump into a cone shape. She pressed it down and brought it back up again, repeating the sequence several times.

She loved the sensual feeling of the clay responding to the pressure of her hands. When it was thoroughly centred and kneaded, she paused.

"How are things with you, Nick?" He was making an enormous pot for a garden plant and it was taking a considerable amount of strength, more than any woman would have.

"I've been in trouble this week," he replied.

"What sort of trouble?"

"Well, my wife and I had our grandchildren to stay at the end of the summer holidays and found them distinctly tiresome. Instead of playing in the garden, climbing trees, making dens and walking the dog, all they wanted to do was watch television all day. They would fight quite viciously over who should have the remote. They were very picky about food and generally disagreeable. Fran was exhausted by the end of the week and we were both very relieved when they left. I mentioned this to some friends last week and Fran was livid. I've been instructed to set the record straight at the earliest opportunity. That is a euphemism for telling these friends a bunch of fibs about how delightful we always find the children and what an absolute joy it was having them to stay."

"I suppose that might be a small price to pay for a return to domestic harmony."

"Yes, but nobody will be fooled and it's completely idiotic."

Connie laughed. This had been an unusually long speech from Nick. She liked him. His beautiful creations ranged from small and delicate vases to massive containers, all churned out with apparent effortlessness. He withheld all judgement on her own efforts and, for this, she was grateful. She knew that some pieces of her work were less bad than others but that all were substandard. He wouldn't insult her with the insincerity of fake praise.

Wetting the clay and with arms resting on the wheel surround, she cupped her hands around the spinning cone with her thumbs on top. Gently, she pushed a thumb into the centre and down towards the base. She pushed the clay away from her to open it up. With her thumb, she evened out and thinned the floor, then released the clay and stopped the wheel.

Wetting the clay again and pressing the pedal, she repositioned her hands so that the fingers of her right hand on the outside wall were opposite those of her left hand on the inside wall. Slowly and smoothly, she lifted the clay into a cylinder shape. All seemed to be going well, but then, it suddenly collapsed.

"Bother!"

"Better luck next time," said Nick as Connie scooped the clay off the wheel, wiped over the wheel with the sponge and reached for the next ball.

She turned to Nick. "Did you know that the earliest ceramic objects found date back to 29,000 BC? I read that recently somewhere."

"No, I didn't know that but I do know that a potter's wheel was in use at least as early as 400 BC."

Connie threw the next ball of clay onto the wheel and started the whole process again. "I have also read that the idea of clay pots probably started in prehistoric times when people would line their woven baskets with clay for carrying water. When these dried out, the clay linings would shrink and could be used as bowls. It was then found that baking the bowls in hot ashes hardened and strengthened them so that they could be used for storing and transporting things."

"That sounds entirely feasible." Nick usually agreed with her.

Connie had better luck with her second attempt and produced an acceptable vase with rounded base, narrow middle and wide-mouthed top. She slipped a cheese wire beneath it and transferred it to a wooden bat. She continued with the next ball of clay and eventually carried four respectable creations on separate bats into the drying room.

She recovered two of the best bowls from the previous week and set about refining them. This process was very enjoyable. With the first bowl centred upside down and secured on the wheel, she used a cutting tool to remove surplus clay and carve out an elegant foot at its base. Much of the crudeness disappeared and the result was pleasing. She repeated the process with the second bowl. These were now ready to be biscuit-fired, glazed, refired and, finally, pronounced complete.

Three completed works of art, started some weeks previously, were carefully wrapped in Matthew's shirt at the end of the session. They'd been glazed with Chun blue and she had even painted on some white flowers. They looked horrible but she would take them home for display, like a child with grotesque daubs from Playgroup. After they had been duly admired, they would be hidden on a shelf at the back of the garage with the other rejects.

~

That evening, they sat around the kitchen table while Connie served up spaghetti bolognaise. The delicious sauce was made of best Aberdeen Angus minced beef, cooked with onions, tomatoes, rich beef stock and herbs. Her three latest bowls containing, respectively, grated parmesan, chopped parsley and finely-sliced spring onions were placed in the middle of the table.

"Mum, I think a Neanderthal would be very proud to eat the fruits of his foraging expedition out of one of your bowls," said Charlie.

"I'll take that as a compliment," replied Connie. "More and more information is coming to light suggesting that Neanderthals were far more advanced and civilised than generally given credit for."

Meals were noisy affairs with the boys trying to outdo each other with feeble jokes. They had enormous appetites. Pudding consisted of large vol-au-vent cases taken out of the freezer, cooked to a crisp and then filled with hot, velvety smooth apple purée made from windfalls collected from under the Bramley tree. Double cream was liberally poured on the top.

The boys went off to do their homework, leaving Matthew and Connie to clear away.

"We've had an invitation," she said.

"That sounds ominous."

"It's on the mantelpiece in the sitting room. That's where one is supposed to put these things. When I went to Pat's house, I saw at least six of them all lined up."

"How terrible." Matthew was genuinely appalled.

They went through with mugs of coffee and he picked up the card.

"So," he said, "a fortieth birthday party for Bella, hosted by her parents and held in a posh London hotel. It says, 'In Costume'. What does that mean?"

"I didn't notice that. It means fancy dress. Oh dear, that complicates things. What on earth are we going to wear?"

"Haven't a clue." What to wear for things was absolutely the lowest item on Matthew's list of priorities.

"I'll think of something." Connie's mind was a total blank. "I'll write and say we're coming. We'll have to buy a present. It will have to be something that Bella hasn't already got, which makes it difficult."

Ten

The first inklings of real dread crept into Connie's mind as she and Matthew climbed a grand staircase leading from the entrance hall of a prestigious London hotel. The couple in front of them were in full evening dress. There must be a different sort of function going on somewhere else.

A seed of anxiety had been sown earlier on. The babysitter had been gratifyingly reassuring. She had laughed out loud and pronounced them definite contenders for first prize. Charlie, torn between outrage at having a babysitter and pleasure at the prospect of playing chess with her, especially as she wasn't very good, said, "You look great in my shirt, Dad."

Jamie, cuddling up to Connie, said, "You look lovely, Mum."

Ned had looked worried. "I think Dad looks a bit stupid."

Inspiration about costumes struck a couple of days after receiving the invitation. Connie, an avid reader, tended to alternate modern fiction with the classics, all of which she'd read in her teens but which yielded up even richer delights when read again twenty years later. She'd just finished *The Forsyte Saga* by John Galsworthy and was replacing it in the bookshelf, which was more or less arranged in alphabetical order, when her eyes rested on her collection of Thomas Hardy novels. She and Matthew would go as Gabriel Oak and Bathsheba Everdene. Everyone she knew had loved the film *Far from the Madding Crowd* with Julie Christie and Alan Bates.

It would be easy. She had the perfect dress for a rustic heroine. She'd found it in a charity shop for five pounds and never worn it. It was a Laura Ashley creation made of blue and white cotton, long, flounced, lace-trimmed, low-necked and small-waisted. She had a most becoming straw hat with a wide brim and trimmed with flowers. This was also from Laura Ashley but had cost five times as much as the dress. At the back of Ned's toy cupboard were several fluffy toy lambs, no longer played with but too sweet to throw out. She would attach these to her waist band with blue ribbon.

Matthew would wear his brown corduroy trousers with string tied below the knees. Charlie owned a baggy, cream, linen, homespun shirt with no collar but just a few buttons below the neck and Matthew could borrow this. Charlie was nearly six feet tall now, so there wouldn't be a problem with size. Perhaps, a cotton scarf casually knotted to set things off. Connie had a suitable hat; brown lambskin, meant to be worn with the brim turned up but, with the brim turned down, it looked like a flowerpot. She briefly wondered about suggesting a brown, curly wig. She'd acquired this on a whim and it was in a cupboard somewhere but she decided that it would stop the hat fitting comfortably. Matthew would wear a low-slung belt with a few more of the little lambs attached.

The couple in front walked along a wide passageway until coming to a door. There were balloons outside and a sign which read 'Bella's Birthday Party'. The couple turned in. A low hum of voices emanated from the interior; no music, no laughter.

Connie clutched Matthew's hand. "I think we'd better turn around and go home before it's too late. I've made a terrible mistake."

"Nonsense," he replied. "I've been looking forward to this. I haven't been to a fancy-dress party since I was a child."

They went into an anteroom which had a rack of coat-hangers on one side and a table for presents on another. Connie put their prettily wrapped parcel, containing an expensive black evening bag, on the pile. She peered through the door into the main room and failed to see anyone else in fancy dress, apart from one or two men dressed as dashing cavaliers and a couple of women in crinolines. Everybody else seemed to be in black ties and elegant evening gowns.

The couple in front were being loudly announced by an usher.

"Mr and Mrs Frederick Philpot."

Connie found herself praying, *Dear God, I rescind all that rubbish about not believing in You. I think we might need a bit of help this evening.*

The usher asked Matthew for their names. "Dr and Mrs Matthew Shaw," he replied. Connie spied Tim and Bella on the far side of the room and they weren't in fancy dress. They were standing next to an elderly couple, presumably Bella's parents. Bella's mother looked straight at them. "Who are those people, Arabella?" Her voice was clearly audible.

"Please don't give those names," Connie whispered urgently to the usher. "Please introduce us as Mr and Mrs Gabriel Oak." In a stentorian voice, he obligingly did as she asked. Connie had had a sudden fear that the press might be there. They did turn up sometimes at society events and Matthew might find himself in trouble for damaging the reputation of his company. She looked inappropriate but he looked ludicrous. He was oblivious to the cruel nature of the social catastrophe. He didn't care; he never noticed what people wore but, also, he had a childlike faith in her judgement about these matters. She had betrayed him.

"Matthew," she said in an undertone. "I can't face that formal reception line-up." She'd seen Tim's expression changing from one of bland politeness to a rictus of pure delight when he'd noticed them. She thought that Bella was looking a bit stony while the parents maintained their air of good breeding. "You'll have to go on your own but I think you should take off your hat. I've already dumped mine and yours is completely beyond the pale."

"I'm keeping it on," he said. "I'd be incomplete without it."

"Okay, but I'm off to find a window to throw myself out of."

"See you later on, then." Connie moved through the crowd. She didn't know anyone but had learned how to cope with people who hadn't the slightest interest in her. She took a glass of wine offered by a smiling waiter. She usually opted for fruit juice but alcohol was a requirement for this evening. She felt acutely stressed. Damn and blast all these complacent morons standing in groups, looking so dignified and confident. Social events were a strange sort of ritualised torture. It was okay for the young and single to have parties.

There was a purpose to it; they would be hunting for a mate and there would be fun and flirtation and pheromones floating around. Try a bit of friendly banter with a married man, however, and the full weight of his wife's disapproval could soon poison the atmosphere.

She wandered around seeking a friendly face or kindly eyes. There would be a few out there but they were difficult to find and most people were huddled in little exclusion zones. People wanted to be thought interesting. How often had she been told about a book that was absolutely fascinating or a place that was simply delightful but, on eagerly tracking them down, had found the reality sadly disappointing.

There were the eye-swivellers; people who couldn't find time to look at you because they were too busy seeking out someone less dull. There were the battering rams who would never let you get a word in edgeways and there were the socially accomplished couples who worked as a team. They would stand very straight, have little smiles and speak through barely open lips, emitting staccato phrases of a singular meaninglessness, giving each other cues to make it seem spontaneous.

People became less entertaining as they grew older. Connie had been to a school reunion recently and chatted to the girl who had been the funniest mimic in the class and had told the rudest jokes. She had evolved into a travesty of her former self and was now conventional and humourless. Connie wandered slowly through the little groupings, all boring each other to death, and admired her surroundings. The room was beautiful with lustrous wood panelling and a soft rose carpet. There were chandeliers and great gilt-framed mirrors. The wall lights were antique brass, dripping with crystal pendants and there were lavishly draped windows down one side. She would go and see what the curtains were lined with.

Their house in High Wycombe had been left in good condition. She and Matthew had put a coat of cream emulsion on all the walls and replaced the carpets. Connie had made new curtains for all the rooms except the sitting room. She had bought the fabric but it needed interlining and she hadn't done that before. She was peeking behind the edge of the gold damask when she heard a soft voice. "Hi, Bathsheba."

Turning, she saw a woman of about her own age smiling at her.

"Hello," she replied. "Thank you for speaking to me. I'd given up hope of anyone doing that."

"I'm Anna Hunt. My husband, Daniel, is a geochemist and knows Tim. I don't know anybody." Her voice had the gentle, undulating cadence of someone from the southern United States.

Connie held out her hand. "I'm Connie Shaw. Matthew and I go back a long way with Tim and Bella."

"When you two came through that door, I felt a bolt of real joy go through me. All the formality, stuffiness and constraint evaporated. It was so funny."

"It was a moment of terrible mortification for me. I don't think I can ever recover. We seem to be the only people here who aren't dressed properly."

Anna was wearing a green velvet evening dress, which would have been stunning on a fuller figure. She had short fair hair, very white teeth and blue eyes which held a look of vulnerability. She appeared under-nourished, physically and spiritually. "I'm from South Carolina," she said. "I met Daniel there when he was on holiday a few years ago. It's a second marriage for us both. So, what are you when you're not Mrs Oak?"

Connie thought for a moment. Could she claim to be a potter or a school teacher? Not really. "After some earnest reflection," she replied, "it pains me to have to admit that I am a 'nothing'. What are you?"

"I'm a fraud." They both laughed. "Back home," she continued, "I was a practicing lawyer. I can't get that sort of work here, so I did a Garden Design course. People pay me to tell them what to plant in their gardens. What I don't tell them is that there are no shortcuts with gardening. Keeping them looking good involves hours of hard labour, grubbing around on hands and knees with a weeding tool, deadheading, watering and so on. My own garden is a disgrace." She paused. "Let me make a guess about you. You have children?"

"Yes, I have three boys."

"And they are all highly intelligent?"

"They are very bright but I don't boast about that."

"Why not?"

"Because it would irritate people."

"You worry about irritating other people?"

"All the time, yes."

"Why?"

"My mother has always been prone to extreme irritability and I've learned how not to provoke it. I live with an intrinsic sense of unworthiness and a fear of being a nuisance but I'm used to it."

"Does your husband make you feel unworthy?"

"Matthew? No, never."

"So, your definition of someone who loves you is someone who never makes you feel unworthy?"

"I've never really thought about it but I think that would be quite a good definition."

"And your boys, do they make you feel unworthy?"

"No, they don't. However, when they grow up and get girlfriends, partners or wives, they'll then find themselves reliably informed that I have been a neglectful parent with all the wrong ideas about nutrition and politics and they'll wonder how on earth they've managed to survive their childhood."

"You are wonderfully cynical."

"No, I'm not; just realistic. How do you find living in Oxford? Have you settled in alright?"

"Yes, I've been fine for the most part. We rent a little house in Summertown. The trouble is, Daniel has a bit of a drink problem which can make life difficult at times. He's half-cut at the moment and will be ogling Bella and making a fool of himself. I don't know why I'm telling you this; I haven't told anyone else. Bella doesn't exactly encourage him but she likes to be admired. Don't we all?"

Connie didn't quite know how to respond. "It's interesting how easy it is to say things to a total stranger that you would never confide to a friend. Have you thought of leaving him?"

"Oh no." Anna's eyes widened in horror. "We've only got each other. I just put up with it."

"Would you like to have lunch with me one day? You could admire all the weeds and poor design in my garden."

"I'd love to," replied Anna. "You Brits are wonderful. I often hear things like 'you must come to dinner' or 'we must get together' but, usually, nothing ever happens."

"Well, good intentions go a long way." Connie laughed.

"But I'm expected to say 'everyone has been so kind'."

"Oh yes, a bit of grovelling gratitude never goes amiss." Connie paused. "I mean it, though. We could meet at the Garden Centre, which is easy to find, have a coffee and a look around. Then, you could follow me home and we'll have lunch. Just something simple, like soup and bread and cheese. Have you got anything to write on?"

Anna fished a notebook and biro out of her bag and they exchanged addresses and telephone numbers.

"I don't like to be pushy," said Connie. "I'll wait for you to ring me. If I haven't heard from you during the next three weeks, I'll ring you. Then, if you feel that you'd rather not come, that'll be fine and I shan't be at all offended."

Anna smiled. An extremely handsome man approached. He gave Connie a little bow and an appraising look while taking Anna's arm in a peremptory way that somehow lacked chivalry. "Come," he said. "There's someone I want you to meet."

~

Connie decided that an exploratory foray to find the ladies powder room might be a good use of time. She wasn't disappointed. It was a haven of pink, scented warmth, with mirrors under flattering lighting, tissues, flowers, bottles of scent and hand cream. There was even an armchair in one corner. If she had a book or some knitting, she would be perfectly happy to spend the rest of the evening in there. She sat in the chair for as long as she decently could but eventually emerged back into the corridor where she saw Tim standing at the far end.

She had a feeling that he'd been waiting for her but, as he had been, at least partly, responsible for her sartorial discomfort, she was in no mood to treat him with anything other than coolness. As she approached, she drew herself up into a haughty posture. Tim was reminded of her regal stance before the Rosa Waltz many years before. He looked at her unsmiling face. She hadn't changed at all over the years. Her deep brown eyes, generous mouth, firm chin and glossy helmet of dark hair were the same. She was as slender as ever but the neckline of her dress showed to advantage her previously unseen opulence of form.

She had an aura of sensual awareness and fulfilment. If he hadn't known better, Tim would have described it as an aura of sensual invitation. She wasn't conscious of it.

"Matthew and I have brought shame and ignominy onto your noble family. I take full responsibility and offer an unreserved apology."

"Connie, if I thought there was an atom of sincerity in your apology, I would be seriously worried."

"You and Bella shouldn't invite people to a fancy-dress party and not bother to make an effort yourselves."

"We have made an effort."

"No, you haven't."

"Yes, we have."

"What are you supposed to be then?"

"I am a demon. If you observe closely, you will see two little black horns sticking out of my head."

Connie hadn't noticed them.

"Bella is an angel. She has diaphanous wings on her back and a halo."

Connie hadn't noticed those either.

"Well," she said. "I think those are pitiful travesties of fancy dress."

"Connie, if you knew how close I was to slitting my throat from boredom before you and Matthew turned up, you would moderate your ferocity. This whole thing was thought up by Bella's parents. She didn't want to hurt their feelings and this is how they like to do parties. Bella thought the 'In Costume' bit would liven things up but it's had the opposite effect. Some people have made an effort. Bella's older brother and his wife are Napoleon and Josephine. Her younger brother and his wife, Cecily, are Charles the First and his queen."

"Well, if she's supposed to be Henrietta Maria, I hope she's got the teeth right. According to Sophia of Hanover, they stuck out of her mouth like tusks."

"Trust you to know something like that."

"Are they still resident in the parental home?"

"Oh no. There was a most upsetting incident which is never alluded to. There was an outbreak of vermin. Cecily woke up one morning to find a mouse on her pillow. They packed their things and moved out immediately."

Connie looked very directly at Tim. He raised his eyebrows with an air of innocence. She smiled and he smiled back.

An angel appeared, one with a silken voice and glittering eyes.

"What are you two doing, loitering in the corridor? Come and join in the fun. We're about to cut the cake."

~

On the way home, Connie said, "I made a new friend this evening."

"Oh, good. I think I managed to lose a few."

"How come?"

"They were jealous of my outfit. Some people just can't take being outshone. Incidentally, I'm absolutely ravenous. There wasn't any food."

"There were a few trays of canapés as well as the birthday cake but you can't expect anything as vulgar as food at a posh party. We'll make a sandwich when we get home."

Eleven

At the end of three weeks, there had been no phone call from Anna. Connie tried ringing her several times but there was no answer. Perhaps, she was on holiday. Connie waited another week, ringing frequently at different times of the day. She didn't want to be thought of as someone who issued bogus invitations.

Eventually, she rang Bella. "There were some friends of yours at the party called Daniel and Anna. I had a long chat with Anna and she's supposed to be coming to lunch but I can't get hold of her. The phone is never answered."

"Anna has left Daniel," replied Bella. "She just packed her things and went back to the States. Daniel has moved out of their rented house and is living in college. He's good fun but I always thought Anna was a bit of a drip."

"I liked her," said Connie. "I don't suppose you have her new address?"

"No, I don't have it and I don't fancy asking Daniel for it. I think he's feeling a bit sensitive at the moment. Incidentally, Connie, what's all this about us going on holiday together next summer?"

"I have absolutely no idea." Connie was bemused.

"Tim met up with Matthew for a beer in their usual pub last week and is now saying that they both agreed on what a good idea it would be to have a joint holiday in Corsica next July. The thing is, we don't normally go on holiday with other people. Marina goes to stay with her cousins at Easter and has a wonderful time; they get on really well but we prefer to be on our own as a family if we go away in the summer."

Connie also preferred not to holiday with anyone else but she didn't say so.

"Perhaps, there's been a misunderstanding. I'll ask Matthew."

He looked a bit sheepish when she raised the subject after the boys had gone to bed later that evening. "I hoped the whole thing would just go away because I knew you wouldn't be keen. In the pub, I told Tim we were thinking of booking up for Corsica again, with a week in the mountains and a week by the sea. I then asked him if he had any plans. He said that Bella was insisting on either

Disneyland or Centre Parcs. He sounded so wretched that I jokingly asked if they would like to come with us instead and he looked like a condemned man who'd suddenly had a reprieve."

Connie looked very doubtful.

"They are our oldest friends after all," he said in what Connie considered to be an unbecomingly sentimental voice. "Tim's also concerned about Marina. She's going through an 'ugly duckling' phase. Half her friends look like famine victims but Marina's a bit tubby and has wild hair, which she refuses to do anything about. Bella gets impatient because she makes no effort to help herself."

"Poor girl," said Connie with feeling, remembering her own adolescence. "I'll have to think about all this."

"Yes, of course," Matthew replied, waving his hand with a magnanimous flourish, reckoning that half the battle was already won with his subtle reference to Marina.

"It could turn out to be a catastrophe and the end of a long friendship," continued Connie. "Also, you'd have to accept the narrative that you begged Tim and his family to come because you couldn't face the boredom of being with your own family once again."

Matthew laughed. "Just give it some thought."

Connie did. In a group, it took only one person to spoil things for the rest of the party. Bella had already struck a sour note by saying that she preferred not to share family holidays. In everyday life but especially on holiday, Connie tried to maintain a mental equilibrium. Negative thoughts, she knew, were part of the human condition. She would acknowledge her own, confront them, analyse them, deal with them, or, if necessary, put up with them. She was prepared to sympathise with such thoughts in others and to help if she could but what she didn't like were random dissatisfactions being weaponised to undermine the happiness of innocent parties.

On holiday, as well as being free from the humdrum activities of daily life, Connie enjoyed not having to appease others with ego massage and the suppression of her own opinions. She liked freedom from superfluous communication and freedom to enjoy, without interruption, the natural beauty and historical significance of her surroundings. She wanted peace, time to read and time to think or not to think. All these selfish wants might be under threat. Various little vignettes from previous holidays passed into Connie's mind.

There had been the young mother with a loutish husband, two little boys and a churlish mother-in-law staying in the Cevennes. The stone hotel was at the economical end of the market but in a beautiful location. The large terrace with a parapet overlooked a dramatic gorge with a thin, silver ribbon of a river weaving along far below. The Shaw family had stopped for a drink and while Matthew admired the scenery, Connie observed the clientèle, which comprised a number of elderly people having fun throwing water out of upstairs windows onto their pals below.

She'd been relieved to see this unusual behaviour, having always understood that idiocy was the preserve of the British. Matthew had told her of an incident during a skiing holiday with some university friends in the French Alps. They'd been having lunch in the sunshine, sitting on the wide veranda of a restaurant, when a young man on skis but completely naked shot past them. The French people on the neighbouring table shrugged their shoulders and did that little popping pout with their lips. "C'est un Anglais," said one of them.

The little family gathered for a modest dinner. The mother had changed into a pretty dress and piled up her blonde hair. She wished for graciousness, conversation, perhaps a little charm, even a bit of glamour. She didn't get them. Husband and mother-in-law slouched sullenly to the table, having made no effort to smarten up; she received no smiles, no compliments. The children were quietly accepting, as that was the only choice open to them. They all ate in silence. Connie had a savage desire to seize the husband and mother-in-law and hurl them both over the parapet. That would teach them a lesson; selfish pigs.

On another holiday, Connie had observed an angelic woman in the airport lounge waiting for the flight home. She must have been in her early forties and looked pale and exhausted. She was playing cards with two young children. Strutting around in the vicinity was a virile and handsome middle-aged man with two beautiful teenage girls in tow. Connie surmised that these were the product of a former marriage. With glowing complexions and lustrous hair, they made a painful contrast with their faded stepmother, who, Connie was convinced, had spent the whole holiday putting the needs of everyone else before her own.

It wasn't always women having a hard time. Strolling around a French street market, having left Matthew and the boys in a café, she heard a young English man say to a woman, "Look, there are some of those pretty plates like the ones in our gîte. Shall we buy one to replace the dish we smashed the other day?"

"No, why should we?" was the whining reply. "We've paid enough for the gîte already." So depressing. A mean-spirited remark like that could blight the happiness of a whole day. To be permanently shackled to such a mindset would result in a life of spiritual deficiency far worse than any material deprivation.

Despite misgivings, Connie was very well aware that now the offer of a shared holiday had been made, it could not be withdrawn without causing offence. The party of eight assembled in the departure lounge of Gatwick Airport the following July.

~

The departure lounge was fairly full by the time the Shaws had passed through security but Connie spotted the Melroses sitting at the far end. She hadn't seen Marina for many months and could now understand why Bella wasn't happy with her daughter's hair. It was wild; a huge mass of dark curls sticking out in all directions, like a busby. There was a tangible cloud of tension around the family, with Tim sitting in the middle as if to keep the peace.

As they approached, Charlie tripped over the laces which had come undone on one of his trainers. Accident-prone and a natural clown, he lay spreadeagled on the floor with no sense of embarrassment or loss of dignity. There was no scrambling up with furtive looks around to see who'd noticed. Marina put her hand in front of her mouth and giggled in a way that Charlie found very pleasing. Bella laughed; a spontaneous and joyous sound. Tim looked at Connie, who was rolling her eyes, his expression a mix of suppressed humour and also something else. It was gratitude.

Matthew, Jamie and Ned stepped over Charlie and found seats. They were used to his antics and ignored them. After a suitably dramatic pause, Charlie stood up and beamed at everyone.

Once on the plane, they bagged four pairs of seats on the left-hand side so that they would get a view of the French Alps. Charlie shot into the seat next to Marina. Bella, who was looking fresh and lovely with a crisp white blouse over her jeans, sat with Tim behind them. They had stayed in the Hilton the night before and were well-rested and full of a good breakfast. Then came Jamie and Ned and at the back were Connie and Matthew.

Connie wasn't feeling glamorous. She was in a short denim skirt and a stripey top; no make-up and no earrings. It had been an early start and there had been no time.

She did up her seatbelt and closed her eyes. Getting the house clean, the garden under control and everyone packed up had been an effort. She was tired. The boys were supposed to do their own packing but she didn't trust them to do it properly. They didn't understand the need to have at least eight days' supply of clean underwear and t-shirts because there would be no access to a washing machine until they reached the villa during the second week.

Ned had grumbled to Matthew. "Dad, Mum seems to think that the most important thing in the world is having clean pants."

"Believe me," replied Matthew, "I know all about this weird fetish. A few years ago, I was at a conference in Washington and sitting around the breakfast table with about eight other guys. Some were businessmen, some were academics and there were one or two really tough-looking fellows off an oil-rig. A uniformed page-boy came in and handed me a parcel, which had arrived by Special Delivery. I opened it in front of everyone and what do you think was in it?"

"No idea."

"Eight pairs of brand-new underpants."

"Gosh. How embarrassing!" Ned was squeaking with shock.

"It most certainly was. They all found it most amusing but I still suffer from post-traumatic stress disorder just thinking about it. Mum had found a pile of my pants in the airing cupboard after I'd left for the airport and freaked out at the thought of me being without them."

It had been a stressful summer for Connie. Matthew's parents had come to stay in the middle of Charlie's GCSEs, just when she'd wanted maximum calm. She wasn't really worried about him because he was clever. Trouble was, he knew he was clever and thought he could get away without doing much work. Despite her pleas and remonstrations, he seemed to spend all his spare time playing computer games, using a gadget called a joystick.

Paul and Laura made no allowances and seemed more demanding than ever. In her twenties, Connie had been anxious to please and happy to indulge them. Now that she was forty, instead of feeling more patient and compassionate due to their advancing years, she was becoming increasingly infuriated at being taken so much for granted. She was handed a bag of sweets when they came through the front door and then treated like an unpaid servant.

It helped to make imaginary plans for retribution. Her exasperation was mostly directed at Matthew's mother. His father was a kindly old buffer whose worst crimes involved hinting about her extravagance. He would interrogate her about the price of sugar and cheap cuts of meat. She had no idea about either. Also, he would keep insisting that Matthew was 'up to his eyes' even when he had nothing to do, while Connie was presumed to be permanently available for the latest demand.

The following summer, Connie was planning to get a job; nothing high-powered but the local Garden Centre was always advertising for people. Then, she would be able to say, in a bright voice, "It will be lovely to see you, as always, but you will have to make your own beds, clean your own rooms, do your own laundry, shopping, cooking and washing-up. If you get bored, there are always things to do in the garden. You won't be able to grumble about having a barbecue instead of a Sunday roast or be rude about my bacon baps because of them having no butter inside.

"You won't be able to raid the fridge and pinch that delicious leftover pudding made of bananas, nuts, chocolate and cream, that I'd saved especially for Jamie, because I wouldn't have made it in the first place. I'm afraid that things are different here now because I'm 'werking', I'm 'werking'."

After this childish internal rant, Connie dozed off until being woken by Matthew saying that they were flying over Paris. Then, coffee and a snack arrived, for which she was pathetically grateful. Her stress levels were dropping.

They rose again at Ajaccio Airport, which seemed ramshackle and primitive after Gatwick. The crowded baggage hall was oppressively hot. Matthew elbowed his way to the carousel while Tim and Connie went in search of trolleys. They eventually found a stack in the middle of the car park and swooped in triumph, only to find them shackled together. "Oh, bugger," said Tim. "I've only got notes." They looked at each other as if to confirm that they'd dealt with worse crises than this one. It was a curiously intimate look.

"Matthew has some ten-franc coins," said Connie. "You wait here and I'll be back in a couple of minutes." She sped off. Tim watched her retreating form, noting that from behind, with her short skirt and slim legs, she didn't look any older than Marina.

After lengthy formalities at the car rental desk, they took possession of a multi-seater Citroen. They circled the car park twice before finding an exit, took an embarrassingly long time working out how to get the barrier to rise and headed off to the main road for Corte.

"Please shut your window, Bella, or the air-conditioning won't work." Matthew was driving and fiddling with knobs on the dashboard.

"But I'm boiling hot. I must have the breeze."

"If you shut your window, the car will very soon feel cool."

"Sorry, but I'll stifle if I shut the window. You're welcome to shut yours but mine stays open."

Tim leaned across and shut it firmly. There was a tense silence for about three minutes and then, "It's freezing in here. You'll have to turn the fan down or it'll play havoc with my sinusitis."

~

They stopped for a late lunch at a roadside pizzeria and sat under large cream parasols and evergreen oaks. Exotic lilies flamed from terracotta urns; service was slow. Tim took over the driving. The road writhed and wriggled up towards the Pass of Vizzavona with Monte d'Oro on their left. The view was spectacular and they stopped in a car park where there were a couple of stalls selling goat's cheese and cold drinks.

The mountain towered over them. "Two thousand three hundred and eighty-nine metres," said Matthew, "but by no means the highest. The highest is Monte Cinto at two thousand seven hundred metres at the top of the Asco Valley."

Tim and Connie exchanged a glance. They both knew about Matthew's obsession and how he knew the exact height of almost every mountain in the world. Bella looked unimpressed. She thought the great mass of granite looked arid and hostile and said so to Connie in an undertone. Connie nodded. "I don't think we're going to be required to climb it."

The crystal clarity of the air and brilliant blue of the sky were exhilarating. They drove on through forests of beech, pine and sweet chestnut until they reached Vivario. Like many Corsican villages, it had a slight air of neglect. Houses in shades of ochre and stone, with unpainted shutters, stood close together on either side of the street. A few small grocery shops displayed their fruit and vegetables on the pavement under awnings. A café was found in a quiet lane, its garden shaded by a pergola of vines; the purple fruit nestling in clusters among the bright foliage. There were no other people. Connie and Bella pulled two tables together and arranged the chairs. They were served with iced drinks and it was peaceful. Everyone was at ease.

Matthew drove the last stretch to Corte. As they rounded the final bend before crossing the Tavignano River, the citadel came into view. Crowning a jagged molar of rock, it looked down over the campanile and the white buildings with their orange roofs forming the Old Town. He slammed on the brakes and leapt out with his camera.

"Fantastic!" He beamed as he climbed back into the driver's seat.

"Very nice but it doesn't warrant sending us all through the windscreen." Bella was frowning but nothing seemed to dent Matthew's good humour. He just laughed and carried on to the hotel in the Restonica Gorge.

~

The old part of the hotel was an uncompromising rectangle made of granite and with a row of shuttered windows on the first floor. The restaurant was an elegant extension attached to one side and overlooking the swimming pool. There was a purpose-built block of bedrooms with modern bathrooms; half of which overlooked the river, the other half overlooking the car park.

They met at half past seven in the lovely dining room with its vaulted, pine-panelled ceiling and windows on three sides. The tables were candlelit, the napkins and cloths of deep rose damask. The plat du jour was chicken fried in garlic butter and they all opted for this. It was served with chips, salad and a huge dish of wild mushrooms. Connie put a large spoonful of these onto Charlie's plate. "Go easy, Mum," he said. "If you give me any more mushroom, there won't be 'mush' room for anything else." Marina cackled loudly. Bella gave her a look. Connie was glad to observe that it was ignored.

Matthew proposed some ideas for the following day and there was general approval. Connie had asked him earlier to suggest that they all did their own thing in the morning. She didn't want to be thought unfriendly but couldn't face being sociable at breakfast.

The boys were all in one room but Marina had a room to herself. She generously offered to share it with Ned, who gave the matter some serious thought. It would depend on how much duffing-up he could take with the inevitable pillow fights.

Later on, Connie and Matthew were ready for bed and Connie was wearing a pretty blue and white cotton wrap. She'd made this before having Charlie, when first-time mothers routinely spent several days in hospital. It had a deep flounce around the hem, ruffles around the sleeves and a ribbon-lined sash around her waist. These days, she kept it for holidays. She stood on the balcony, gazing at the stars and crescent moon. She inhaled the resinous scent from the pine trees mingled with a sweet aroma of tobacco wafting up from the terrace. Matthew came and stood beside her.

"Are you okay?" he asked. "I thought today went pretty well."

"I'm fine," she replied. "I'm going to make some tea. Would you like some?"

"No, thanks. I'm just going to crash out."

Connie unzipped a small cuboid PVC bag. It was green and white striped and held a travelling kettle with adaptor, mugs wrapped in a tea towel, teabags, teaspoons and dried milk. There was a little fridge in the room, full of cold drinks. Tomorrow, she would buy some fresh milk but for now, she would make do with Coffee Mate. She plugged in the kettle.

Sitting on the balcony with her feet resting on the lower strut of the balustrade, Connie sipped her tea and relished the peace and solitude. Looking around, she noticed that almost all the windows had metal security shutters firmly in place. It wasn't enough to close the windows and pull the curtains. She couldn't understand this aversion to fresh nocturnal air. She listened to the water gushing and gurgling in the river. The day had gone smoothly and she was okay but she wasn't properly relaxed; she hadn't yet experienced the feelings of euphoria normally associated with the start of a holiday.

She let her thoughts roam and become untangled. It was time to admit that their happy foursome was feeling some strain. Tim and Matthew were like brothers. She had a bond with Tim that was as unspoken as it was potent and durable. Bella was always at ease with Matthew, whose accepting amiability gently flattered her. She and Bella, however, having once been close, were now playacting as friends. Connie was occasionally aware of active dislike from the other woman and it was difficult to ignore.

Their socialising over the years had been restricted to periods of a few hours, never more than one day. Being on holiday together was different. Connie could feel that her nervous system was in a state of low-level alert; she was ready for trouble, ready for attack. She could express no unworthy thought and make no harmless joke that might be open to misinterpretation. She could hear Bella saying to Tim, 'You know, Connie isn't really a very nice person. She says the unkindest things about her poor mother-in-law'.

Bella played the game that even the most ungenerous of women could manage. It was the pretence that they were good, kind and universally caring. Everyone knew the fundamentals of good manners but even these were subject to variation depending on circumstances.

Before Matthew had gone to Australia, he told her that his parents in Kenya had horses and always dressed for dinner. When they went out to stay before the boys were born, Connie was amused to see a couple of fragile old creatures grazing in a field. They both looked as if they would collapse under the weight of a saddle let alone a rider. Also, she certainly couldn't recall any dress formality with their modest evening meals.

When challenged about his mendacity, Matthew thought for a few moments. He explained that it had been partly a matter of trying to impress her because he wanted her to marry him but it wasn't only that. He'd been brought up to regard it as normal to boast without seeming to boast. It would have been unthinkable not to claim that everyone was doing terribly well. Unthinkable not to agree that tennis was super fun and unthinkable to upset the applecart over politics. Nobody ever admitted to weakness or failure or misery. It was the accepted way to behave and it was why he didn't like parties and always tried to avoid social gatherings with his relations.

There was the well-meaning guidance about treating others as you would like them to treat you but this could end up with being had for a mug. There was the old stricture about either saying something pleasant or saying nothing at all, but this could result in such blandness of discourse that silence would be preferable. Once trust had gone, conversational options diminished, especially as you couldn't tell the truth because, apparently, it always hurt.

Connie hadn't mentioned to Bella that she'd heard from Anna Hunt. A late Christmas card had arrived in February; there was no address but it came from the United States. Connie knew that there would have been scant interest or sympathy from Bella. The message was short.

Hi Bathsheba,
I've left him. He was a drunkard, a bully and a pig.
Now, I'm free. Hoorah!
Thank you, Connie.
Love, Anna

Perhaps, a half-hearted friendship was better than no friendship at all. Connie finished her tea. She and Bella would carry on playacting and work things out somehow. So much of life was compromise; yet another platitude. She would go and check on the boys.

They were asleep but, on coming out of their room and shutting the door very quietly, she saw Tim emerging from Marina's room next door. He looked pleased to see her. "Marina's wide awake," he said. "She's reading *The Hunchback of Notre Dame.*"

"That's a terrible story," replied Connie, "but I remember enjoying it when I was Marina's age. So, things are all right at your end, then?"

"Everything's fine, thanks. Bella likes the hotel. We have a spacious modern bathroom, a big comfortable bed and good reading lights. She's happy."

They would have liked to linger but there was no good reason to do so. There was every good reason not to do so. They wished each other a good night.

Twelve

The awesomeness of the untamed river plunging and whirling down the gorge, of the pines clutching the valley sides while cradling the crags and pinnacles of the mountains beyond was reduced almost to insignificance by the terror inspired by the one-track road. Chunks from the edge had slipped and crashed into the depths, giving it a nibbled appearance. Many of the passing-places were on the edge of precipices; cars squeezed painfully past each other with millimetres to spare, the drivers sweating, passengers pop-eyed with fear.

Matthew knew where he was going and Tim was unfazed. The two men were cracking jokes while everyone else was silent.

Breakfast had been served on the terrace to the sound of rushing river and birdsong. Everything looked clean and invigorated, including the freshly watered geraniums. There had been orange juice, one croissant each and several rounds of French bread with generous portions of butter and jam. There had been café au lait, not quite enough but a feeling that to ask for more would risk frissons of disapproval. The plan for the day was to explore the Restonica Gorge and find themselves a rock pool. They'd bought a substantial picnic from a supermarket on the way.

Matthew managed to locate the spot his family had been to before. They left the car on a small, sloping spur and picked their way, carefully, in single file down a narrow path matted with pine needles, weaving between rocks, roots and clumps of bilberry. At the bottom, all were captivated by the loveliness of everything in sight; the vast turquoise pool, the waterfalls cascading over the white granite rock, the pines with their resinous scent.

"This is heavenly," said Bella. "I've never seen water like this before; such a glorious colour." She dabbled her hands under a cascade. "It's cold, though."

"Yes, it's freezing." Connie put her hand in the water. "Two minutes in that will be enough for me. But you like it here?"

"Oh yes, it's beautiful. And we have it all to ourselves. Quite magical."

"Choose your own sunbathing rock," said Matthew. "I'm staying here, under this alder tree." He dumped his rucksack, unpacked the drinks and wedged them in the water to stay cool.

Connie spread her towel on a flat rock with an upright bit for a backrest. It was under a pine tree. She unpacked a large sunhat, a bottle of sun cream and a fat book while settling down peacefully for a lengthy reading session.

Rather shyly, Marina established her position not far away, slipping out of a cotton tunic and stretching out in an emerald bathing costume. Connie noted that she wasn't at all tubby. She looked across at Connie's book.

"What are you reading?"

"*The Idiot* by Dostoevsky. I like to bring something challenging on holiday because there is usually plenty of time to get properly 'stuck in'."

"Strange title for a book?"

"Yes," replied Connie. "It's about a man called Myshkin and he's not an idiot in the way Charlie is. I've only read the first couple of chapters, so I can't speak with any authority but, having read the introduction, I think there were two reasons for it. One was that he suffered from epileptic fits which were associated with mental problems. The other was that he always behaved with honesty and simplicity. He was genuinely good. There was no guile, no artifice about him. He assumed that other people were the same and it was his innocence which caused others to think him an idiot."

"Are you enjoying it?" Marina asked.

"I'm finding it compelling," answered Connie with a smile. "But I think it's going to be quite sad."

Charlie, Jamie and Ned were swimming, splashing each other and laughing. Bella was also in the pool, keeping her distance from the boys and letting the waterfalls play on her shoulders. Tim went on an exploratory foray, loping from rock to rock until he was out of sight. He insisted that Corsican granite was officially pink but, to the untrained eye, it looked white. Matthew had dozed off. Peacock blue dragonflies shimmered and hovered. Tiny lizards would appear, lie motionless on the rock and then vanish. The constant, muted roar of the water soothed and lulled, making conversation unnecessary.

Lunch was baguette, soft cheese, nuts, chocolate and peaches. The hours slipped by; no one invaded or disturbed their territory. They all alternated dips in the pool with resting on the rocks. When finally, by putting on his shirt and looking at his watch, Matthew conveyed to the others that it was time to return to the hotel, all was peaceful acquiescence. Even the challenge of the downhill drive was met with stoicism and calm.

~

Early that evening, Connie was sitting on the hotel terrace watching her sons. They were taking advantage of the quiet period of the day to have the swimming pool to themselves. There was much maternal fondness in her expression; she took pride in their strong, lithe, beautiful bodies plunging and streaking in the water. She had enjoyed a leisurely beauty routine and was looking groomed and refreshed in a white top and a long, crinkle fabric, Indian skirt in shades of amber and gold.

Bella crossed the terrace and sat down beside her.

"You look nice, Bella," said Connie admiring the pale blue shift and white beads.

"You do, too." Bella smiled.

"Thank you. I feel we have a duty to uphold the reputation of British women and prove to the world that we are every bit as glamorous as French women, if not more so."

"Quite right," said Bella. "Marina's reading in her room. Where are Tim and Matthew?"

"They've gone for a stroll and will be back at seven."

"Ned's a funny little chap," remarked Bella, casually.

"He's a darling." Connie was unprepared for what came next despite the sudden silken tone.

"He blinks a lot and has a habit of avoiding eye contact. I'm wondering if he's slightly autistic."

"No, I can assure you that he is not. I know about the blinking and asked our doctor for advice. He said that Ned would grow out of it. It was nothing to worry about and we shouldn't draw attention to it. As for the lack of eye contact, I'm totally unaware of it but he is quite a shy child."

"It's just that I know a bit about these things," said Bella. "It might be worth keeping an eye on him."

Connie stood and, on the pretext of asking the boys to come out of the pool and get dressed for dinner, she moved away from Bella. She felt shocked and distressed, not so much because of what Bella had said; she knew it to be irresponsible and wrong, but because it had been a deliberate attempt to cause hurt and upset.

Connie didn't enjoy her dinner. She sat as far away from Bella as she could and, while obeying all the rules of decorum, managed to avoid talking to her. Connie wasn't a sentimentalist but her reserves of emotion went very deep. Like any mother facing an attack on her child, powerfully instinctive feelings of love and protectiveness were aroused, not to mention a fierceness that was quite difficult to conceal.

That night, when she and Matthew were drinking tea on their balcony, Connie told him what Bella had said.

"She's just trying to wind you up." Matthew was perfectly calm. "She did a psychology degree at Bangor and, like many people with a small amount of knowledge, she takes a simplistic approach to complex matters. People like Bella are harmless unless they get into positions of power, whereupon they can cause havoc and ruin lives.

"The reason Ned has been avoiding eye contact with Bella is because he doesn't like her very much. She told him that the book he was reading was rubbish. A bit rich, really, coming from someone who was reading a Mills & Boon on the plane."

"I've read a Mills & Boon," said Connie. "I rather enjoyed it; it was well-written."

"Well, that's good to know." Matthew paused. "It might or might not be a comfort to you to know that I was exactly like Ned when I was his age. I didn't keep blinking but I had a sort of facial tic. I was teased about it at school but eventually it went of its own accord. My advice to you is not to give Bella the satisfaction of knowing she has upset you. Ned isn't remotely autistic."

They were silent for a while, listening to the musical sound of the river.

"I don't think you ever met Erik," remarked Matthew. "I was having lunch with him in Oxford, along with Tim and Bella, before I had actually met you. He was a Swedish structural geologist from Uppsala University; extremely bright and full of energy and enthusiasm. He could never stop talking but he was always interesting and highly amusing. He lacked a certain polish, I suppose. I remember him blowing his nose on his table napkin. Don't worry, it was a paper one," he added, seeing Connie's horrified expression.

"Despite that, he was one of the most decent men I have ever come across; honest, kind and generous. During lunch, he was telling us about something that happened when he was doing fieldwork in the Highlands, on Speyside. He was looking at a rock outcrop which continued beyond a high fence. He decided to climb over the fence and was continuing with his scrutiny and measurements when he heard a sort of wet, snuffling noise coming from behind. He turned and saw a great African buffalo a few metres away, staring at him. He climbed back over the fence in short order. It turned out that he had illicitly entered a wild life park. He got quite carried away, telling this story, and we were all laughing.

"Anyway, when he'd left after the lunch, Bella announced that Erik was psychotic because he ate with his mouth open. Of course, he didn't do this routinely but only when he had so much to say that there wasn't time to swallow his food before saying it. He most definitely was not psychotic. He was and still is the sanest man in the world."

For someone whose interest in human behaviour was minimal, Matthew was waxing quite loquacious. He continued. "Bella has her good points but she belongs to a class I think of as the 'bitterati'. These are people who suffer from contentment deficit syndrome and there are a lot of them about. Bella takes it one stage further, always casting around to find instances of the elusive happiness factor; whereupon she does her best to nip them in the bud."

Connie laughed.

Thirteen

It was generally agreed that the following day, Monday, was going to be a restful affair. A strenuous expedition was being planned for Tuesday involving a hike up to the upper valley of the Restonica River to see the glacial lakes of Melo and Capitello.

They drove into Corte town with the intention of walking up to the citadel. Connie, who'd seen it before and remembered a lot of steps, some unremarkable buildings at the top and some very fine views, decided to opt out. She always relished the luxury of peaceful solitude. Marina chose to stay with her and the two of them were happily established under a parasol in the main square as the others set off up the hill. Connie asked for a large café au lait, to make up for the deficiency at breakfast, while Marina had a coke.

The square was cobbled and surrounded by five-storey buildings with rows of shuttered windows. They mostly looked as if they could do with a coat of paint. There were some ornamental lamp posts and a few shrubs in tubs dotted around. In the centre, on a plinth, was a statue of a fine-looking man in eighteenth-century garb. Marina had glanced at the engraving on the plinth. "Who was Pasquale Paoli?" she asked.

Connie consulted her guide book. "He was a patriot and founding father of the Corsican Republic," she read out. "He declared independence from the French and Genoese in 1755, introduced a modern constitution and founded a university in 1765. However, independence only lasted for fourteen years because in 1769, Paoli was defeated at Ponte Nuovo. The French and Genoese took back control but the Genoese then ceded their share to the French. Paoli was exiled to England."

Connie noticed that Marina was only half-listening. She put away her guide book and sat silently. She felt an affinity with the trusting, gentle girl beside her.

Marina said, for no apparent reason, "Mum told me I should find someone I admired and model myself on them."

"I remember my own mother giving me advice like that."

"Did you follow it?"

"Certainly not."

"Why not?"

Connie pondered. "Basically, because it stops you working things out for yourself. Everyone's a messy mixture of good and bad, weak and strong. It helps to learn from other people but not to copy them. Apart from the fear of being found out, pretending to be something you are not can land you in trouble."

"What sort of trouble?"

Connie laughed as she thought about all the inadequacies, embarrassments, disappointments and failures that made up episodes of trouble in life. "Well, at the harmless end of the scale, when we were visiting my mother at Easter, we rang the doorbell. She opened the door and behaved in a way that was totally out of character. She made a theatrical sweeping gesture with her arm and said 'Welcome' in a loud voice. It was obvious that she'd observed someone else doing this and thought it looked good. But it was just embarrassing. On another occasion, she tried to emulate a French woman she'd met and admired. That involved a lot of gesturing with her hands, in what she thought was a graceful and Gallic way, whenever she spoke. That was also embarrassing."

"At the more serious end of the scale, I nearly ended up dead because I pretended to know how to ride a horse. Some people are born with confidence and others aren't. People without confidence look to others for approval by trying to please or by being self-deprecating. It never works; I've tried it."

"How do you become confident?"

"I wish I knew."

"What happened with the horse?"

Connie had been scanning the square and noticed a hairdresser tucked between two shops.

"Marina, would you like to give Mum a terrible shock?"

"Ooh, yes."

"What I mean is, would you like to give Bella a really nice surprise?"

"Maybe."

"I'm going to see if that hairdresser over there will give me a quick cut because I didn't have time to get it done last week. How about having your hair trimmed? If you had a simple bob, not only would you look stunning but it would be cooler and swimming would easier."

"Okay," said Marina. "I think I'd like that but first, you must tell me about how you were nearly killed."

"I was fifteen. A school friend had an aunt and uncle with a farm. We went there one day and I met her cousin, a very handsome chap of about eighteen. I really fancied him and when he asked if I could ride, I replied 'Of course I can'. However, I had only ever plodded around a country lane on a fat little pony who could hardly manage a trot let alone anything faster.

"Anyway, I found myself saddled up on a spirited animal, who instantly recognised that I was an imposter and decided to bolt. It shot off down the track like a rocket. It was completely terrifying and I don't know how I managed to stay on. I was slithering from side to side and didn't have a clue what to do. Eventually, we reached a T-junction and came to a juddering halt in a clump of trees. I flew off the back and saw this great rump about to squash me. I was rescued then by the handsome cousin and might have enjoyed being lifted onto his horse and ridden back if it hadn't been for the split lip and bleeding nose obscuring my charms. I haven't been near a horse since."

~

The coiffeuse looked at Marina's massive head with a suitably dispassionate Gallic air. "Un peu trop, n'est-ce pas?" She set to with her scissors. It was almost like watching a sculptor at work but, instead of chips of clay or marble flying around, there were ringlets cascading in a steady stream to the floor until a great soft brown carpet piled up around the chair.

The end result was astounding. Curls framed the delicate face and pretty ears. A high, slightly rounded forehead was on view. The blue eyes looked bigger; the slender neck looked longer. All the heaviness had gone. Marina looked exquisite.

Madame was clearly pleased with her own handiwork. "Très, très jolie," she said with satisfaction. Connie paid the bill with a large tip and then steered Marina over to a gift shop full of trinkets and jewellery. They bought some gold hoop earrings. When the others returned from the citadel, Connie and Marina were back under their parasol, innocently tucking into dishes of ice cream.

Connie was a little worried about Bella's reaction. She knew there had been tension between mother and daughter over the hair but she also knew that Bella would find it hard to feel triumph in anything for which she couldn't take credit. In the event, Bella was sensible. She neither over-reacted nor under-reacted. She smiled, although not at Connie. Tim's expression was inscrutable and he, also, avoided looking at Connie. The boys just stared.

It was Matthew who eased the tension. "Well, I don't know. We turn our backs for five minutes and Marina changes from a normal girl into a glamorous film star. I can't understand it. I think we could all do with some of that ice cream."

A waiter approached.

Fourteen

There was a palpable air of exhilaration and harmony when they clambered out of the car at the Bergeries de Grotelle, the starting point for the trail, and saw wild ponies grazing around the carpark. The harmony was only slightly dented when Connie produced hats for the boys.

"Mum, I'm not wearing a stupid hat."

Connie, at five foot three inches, stared up at her eldest son, who had recently topped six foot, and decided that it would be undignified to fight a battle she couldn't win.

"I'm not wearing a hat either," said Jamie.

"Nor am I," said Ned.

"Okay. When you all get carted off in an ambulance with severe sunstroke, don't blame me. However," Connie continued in a deceptively mild tone, "until you have all put sun cream on the bits of you which aren't covered up, we're not going anywhere."

Marina looked on, smiling, her hat securely in place. She was enjoying the undivided attention of the boys. Gentle, dreamy Jamie was the same age as her and easy to talk to. Ned invoked motherly feelings and, with Charlie, there was a definite spark. His mission was to make her laugh.

They all wore shorts and hiking boots but carried extra clothes. The weather could change higher up. They'd packed plenty of drinks and lots of food. The first part of the trail was gentle; meandering through pine trees, rocks, juniper, leafy shrubs and scrubby grass. It became steadily steeper and, after about half an hour, they reached the Bergerie de Melo where the path forked. After consulting a guidebook, they opted for the more challenging route which involved clinging onto the chains and climbing the ladders which had been bolted into the rock. The scenery was staggeringly beautiful.

Matthew and Bella led the way, followed by Tim and the boys. Connie and Marina brought up the rear. At the top of a particularly vertiginous and challenging bit of trail, Connie announced that she was going to have a little rest. She and Marina sat on a large rock and shared a bar of chocolate.

"Connie, do you think I'm fat?"

"No, I don't. You are absolutely and most emphatically not fat. You have a very beautiful figure. You are perfect and very lucky. Don't ever be tempted by any stupid diets or you'll end up with osteoporosis in middle-age."

Just then, they were distracted by a figure coming down the hill towards them at some speed; someone with a strange uneven gait and with one shoulder twisted up and higher than the other. As the figure approached, they could see that it had a hideous visage with bulging eyes and a tongue distorting one side. Connie, who needed glasses for distant vision, was alarmed but Marina collapsed in helpless laughter.

"It's Charlie," she said. "He's pretending to be Quasimodo coming to rescue me from the wicked Archdeacon Claude Frollo."

"I've been sent all the way down here," he said cheerfully, "to find out what is taking you two so long. There is a heated debate raging up there as to whether we should have lunch at the first lake or stagger on up to the second. I favour the former."

Connie coolly appraised her son in his cut-off jeans, with his mop of fair hair and broad shoulders. "In my opinion, which I know does not command universal respect, it would be the height of self-indulgence to have lunch before we get to the top."

"I knew you'd say that, Mum, and I presume Marina agrees." She nodded. "I have, therefore, just been outvoted by seven to one."

He set off at a jog back up the flower-filled meadow. Connie and Marina followed.

The glacial Lac de Melo was a neat circle of water in a basin of sloping pastureland. It reflected the greens of the surrounding vegetation. There were no pines here; just a few stunted deciduous trees. It was a place of peace and beauty with the jagged peaks of the Rotondo Massif rising all around. The sun blazed down but the air was becoming fresher.

They walked on up to the Lac de Capitello at nearly two thousand metres. It was chilly here and they all put on sweaters. There was an austere beauty about the massive, vertical walls of granite dropping into the deep blue water and the brilliant, cloudless sky above. Apart from a few patches of scrub, there was no greenery.

Connie and Tim sat on a rock in a state of awe. The velvety silence was broken by the sounds of the others by the water's edge. The boys were chucking rocks into the lake and laughing. The majesty and grandeur had a purifying effect on the spirit. Minor irritations and petty thoughts melted away. Tim was scanning the surroundings through a pair of binoculars, hoping to spot a golden eagle.

"I'm trying to think of something profound to say," remarked Connie, "but words seem so inadequate."

With his eyes still trained on the skyline, Tim replied, "You and I don't need words, Connie."

~

On the way down, Connie once again found herself walking with Marina. "Bella told me that you have a lovely time staying with cousins every Easter."

"It's okay. I don't hate them or anything."

"What do you do?"

"Not very much. I get a bit bored, actually. Caroline and Linda are into clothes, make-up and shopping. They watch a lot of videos. I like to read but they don't. Paul ignores us and plays games on his computer all day long. The house is nice with a huge garden and they have dogs. I really love the dogs. One thing I do hate, though, is the fact that the loos and bathrooms don't have locks on the doors. I asked them about this one day and Paul said that only lower-class people worry about such things."

Connie laughed. "That very neatly illustrates what we were talking about yesterday."

"How d'you mean?"

"Well, Paul had obviously heard someone else make that remark; perhaps, someone he was modelling himself on. Perhaps, it just made him feel superior. Instead of analysing it and realising how insultingly offensive as well as intellectually vacuous it was, he chose to repeat it. He probably thought he was being worldly and wise."

Bella was not far behind and it might have been that she overheard some or all of this exchange. On the last lap of the walk, when Connie was by herself, she approached and in a tone which was quiet but distinctly aggressive, she launched an attack.

"I hope you're not filling Marina's head with a load of subversive nonsense. I know you try to be nice to everyone and that, of course, is very sweet and touching but I'll thank you to back off from my daughter."

Connie was shocked. She felt upset and oddly guilty but stayed calm.

"Fine," she replied with a little shrug. "The next time Marina speaks to me, I'll tell her to go away."

"Don't be silly, Connie."

"It's you who are being silly, Bella."

~

That night, Matthew was feeling amorous. Connie was tired and a little depressed following the latest tiff with Bella. She didn't reject him but wasn't unduly responsive.

She'd been thinking about sitting with Tim by the upper lake and it triggered something in her brain. Suddenly, it was another's long, sensitive fingers caressing her, another's soft lips pressing on her own, another's powerful body gliding onto hers, another's limbs entangling with and gently guiding hers. Her body ignited into sort of frenzy.

Matthew was happy. He hadn't had such wild sex for months. He put it down to the oysters at dinner. Connie had pronounced them disgusting but they'd had an effect.

~

The two women behaved with impeccable politeness towards each other over the next few days. They had both scented danger and were playing safe. Connie had often wondered if such a thing as genuine friendship had ever existed; a state of being without competition, false admiration or concealment. There seemed always such a need for flattery; such care had to be taken not to offend and not to disappoint. Always a fear of inadequacy, of not being 'nice' enough. If you breached any rules in the quest for trust or humour or informality, you ran the risk of being pronounced 'rude'. It was hopeless.

There was so much official advice on how to achieve optimal health and happiness, mostly revolving around social relationships; being with people, talking to people, grinning at people, clinking glasses with people. It didn't work.

There were pockets of generosity of spirit to be found but they were rare and so much in demand that there were never enough to go around.

Each evening, after dinner, Connie would leave the others to their nightcaps and conversation and go up to the bedroom. The boys and Marina looked after themselves. She relied heavily on this period of solitude to maintain her equilibrium. She would undress, put on her beautiful gown, make tea and sit on the balcony. Her mind would meander and muse until she felt at peace. Only then would she lose herself in the world of Myshkin with his tortured conversations and misunderstandings.

The remaining three days passed pleasantly, two of them by rock pools in the Restonica Valley, one upstream and the other downstream from the one they'd bagged on the first day. On the day in between, they walked up the gorge along the Tavignano River from Corte. The path was a medieval mule track, meandering but pleasant underfoot. Dark blue lavender and herbs grew on either side. The scent was intoxicating. There were rock roses and curry plants. The gorge was deep and enclosed with glimpses of rock pools far below; the scenery was dramatic.

After about a mile or so, they came to a gate and a small garden with a picnic table. There was a little chapel and a spring where they could top up their water bottles. It was charming but they didn't linger long because they had another five miles to go before reaching their destination, the Russulinu suspension bridge. Once there, they had a picnic and then retraced their steps. It was an exhausting but satisfying day. Tim spotted a golden eagle.

On their last evening, the hotel laid on a barbecue; a great feast of grilled meats and fish served with a variety of salads and crusty bread. The terrace and pool were lit up, wine and beer flowed. There was music and, after the food, dancing.

Marina and the boys joined in, flinging themselves around with great abandon. It delighted Connie to see their lack of inhibition. At their age, she had been crippled by it. Matthew asked her to dance and she declined but Bella willingly joined him in the merriment of the gyrating crowd. Connie and Tim were left sitting at the table.

"Will you dance with me?" he asked.

She shook her head. "No, I think I won't." She laughed.

"Please." Tim looked beseeching. "We can do a simple shuffle, nothing embarrassing."

They stood and he held her. "You look extremely fetching this evening."

Connie knew that this was true. She nodded and smiled.

"As Matthew has grabbed my wife, it gives me a perfect excuse to seize his. An opportunity that I have no intention of wasting."

She smiled again.

"It's been a wonderful week, Connie. I've never known Marina so happy and at ease. I've enjoyed every minute."

"It has been good," she agreed.

"Don't worry about Bella. She can be a bit spiky but she still regards you as her dearest friend."

Connie wondered just how many poisoned droplets had reached his ears. She'd had more wine than usual this evening and didn't care. Tim chatted on. The music changed from 'disco-pop' to what she thought of as French café music; a smoky, husky bass voice crooning suggestively. Tim had all the qualities she looked for in a friend; he was always pleased to see her, happy to talk to her and quite unshockable. She was finding dancing with him very enjoyable. It had always surprised her that the standard ballroom dancing hold was considered perfectly proper. To be physically close to Tim, to have one of his hands in hers and his arm around her back implied a form of possession, which was by no means displeasing.

The potential for intimacy made it exciting even when the utmost decorum was being practiced. In fact, the more decorum, the greater the thrill. She was suffused with languorously agreeable sensations. She didn't want to stop dancing and nor did Tim.

"What was the matter with Bella?" Connie asked when she and Matthew were in their room.

"I hope you've enjoyed your evening, Connie." The voice had been dangerously icy as Bella glared at her with eyes as hard as chunks of polished quartz, her mouth twisted with loathing.

Normally, Matthew could be relied upon for unwavering support and approval. Connie looked at him. "You and she were frolicking around like a pair of hysterical lovebirds while Tim and I could hardly have been more staid and more boring." Just at the moment, he was looking uneasy and distinctly ill-tempered.

"Yes, Bella and I were frolicking around, the key word being 'frolicking'. You and Tim were behaving like a long-married couple who still had the good fortune to be in love. I felt a bit funny watching you and I'm not surprised Bella is fed up. You're not always quite as subtle as you think you are, Connie."

Fifteen

"The pink rock is granite," said Matthew in a loud voice, "and these bays on the west coast are very deep continuations of the valleys. They're a legacy of the Miocene period, fifteen million years ago, when the Mediterranean was a vast, dried-up salt pan, cut off from the Atlantic and Indian Ocean. The Corsican mountains were just an isolated range then with rivers flowing down towards the plain."

"You might as well save your breath, Matt; they're all asleep." They were winding along a spectacular bit of road between Evisa and Porto; great pink rock spikes on their left and a deep canyon on their right. Tim looked amused.

"Scandalous ingratitude! I think we'll stop in Porto, have a cold drink to wake everyone up, because then I'd like to drive west to Cape Rosso so that we can see the Calanches de Piana. They're magnificent. You can take a turn at the wheel if you like."

Connie wasn't asleep. She was sitting quietly at the back of the car. Matthew's terseness had evaporated overnight but she'd woken up feeling subdued and mutinous. She'd had enough of being out of favour and had been mulling over scenarios involving getting an early flight home or booking herself into alternative accommodation; both ludicrous and logistically impossible but just thinking about them improved her state of mind.

It took very little energy or imagination to make someone unhappy. To be cooped up in a car for several hours with a misery-monger and then be obliged to share a house with her wasn't a prospect she relished but there was no escape. To make matters worse, Tim and Bella had looked unusually cheerful when they came down to breakfast that morning.

Matthew was gratified by the general appreciation of the Calanches, which were truly imposing. They turned south, heading for Cargese and then on to Ajaccio. Their villa was at the southern end of the Bay of Ajaccio at the Plage de l'Isolella. On the last lap of the drive, they could look down from the road over an uneven tapestry of trees to the sea; sapphire with stretches of translucent aquamarine, randomly dotted with motionless white yachts.

They stopped at a large supermarket and loaded up with supplies. Connie threw in washing powder, softener and sundry cleaning materials. She'd read countless novels based on exotic holiday houses; invariably they included a woman, benevolent and kind, who just somehow materialised and produced delicious meals while doing all the cleaning and laundry. There would be no such entity in their villa, despite its high-grade rating and full quota of mod-cons.

~

Connie opened the white wooden gate and passed from the dusty lane through to enchantment. Standing still in the afternoon heat, she felt a lavender-scented breeze caressing her neck, easing the tension. All around was colour; plumbago, oleander, bougainvillea, lantana, roses. There was freshly watered grass and an almond tree, beneath which was a cushioned swing-seat. The villa was apricot with blue shutters; there was a covered veranda and terrace, both tiled in cream. She put down her carrier bag of bottles and cartons and sat under the tree.

Car doors were slamming and the others appeared, carrying bags and cases.

"I thought you were supposed to be unlocking the house and preparing some drinks," said Matthew. He had done most of the driving, choosing the longer route in order that everyone might enjoy the spectacular mountain and coastal scenery. He was wondering whether he should have saved himself the trouble. There had been complaints about the picnic site where they'd stopped for lunch. Bella had pronounced it disgusting, with bits of tissue everywhere.

"You forgot to give me the key," replied Connie, gently rocking back and forth on her seat.

"I gave it to someone."

"I seem to have it my pocket," said Tim. "Sorry about that, everyone." His face creased in an amiable grin, imperturbable good nature radiating from his stocky frame.

They entered the shuttered dimness of a large living area and were soothed by what they could see; white walls, white hydrangeas in an earthenware vase on a round pine table, easy chairs with blue cotton cushions, a dresser full of pretty crockery, lamps with apricot shades. Through an archway with a bead curtain at the back of the room was a kitchen.

Connie went through and gratefully washed her hands with the soap and paper towels provided. She found a jug and some glasses, then opened the fridge to look for ice. It was a celestial vision of bright light and shelves packed with good things; wine, orange juice, milk, butter, cheese, eggs, tomatoes and slices of cooked ham. She'd forgotten they'd asked for a 'welcome pack'.

She emptied the ice tray into her jug, followed by the orange juice and a bottle of lemonade from her shopping bag. She found a tray, noticing two baguettes on a ledge, and carried it all through to the pine table. With her spirits rising, she found Bella and asked her to choose which of the four bedrooms she and Tim would like and then wandered outside to explore. She found a sandy path leading directly to the beach at the bottom of the garden. It was private, leading through scrubby maquis for about fifty yards. To the side of the house, at a lower level, was the swimming pool, sparkling and pristine.

There were loungers and parasols on the generous paved surround and the whole thing was set in a lemon grove with an abundance of ripe fruit waiting to be picked. There would be no more need for sugary rubbish out of supermarket bottles. Jamie and Ned were already splashing around while Matthew was asleep on a lounger.

She spotted Charlie and Marina emerging from behind the house, carrying a couple of hammocks. "Would you like a useful job?" she called out.

"We were just hoping you'd suggest something like that." Charlie grimaced.

"We could do with someone to unpack all the food shopping and then make afternoon tea."

A little later on, she heard laughter coming from the kitchen. She paused to listen. Charlie was pretending to be a French onion man and was speaking in a deep, guttural voice with an appalling accent. Every time he repeated the words 'les oignons' with a horrible nasal twang, a fresh peal of mirth would ring out. Connie noticed that Tim had emerged from somewhere and was also listening. A head poked through the bead curtain.

"Mum, I thought I heard you. I'm sorry to report that I have very bad news. There are hundreds of tiny coffee cups and hundreds of glasses but no teacups, no mugs and, worst of all, no teapot."

"This calls for emergency action," said Tim. "Quickly, Connie, out to the car. Charlie, please tell the others we've gone in search of a teapot. We won't be long."

~

"This is fun," said Tim, glancing across at her. "How long can we spin it out?"

"Not for very long." It did feel like fun. There was something ridiculous about racing off to find a teapot; something clandestine as well. Tim's good humour made everything enjoyable. It was only a few miles to the supermarket, where they parked under a tree in the vain hope that the car would remain cool. They grabbed a trolley and headed for the homeware department which had a large array of cheap, brightly patterned crockery, including teapots.

"Mugs or cups and saucers?" Tim asked. They all came in packs of six.

"Let's keep things simple and get two dozen mugs, two milk jugs and two teapots."

Emboldened by their success, they moved on to the confectioner's counter. Connie gazed in awe at the artistry of the exquisite tartlets, pastries and cakes. Some were piled high with glazed berries and others oozed with creamy fillings.

"Tim," she said, "I'm going to leave you to choose a selection of these; one each will be enough. I've just remembered something very important and I'll meet you back here. Please don't move or I'll never find you again." She raced off.

He waited patiently until, coming towards him, he noticed an enormous cuboid package beneath which a pair of brown legs, encased in a swirl of duck egg blue, moved swiftly. "Sorry to take so long. It took ages to find and I couldn't think of the French word for loo paper." She jettisoned the package into the trolley with Tim rescuing his box of cakes just in time.

"Let's go."

Connie and Tim washed everything in an old-fashioned porcelain sink. On the veranda was a long wooden table with what looked like an old church pew behind. There was a stack of green plastic chairs for arranging in front. Connie found a blue and white check vinyl tablecloth, exactly the right size. She laid everything out while Tim went in search of the others.

Connie was braced for another dose of froideur and was almost taken aback when Bella cooed with pleasure and approval over the offerings.

"You have been working hard, Connie. Well done. How absolutely lovely. Thank you so much."

The charm offensive continued. Bella had bagged the best room but was at pains to insist that really Connie should have had it. She was round-eyed with wonder at the perfection of everything and each mouthful of tartlet was accompanied by a sigh of blissful contentment. Connie wondered if anyone else had noticed this odd behaviour. She glanced around the table and caught Marina's eye. A brief look of complicity passed between them and Connie felt less alone.

She was very happy with the sleeping arrangements and didn't begrudge Bella's taking possession of the master bedroom. The boys had a large room containing two sets of bunk beds; Marina was delighted to have a double bed and shower room all to herself. The house had obviously been extended and she and Matthew had a room in the original part of the building. It was very simple with whitewashed walls and a tiled floor. Behind gauzy drapes were a window and a door which opened out onto a small terrace and a grove of peach trees. The big white bed had a table and lamp on each side and behind a broderie anglaise curtain, which extended the full length of a side wall, were generous shelves and hanging space.

The most thrilling aspect was the spacious bathroom. The shower was set in one corner with a low wall to contain the water within a quadrant, the radius of which was at least two metres wide. There was no requirement for any form of enclosure. The water pressure would prove to be powerful and the user could enjoy a lovely view through the window during ablutions. It was primitive and glorious.

They lingered around the tea table until the boys wandered off with Marina. Bella insisted on clearing away and Connie left to unpack her cases and investigate the facilities in the little wash house at the back. There had been a general consensus that they should eat out in the evenings but no one felt like exploring further on their first day. They prepared a simple meal from what was in the fridge. Bella arranged the ham on a platter and hard-boiled some eggs. Connie sliced the huge tomatoes and sprinkled herbs and olive oil on top. She sliced up the ripe peaches and filled a bowl with yogurt. The baguettes were cut into chunks and put on the table with butter and cheeses.

They assembled once again around the veranda table and poured out chilled rosé wine. To a chorus of cicadas, they watched the sun sink below a distant headland, leaving an apricot haze to merge with the silvered sea. The yachts, sails now furled, were delicate silhouettes.

~

Lying in bed that night, Matthew was dozing off when Connie asked, "Are you happy?"

"How could I be anything else when I'm with you. Are you happy?"

"Moderately so."

"What's the problem?"

"I can't understand what's happening with Bella. She's being excessively agreeable and it makes me uneasy. She's like a chameleon. Haven't you noticed?"

"No, not really. Do you think Tim has noticed?"

"Probably not. He's just as obtuse as you are about these things."

"No need to be impolite." Matthew was unruffled. "You know how hard we try to understand the complexities of female angst."

There was silence for a while.

"Do you remember telling me about your aunt and uncle, Verity and Ted?" Connie asked.

"Not really. What did I say about them?"

"You told me that they had a long and happy marriage with no children and that when Ted died, Verity inherited his money in the normal way. At that point, Ted's sister, who had not been especially fond of Verity, became very warm and friendly. The sister had children and grandchildren and began to include Verity in the various family events, asking her to stay and so on. Verity was grateful and gladly responded, assuming it was a form of natural sympathy and affection.

"However, she was horribly disillusioned a couple of years later to receive a letter from the sister's solicitor. The letter was phrased with great tact and delicacy, saying that, although there could be no legal duress, Verity was invited to leave all money and assets accruing from Ted to the sister's offspring rather than to her own extended family, when making her Will."

"I do remember all that," said Matthew, "but what on earth does it have to do with Bella?"

"Nothing at all. It's just that there is sometimes an underlying motive for a sudden onset of goodwill."

Sixteen

The incident occurred shortly before they were due to fly home. Connie told Matthew about it but he didn't believe her and she never spoke of it again.

The days had passed pleasantly and without friction. They would start with a leisurely breakfast on the veranda. Tim and Matthew took it in turns early each morning to walk to a local patisserie to buy rolls, croissants, baguettes and teatime treats. They would sit around the table, in their own time, and help themselves to orange juice and slices of sweet melon. In the kitchen was a wonderful gadget with flasks on two hotplates; one for fresh coffee and the other for hot milk. There was creamy French butter and lots of jam and honey.

For lunch, there would be bread served with cheese or pâté or cold ham. There were tomatoes and salad leaves. Bella and Connie would make a jug of fresh lemonade with fruit from the garden. There would be peaches, nectarines and grapes. "Are you sure it's okay for us to be nicking all the owner's lemons?" Matthew queried, looking a bit worried.

"I asked the gardener," replied Connie, "and he said it was fine. He said they would be wasted if guests didn't use them."

Afternoon tea became a regular ritual, usually organised by Charlie and Marina. In the cool of the evenings, they would stroll to the village and choose from a selection of eateries. Connie's favourite was a fish restaurant set in a sort of cellar with a ramshackle arrangement of tables and chairs. She had a suspicion that levels of hygiene in the kitchen were not of the highest order but the bouillabaisse served in large tureens was delectable beyond description. It induced a form of gastronomic ecstasy which was addictive.

The large pool was in constant use but Bella and Marina, both powerful swimmers, would strike out from the sandy beach far into the bay. Bella's muscled shoulders were testament to her prowess; she looked Junoesque in her bathing suit. Connie swam in the sea every day but stayed close to the shore. There were many sailing boats moored by the beach, within wading reach of their owners. She would weave her way between them, enjoying the tranquillity and warmth of the water.

~

In a clearing reached by the pathway leading downhill from the ticket office, a cluster of people stood around a stone monument. There was a tall man and a stocky, broad-chested man, both in shorts and shirts. There were three boys in shorts and t-shirts and a girl in a mini skirt. There were two women; one blonde, wearing huge sunglasses and a striking, deep pink sundress. The other was dark-haired and wore clothes with an oriental look—blue, filmy palazzo pants gathered around the ankles, a white embroidered cotton top with long sleeves tapering from slender at the shoulder to bell-shaped and gathered around the wrists. She wore a soft white sunhat with the brim turned up in front to reveal some blue lining. She moved away from the group and walked on along a path.

After a minute or so, the stocky man followed her. The blonde woman's head turned to watch him go but she stayed where she was.

Tim often thought that, although Matthew seemed content with mineral exploration and a fat salary, he should have stayed in academia. Apart from geology, Matthew had a fascination with a variety of other subjects including history, geography, archaeology and astronomy. He loved holding forth in front of an audience and, just now, was expounding on megalithic sites, the Stone Age, the Bronze Age, a pastoral people being invaded by a war-like tribe called the Torreens, who came from the eastern Mediterranean and were probably responsible for introducing swords and daggers, such as the ones depicted on the menhir, Filitosa V, in front of them.

Tim was not in the mood for scholarly pontification and preferred the idea of a comfortable chat with Connie. He caught her up. "This place has a definite atmosphere," he said, looking around at the great granite slabs and several other menhirs.

"Yes, it does but I think it would look better in spring or autumn. I know there are olive trees and evergreen oaks dotted around but the grass is dead and everything looks pinky-brown and lifeless. It's like a desert and I find it withering to the spirit. It's extremely hot and I'm heading for some shade and a cold drink in the café. I'm glad we came though; it is interesting and it wouldn't do to sound unappreciative."

They strolled along the dusty track, at ease with each other.

"How are things with your mother?" Tim asked.

"She's fine, thanks. We all go down to Dorset for a week at Easter and again in the summer. We rent a cottage. She likes to cook some meals for us and we cook some for her. We take her out for picnics and expeditions, which she enjoys, and we usually have a couple of days to ourselves. It works very well. My brother and his family are only thirty miles away, within easy driving distance if there's a problem. They see her quite often and have her at Christmas, which is a relief to me because I don't find her the easiest of companions. Theoretically, she's always welcome to come and stay but she won't drive on motorways, so it doesn't happen.

"She made me laugh the last time we saw her. She told me in all seriousness that she'd come across something called 'The Distressed Gentlefolk's Association' and got in touch with them in the hope that they'd send her some money. However, she was absolutely outraged when all she received was a request from them for a donation towards Christmas hampers for the genuinely distressed."

Tim chuckled.

"How about your parents? Durham is a long way off."

"My parents would like to see more of us, especially Marina, but I also have a brother who lives quite close to them and this lets me off the hook. We left Marina with them for a week when she was nine while Bella and I went on to Scotland for a holiday. It was a field work sort of holiday. Marina had a lovely time; she told me so. My parents did everything they could think of to make her happy. There was a trip to a zoo, playgrounds, donkey rides. They played games, read stories, made cakes. My mother taught Marina how to knit and crochet and it was clearly a joyous time for them all.

"However, Bella was jealous. She was very polite to my mother. Bella knows how to speak with perfect courtesy and shrivel people up at the same time. I find that good manners can be deployed in a way that is very chilling. Anyway, very charmingly, she let my mother think that Marina hadn't enjoyed herself all that much and didn't want to stay again. It made me angry because my mother was clearly hurt, although she tried not to show it. There was nothing I could do."

"What a shame," murmured Connie.

"Before Bella and I married, Mum gave me some advice. She said that, if ever there was a disagreement between my mother and my wife, I should always back my wife even if I knew my mother was in the right. She said it was the only way to avoid serious trouble."

"So, she's been 'hoist with her own petard' after a fashion?"

"You could say that, yes." Tim laughed. "The trouble is, I've never known a woman be as jealous as Bella is. It's almost pathological and can make life difficult. I know I'm being disloyal, speaking like this, but I trust you, Connie."

~

Further south down the coast from their villa was a small town called Propriano. A guidebook suggested that the charm of this once quiet fishing village had been destroyed by the trappings of tourism but this wasn't the opinion of the two families from the Plage de l'Isolella, as they walked down to the seafront.

Aware that it might be cumbersome and unsatisfactory to explore in a gaggle of eight, Matthew stopped in front of a restaurant. "I think we should split up and meet back here in about an hour for some lunch. I'm going to stroll around the harbour and admire the boats. Who'd like to come with me?"

The boys volunteered to go with him and so did Marina, who always opted to be where Charlie was and Bella wasn't. They set off.

Bella tucked her arm firmly around Tim's. She gave Connie a little smile and a look, which could only be interpreted as an unspoken dismissal. It gave Connie the perfect excuse to wave merrily and say, "See you later." Tim looked uncomfortable but there was nothing she could do about it. She headed towards the main street which was full of shops and cafés. Being on her own was a treat. She was wearing her favourite dress—a cheap, cotton, high-waisted midi bought from C&A years before. It had a short-sleeved, denim bodice and a blue and white checked skirt. It made her feel young, pretty and carefree.

The shops were inviting and buzzing with cheerful activity. There were beach clothes, casual clothes and smart clothes. There were shops full of leather goods and the delicious scent that went with them. There were shoe shops full of pretty sandals and jewellery shops with displays of beads, bracelets and earrings. There were bright scarves, hats and vibrant colours everywhere. People were admiring window displays of confectionery and gathering outside the ice cream sellers. Most of the merchandise was of good quality and the shopkeepers uniformly charming.

Connie lingered in a boutique for some time, with the luxury of knowing she wasn't holding anyone up. She eventually bought a sarong; not just a rectangle of cloth to be knotted over a swimming suit, but a long wrap-over skirt, shaped to fit the hips and with an extended waist band to tie around the middle. It was a rich aubergine colour and very elegant.

She retraced her steps to the harbour, which was backed by tall houses painted in soft pastel colours. There were cultivated lawns, date palms and a wonderful view out into the bay. She sat on a bench. A young and very attractive dark-haired couple had taken up station beneath a nearby tree. They started to sing arias from La Bohème. They were the personification of Mimi and Rodolfo; their pure, thrilling voices reverberating with passion and doomed love. Connie was entranced and emotionally moved; she loved opera. She was conscious of being in a rare state of exquisite happiness.

It didn't last. Bella plonked herself down on the bench.

"Where's Tim?" Connie asked.

"He's gone to find the others; they're all on their way." She pointed in the direction of the group heading towards them.

"I've been enjoying the opera."

"Well, it's very nice but, to be honest, I can take it or leave it."

~

On Thursday, Matthew proposed a trip to Ajaccio to see the Maison Bonaparte, Napoleon's family home. Connie disliked busy cities with their crowds and traffic and opted to stay behind. She liked the thought of a day on her own, with a book and the tapestry which she'd brought but had remained untouched in its bag. The only visitor would be the leathery-skinned man who had been so helpful about the lemons. He was called Xavier and came every day to check the pool and water the garden. He wasn't talkative but smiled a lot, exuding goodwill. She managed to hide her disappointment when Bella announced that she, also, would prefer to stay behind.

The car took off. Connie pottered around for a bit before laying a towel on a lounger and settling down luxuriously by the pool. She was shaded by a parasol; her book and a glass of lemonade were on a small table to one side. She closed her eyes.

"Connie, we can't stay here all day, lounging around and doing nothing." Bella's voice was bordering on the bossy.

"Why not?"

"It would be dull and a wasted opportunity. I'd like us to swim across the bay and walk back along the beach. I did it the other day and it was heavenly."

"I honestly think that would be too far for me. You're an experienced swimmer but I'm not. I'll stay here."

"Connie, don't be such a wet blanket. It's not difficult and you'll enjoy it."

Connie didn't want to go anywhere but Bella had been friendly all week, girly and giggly; it had been quite like old times. Connie valued friendship; it was a rare and wonderful thing. Even a pretence of it was better than nothing. She also knew it had to be a two-way process. Bella had clearly been making an effort to be pleasant and Connie didn't want to appear churlish and ungenerous.

"Oh, all right, then. We'll lock the house, hide the key and just go."

They trooped down the sandy path and plunged into sparkling sea. The bay was a semi-circle. At one end was their villa and on a point at the other end were two charming islets, both with trees and one having a little house. They were attached to the mainland with a walkway. Bella proposed to swim in a straight line from villa to islets.

About halfway across, a feeling of uneasiness stole over Connie. She was not just tired; she was exhausted. She kept going but the gradual realisation that she could not manage much more slowly dawned on her and then filled her with alarm. Bella was a long way ahead, scarcely visible. To call out would be futile. Connie looked around; she was more or less equidistant from any bit of shore. There was nobody anywhere nearby. She willed herself to stay calm but an unspeakable dread began to take hold. She had never before felt so alone, surrounded by empty sea, usually so beautiful but now full of deadly menace. Her limbs felt heavy, as if weighted down, and she could hardly move them.

She knew that she was in the grip of panic and decided to try floating. She turned on her back. She'd read somewhere what to do, but it didn't work. Either her head went down, causing her to swallow seawater, or her legs sank. A horrible, visceral terror seized hold of her. More hideous than anything was the thought of the vast emptiness waiting beneath her. She began to pray.

"On peut vous aider, Madame?"

A little sailing boat was floating beside her and a bespectacled man held out a pole for her to grasp. Somehow, he manoeuvred the vessel so that she could climb a little set of steps at the stern. In fact, she was so weak that he had to haul her up. Undignified but she was well past caring.

"Merci," she said.

"Anglaise?"

"Oui, I'm Connie."

"I'm Pierre. Where can I take you?"

"La bas, s'il vous plaît, par les arbres."

Why was she speaking French when Pierre spoke perfect English? She tried to smile but her lips were quivering so much, she couldn't move them into position. She pressed them together. He could see that she was in a state of deep shock and asked no questions but passed her a small silver flask. Connie never touched spirits but she gulped at whatever was in the flask and an explosion went off in her head. She had some more, then handed it back. "Thank you."

When they reached the shore, Pierre helped her out of the boat and insisted on escorting her up the path to the front door. She got the key from under the mat and unlocked it. Her natural courtesy asserted itself. "Would you like to come in for a glass of wine or a cup of tea?"

He shook his head. Connie put out her hand. "Thank you, Pierre." She looked into his concerned brown eyes. Without thinking rationally, she said, "I have three sons." She could tell that he understood her anguish and agonising train of thought; she began to cry. He gestured for her to go inside and then waved goodbye.

Once she'd started, Connie couldn't stop crying. She sobbed hysterically as she peeled off her bathing suit and stepped under the thunderous shower. She soaped, shampooed and conditioned, her tears mingling with the water. Finally, she calmed, turned off the tap and dried herself. She applied moisturiser and after sun lotion. She blow dried her hair and gave it extra bounce with a hot brush. From the shelf behind the curtain in the bedroom, she took out some sexy black knickers and a top which she hadn't yet worn. It was white cotton, shaped and boned in front with elasticated shirring at the back; no sleeves and no straps. She slipped it over her head and liked the way it fitted snugly over her breasts, with just the right amount of fullness on show to look luscious rather than vulgar.

She put on her new sarong. It draped beautifully over her hips. It was a little too long and would need turning up when she got home but, for now, some high-heeled mules would balance things out.

She made up her eyes and applied lip gloss; she sprayed herself with Diorissimo and put on some dangly earrings. The golden skin of her graceful neck and shoulders looked lustrous, her hair shone, her shapely, slender figure was alluring. From now on, there would be no more modest self-effacement. She walked with a regal bearing into the kitchen and made herself a cup of tea. She carried it out to the veranda and sat, waiting.

The Ajaccio contingent was the first and noisiest to arrive. She gathered that the great emperor's birthplace had been underwhelming but worth a visit. Soon after, Bella trudged up the path. Connie looked carefully for signs of disappointment or guilt. There were none, just an air of irritation.

"Oh, there you are, Connie. I was wondering what happened to you." She went indoors.

Charlie and Marina went to make the tea while Jamie and Ned headed for the pool. Connie could feel both men looking at her with appreciative eyes. She ignored them. She felt strangely removed from what was happening around her and couldn't behave naturally.

The sun was going down and they were all assembled on the terrace, dressed and ready to go in search of dinner. The white gate opened and a courier came in with an enormous bouquet of flowers. The card said, 'To Madame Connie, from Pierre, with my good wishes'.

"What have you been up to?" Matthew asked.

"Pierre rescued me earlier and brought me home."

"Well, aren't you the lucky one," said Bella in a sing-song voice.

Connie felt her carefully cultivated composure beginning to fracture. Wordlessly, she stood and carried the flowers inside. She took the wilting hydrangeas out to the bins at the back, rinsed the vase and filled it with fresh water. With kitchen scissors, she trimmed the stems from the fragrant lilies and roses. One by one, she gently placed them in the vase, each stem accompanied with a prayer of thanks to Pierre. He wasn't a handsome man; he had a poor physique, poor teeth and acne scars. To her, though, he was an Olympian god who would be revered and worshipped for the rest of her life.

When Connie and Matthew were alone before going to bed, she asked him, "How can you make a sailing boat stop in the sea?"

"Not being a sailor, I don't know. I think it involves jibs and rudders."

In a light and conversational tone, she said, "Bella tried to kill me today."

"Don't be silly, Connie." He knew something had upset her and his voice was gentle.

"It's true. She knew I wouldn't be able to manage that swim. It would have been the perfect crime. No one would ever have suspected a thing."

"That's an appalling thing to say."

Matthew wanted her that night but she turned away from him. He hadn't believed her and he'd called her silly and appalling. Perhaps, it was just as well. For the first time, Connie admitted to herself that, although she could never have him, she wanted another woman's husband. On some unfathomable level, that woman understood this all too well.

Seventeen
1996

The comfortable balance of life in the Shaw household had shifted. Charlie had left home to read engineering at Oxford and was installed in a room at the top of a tower overlooking a quad at University College. The room was equipped with a rope ladder, in case of fire. This would allow him to escape through the window to avoid incineration but it deliberately stopped too short to facilitate an illegal entry.

Connie was unprepared for the desolation that overwhelmed her. The pain of his absence was excruciating but she couldn't share it with Matthew, Jamie or Ned in case it made them feel they weren't enough to fill the void. She felt unwell for weeks and this was compounded by the presence of Matthew's parents, who'd arrived in June and showed no signs of wanting to leave.

She blamed them for an upsetting feeling that she'd let Charlie down. He'd come to her with a letter detailing all the things he'd probably need for his first term. So distracted and tired had she been with the incessant demands from Paul and Laura that she told her son to sort it out for himself. Guiltily, she'd asked Charlie about it later but he'd taken offence and wouldn't discuss it. Even worse than that was when Charlie told her that his schoolmate, Adam, who had also been offered a place at Oxford, was receiving much more parental support than he himself was. Adam's parents had filled a crate with tinned food, supplied a toaster as well as a kettle and had made a special journey into Oxford town centre to fit him out with sub-fusc.

Connie told Matthew of these painful instances of inadequacy but his response had been robust. "At some stage, Connie, this adult offspring of ours is going to have to realise that he is no longer a child. He must stand on his own two feet. You've probably done him a favour."

Charlie's interview had been the previous winter. There had been snow on the ground and the trains weren't reliable, so he spent the night before with a friend who lived within walking distance of the college. He was supposed to wear a smart, grey suit, which was also his school uniform but, when he arrived home that evening, he was in an extremely scruffy pair of jeans.

"Why aren't you in your suit?" Connie asked.

"I decided not to wear it."

"But you look like an old tramp with a drink problem."

"That's exactly the sort of person they want at Oxford these days."

"What did they ask you in the interview?"

"First, they asked me to describe what I was wearing in French."

"You could manage that, I presume."

"Yes, of course."

"What else?"

"They asked me to work out the square root of 'i'."

"How can a letter have a square root?"

"'I' is not a letter. It is a symbol for minus 1."

"Could you do that?"

"No, but I tried to."

"Then what?"

"They asked me to state, if I was in a position to propose a bill to go through parliament, what that bill would be."

"And what did you say?"

"I said that I would propose legalising the use of cocaine for recreational purposes."

Connie looked shocked and furious. "That's not funny, Charlie. They're not going to want you now. You are a complete nincompoop."

"It was a joke, Mum. I didn't really say that. I said that I would propose a substantial increase in funding for infrastructure projects around the country. Now that the Channel Tunnel has been up and running for a couple of years, we could extend the high-speed rail line from London, St Pancras, through Birmingham, Manchester, Leeds, Newcastle and Edinburgh to Glasgow.

"We could dam The Wash to protect the land behind from being flooded by North Sea tidal surges, harnessing the tidal hydropower at the same time. There could be a barrage across the Solway Firth with a motorway passing over it, passing west of the Lake District and linking with the M6, thus shortening journey times to the West Cumbrian industrial towns and beyond to Stranraer. Again, it would harness tidal hydropower. All these would be fantastic projects but they'd all need funding."

"Were they impressed?"

"No, of course, they weren't."

However, they offered him a place.

~

Matthew's parents had sold their lovely house with its land outside Nairobi because they no longer felt safe there. They had the good fortune to sell it to a government official, rich enough to afford it and sufficiently corrupt to break the law of the land by depositing the money out of the country and into a Swiss bank account. Many less fortunate ex-pats had returned to Britain in a state of penury.

Their belongings were in store and the plan was to buy a small house near their son and his family and to settle down to a simple but secure life. It had been a difficult and anxious time for them, both in their early seventies, and Connie had done her best to welcome them and make them comfortable. She made them too comfortable. She drove them around for countless viewings of properties on the market but none was thought suitable. They had looked at some lovely apartments in a newly established retirement village with all sorts of facilities but there were concerns about proximity to the neighbours.

When first married, Connie had been invited to address her parents-in-law as 'Mama' and 'Papa', first names being thought too familiar. She rebelled and called them Paul and Laura and there was nothing they could do about it. Laura was a pretty woman with pearly white hair, which had once been blonde, and cornflower blue eyes which held a fragile expression. She used them to full advantage but Connie wasn't taken in. She had always preferred the male of the species, deeming him to be the more trustworthy, but when it came to women, she thought that a blonde was more to be feared than a brunette.

Laura wore bright lipstick, had a refined manner and always spoke with the utmost courtesy. Connie reminded herself that well-bred people always tried to be nice to the servants. She had also discovered that Laura could be amused by the unconventional. She was ironing one day, to the strains of Bellini, when Laura came into the utility room. "Would you mind, Connie dear, if I turn off this awful racket?"

"Yes, I most certainly would mind; this is my favourite aria." Laura had laughed.

"Connie, I thought I should let you know that our bath tap is leaking. Also, when Paul brought up my breakfast tray this morning, there was brown toast instead of white. You know I prefer white."

"Sorry about that."

"Do you think you could run me into town, please? I need some things from Boots."

"Now, this minute or might it wait until tomorrow? I'll be going in for a Sainsbury's shop and I could drop you off."

"Whenever would be most convenient for you. Thank you so very much."

~

Another cloud for Connie was her own mother's resentment over the perceived attention being received by Paul and Laura. There had been no independent holiday for the Shaws that summer and the week in Dorset had been cancelled. Deidre was furious.

She and Connie regularly exchanged letters. Connie kept hers light and neutral, carefully avoiding anything too cheerful. Deirdre's were becoming increasingly embittered with frequent references to her Will: *I know you neither need nor want anything, so I'm thinking of leaving my jewellery and mink coat to your cousin, Emma. She has been very kind to me recently.*

Connie felt insulted by the suggestion that she could be influenced in this way and just ignored it. However, when Deirdre started asking which bits of furniture the boys might like, in order that she could put little stickers on them like the fruit in the supermarket, Connie drew the line. In her next letter, she wrote at the end: *PS I have told the boys to give anyone who talks about their Will a wide berth.*

There was a longer than usual wait before the next letter.

~

It was Saturday in late October and the peaceful period between serving afternoon tea and supper. Connie sought refuge in her bedroom because it was the only place she could be alone. The room soothed her with its pale gold carpet and ivory furniture. The curtains were cream with tendrils of leafy honeysuckle weaving their way upwards, the flowers a delicate apricot and pale yellow. She had gilt-framed baby photographs of her boys around the walls and alabaster bedside lamps with rosy shades. The view out of the window was a different matter. The garden looked unkempt and sad, reflecting her own dishevelled state of mind.

Laura had complained, very discreetly, about the noise Jamie and Ned had been making, while playing football outside. It had disturbed her afternoon nap. She had then asked if Paul could move into Charlie's room because his snoring kept her awake at night. How could she not understand the impossibility of such a thing? When Connie had gently but emphatically refused this request, she'd been met with a haughty coldness. This reinforced her awareness of the shallowness of Laura's affection, if it existed at all under the veneer of civilised sweetness.

Another irritant, admittedly trivial, was the way Laura would deliver regular little homilies on household economy despite filling her own bath so full of hot water every night that it could be heard sloshing out of the overflow pipe.

Connie was aware of the concept of duty and obligation to elderly parents but the current situation could go on for another twenty years, if allowed to. That would kill her. She couldn't understand why Paul and Laura weren't desperate for independence and their own establishment. They were perfectly fit and able to drive. They had talked about getting a car but done nothing about it. They didn't do anything; their lives revolved around meals which she was expected to provide, endlessly.

Connie wondered if she would feel more charitable if they were ill or incapacitated in some way but was relieved that she didn't have to put this to the test.

She was doing things for them that they were perfectly well able to do for themselves. It was impossible to relax properly. She pretended to be at ease in the evenings, when they were sitting around the log stove, but she was in a permanent state of tension. Matthew was, too. A certain level of courtesy had to be always maintained and an air of interest in the most boring and regularly repeated conversations. Paul's political opinions were fairly extreme and Laura's were even worse.

Paul was ex-military and in the habit of demonstrating his leadership qualities by giving orders. He was quietly resigned to having no means of obliging anyone to carry them out but made up for this with offerings of shrewd judgement, sage advice and worldly wisdom. Connie was very fond of him and he of her. She had, after all, provided him with three fine grandsons.

Connie and Matthew weren't in the habit of swearing but the occasional expletive would have been a relief. That was out of the question. Every evening, as the clock ticked towards nine, Paul would say, "Shall we have the news?" He pronounced news as 'niooze' and it was beginning to drive Connie to a frenzy. Her own social life had imploded; she couldn't ask her friends around for coffee or tea. She and Matthew couldn't invite friends for dinner. She never had the house to herself. All her creative projects and hobbies were set on one side.

If Paul and Laura had their own home somewhere nearby, Connie would do almost anything to help them as long as she was free to return to the peace and solitude of her own house afterwards. She still had ambitions for some sort of career. She was still young and Ned was now fourteen. Her brief experience of teaching convinced her that she had the ability but it was beginning to seem as if she would never get the chance.

Sitting up in bed that night before turning off her lamp, Connie said to Matthew, "We have to do something."

"I know. I've been thinking about it."

"I feel as if my soul has been squeezed dry of every drop of optimism and energy. I feel worthless, drained of creativity and devoid of humour. And I miss Charlie."

"I miss him, too. My mother's behaviour is driving me crazy and Dad still can't bring himself to acknowledge that I've done anything useful since I left school."

"We can't go on like this."

"I agree and I have a plan. I've been making a few enquiries. When we first moved into this house, we were going to extend the kitchen. An architect drew up a design, we successfully applied for planning permission and we even had a builder lined up. Then, we decided that we couldn't cope with the upheaval."

"Yes, I remember. Are you suggesting we resurrect the idea?"

"I've been in touch with the architect who says he can get the planning permission updated. I've also been in touch with the builder who says he could start next month. If you're in favour of the idea, Connie, I'll give my parents an ultimatum. They must decide on the retirement village or a hotel within the next two weeks. We'll try a bit of reverse emotional blackmail and make a big thing about the sacrifice we've been making, generously putting things off so that we could take care of them. I'll also let them know that, if we delay any longer, we'll lose the time slot offered by the builder. What do you think?"

"I think you're a genius."

~

Events moved rapidly. A departure date was set for Friday in the third week of November with the builders coming in to start on the kitchen the following Monday. Anticipating a lot of fuss and reasons for delay, Connie had asked Matthew to book lunch for himself and his parents in the restaurant at the retirement village, which was called Maple Manor. A time schedule would concentrate the minds. The food there was excellent and she also suggested that he book all seven of them in for Christmas Day lunch, as her own kitchen was going to be out of commission. They could work out who paid later.

As the leaving day approached, Connie felt more and more guilty and she was positively emotional when the moment came for them to leave. Matthew had taken the day off work and was being very calm and business-like. Absolutely everything was ready in the apartment. It was just a question of packing up their last few remaining personal belongings. Nonetheless, there was a lot of banging about and slamming of doors. As Matthew finally managed to usher his parents out of the front door, Connie kissed them goodbye.

"I know you've done your best, Connie," said Laura, "but it's been hard for us staying here and we're glad to be going."

Connie waved until the car was out of sight. She shut the door, went to the kitchen and made herself a cup of coffee. *Thank you for that, Laura, thank you so very much. I can now feel spiritually as well as physically free of you.* She sat in the rocking chair by the window. There were newspapers piled up on the windowsill. She and Matthew liked *The Independent* but she'd asked to have *The Telegraph* delivered for Paul and *The Mail* for Laura. They'd forgotten to take them; she must ring the newsagent and cancel the order. Usually, she was an avid follower of world affairs. This month had seen royal divorces, a fire in the Channel Tunnel, the re-election of Bill Clinton, Mad Cow Disease and the birth of Dolly, the sheep. Just at the moment, she couldn't get worked up about any of it.

She rocked gently back and forth. The house was like a furnace because the heating had been on full blast since September. She must switch off the radiators but she couldn't summon the energy. There was none to summon; the cistern was empty. She knew it would trickle back slowly but the process hadn't yet started.

Despite her bravado, Connie was wounded; engulfed with feelings of inadequacy and deprivation. She didn't know why but inadequacy was a default part of her normal condition along with the constant need to please other people and a fear of letting them down. It was a mug's game; a waste of time and she was going to stop doing it forthwith.

Deprivation was a different matter and required some analysis. She sipped her coffee and looked out of the window. Most of the leaves were down; the trees looked bare and vulnerable. She hadn't expected gratitude from Laura but some token of affection would have been welcome. It was the lack of motherliness which pained her; it was just the same with her own mother. Deirdre could put on a show of maternal benevolence if there was an audience. The act was the main component of the whole business. She had an act for every occasion, often accompanied by a sentimental narrative of her own imagining.

It was horrible to be snubbed one minute and wooed back the next with purring platitudes, as if you were too stupid to discriminate between fake and genuine. It wasn't the absence of people that induced loneliness but the thinly veiled indifference and narcissism often encountered when with them.

She should be happy. She'd just been released from a great burden. She must stop this self-pitying nonsense.

~

Several weeks earlier, Paul and Laura's furniture had been moved out of store and deposited on the floor of the Shaw's double garage. Connie looked at it, trying to fight off a sense of desperation. Laura stood beside her, helpless and complaining of cold, despite wearing a thick coat. A grand piano and some massive wardrobes were the only items that had been, mercifully, left behind in the old house.

Some of the stuff was beautiful but much of it wasn't and all of it was sadly neglected and suffering damage from white ants and woodworm. There was a musty smell. The beds were particularly dispiriting; heavy, scratched wooden bases and headboards with ancient mattresses, probably home to trillions of dust mites and gallons of dried-up bodily fluids. There were heaps of curtains, edges in shreds from sunlight, linings grubby and rain-stained.

Sofas and armchairs, once welcoming and comfortable, now looked sagging and shabby. A huge refectory table surrounded by ten clumsy chairs had boxes of china and glassware piled on top. The china might have been valuable but was unsuitable for a dishwasher. Much of it was broken and crudely glued back together. Paul and Laura had lived with the frugal habits of the wartime generation.

Connie was knowledgeable about old furniture. Her father had loved antiques and she'd gone with him to auction sales. The new apartment was one of the largest on offer. It had a generous living room, two spacious bedrooms, each with its own bathroom and fitted cupboards, a good-sized kitchen with separate utility room and an airy hall. However, Connie could tell at a glance that most of the stuff in the garage wasn't going to fit.

There was a Welsh dresser, a massive sideboard, a few heavily carved Jacobean chests of drawers, several occasional tables, a heap of moth-eaten oriental rugs, a Wellington chest with a cunning locking mechanism down one side and drawers stuffed with old bits of used wrapping paper and sundry pieces of general rubbish.

"You must be very attached to all these things, Laura," said Connie gently. "An important part of your life is spread around in here."

"No, I'm not remotely attached to it. I hate most of the dismal, brown, depressing load of junk. I didn't choose it. It all came from Paul's family. When we were young, it didn't occur to us to pick and choose; we just used whatever was going. When we moved house, we didn't automatically change things; we accepted things as they were and got on with it. There was never any nonsense about new kitchens and new bathrooms and ridiculous extensions. And we looked after our elderly parents."

"I don't remember you and Paul doing that," replied Connie.

"Of course, we did," snapped Laura.

"Well," said Connie, "if you don't care too deeply about most of this, our task will be much easier. Some of these things are very lovely and will fit perfectly in your drawing room. This bow-fronted chest of drawers is Hepplewhite; that mahogany corner cupboard is Sheraton, the beautiful leather-topped desk will be just the thing for Paul's new computer and printer. Matthew has booked him in for the beginner's class at the local college. You might like to go along, too. Paul is planning to write his military memoirs down in a professional format.

"The small mahogany dining table will fit, especially as the top folds down from horizontal to vertical when you release the bolt. It's brilliant. We'll have to look for some daintier chairs and I've seen a set in a local antique shop which you might like. This canteen of silver cutlery is magnificent but you'll need some everyday stainless-steel knives and forks for your dishwasher.

"If you agree, more or less, with what I'm suggesting and clear it with Paul, I'll arrange for the things you'd like to keep to go to a furniture restorer. He'll polish it all up, repair any damage and treat any woodworm. The rest of the stuff can go to the auction rooms."

Laura looked glum. "What about the pictures?"

"I'm sure you'll want to keep those but, perhaps, we should buy some new mirrors. What's under here?" Connie lifted up an old candlewick bedspread. "Oh, this is pretty. It's an envelope table. The four flaps open out, swivel around and form a card table."

"Yes, I know," replied Laura. "We used to play bridge on it."

"The green baize is all mildewed but we can get that replaced easily. This is Adam style and the wood is ripple mahogany with classical inlays and it has a little drawer for cards. It's exquisite and delicate. You can't part with this."

"No, we'll hang on to that. Connie, what will Paul and I do all day in this wretched flat?"

"You'll be free to do whatever you want. You won't have to stay inside all day, you'll have a car. Matthew and Paul have gone for a test drive today. You'll be able to explore the local area and then go further afield. You can book up for short breaks all over the country. There's so much to see and so many places to visit. You can become a member of the National Trust and English Heritage."

"I don't want to be a member of anything." Laura's tone was so redolent of disgust when repeating the word 'member', that Connie had to suppress a laugh.

"It just means that you can visit lots of beautiful stately homes without paying each time. It's well worth it but, apart from that, there are all sorts of events and outings laid on by a committee at Maple Manor. You and Paul have always been sociable, far more so than Matthew and I have. There'll be people to talk to, play bridge with, have meals with, walk with, if you want to. You won't be bosom buddies with everybody but you'll soon find some congenial people. And then, there is everything that London has to offer. It would be easy to hop on a train and take advantage of some of the culture.

"In fact, I think you and I should have a trip into London. We'll go to Harrod's, John Lewis and Liberty's and have some fun. We'll choose curtains, carpets, new beds, duvets, sheets, towels and, definitely, some new sofas."

"It's all such an effort. I don't think I can be bothered and the weather is so cold and miserable. I do miss the African sunshine; everything is gloomy here."

Connie began to feel her patience wearing thin. "Laura, just imagine being given a terminal diagnosis tomorrow and told that you only had three months to live. You would say to yourself, 'How I wish I could be back in that freezing garage full of shabby furniture, with my tiresome daughter-in-law. I was in a state of good health and making exciting plans for the future and had nothing to worry about'."

"Connie, are you implying that I should be counting my blessings?"

"Certainly not."

"Good. Because that would have been extremely aggravating."

There was a pause and then Laura laughed. "You have a point, though, and I like the sound of a shopping spree in London. Will we have time to take in an art gallery?"

"I very much doubt it."

Eighteen

A tall, thin, upright figure was a regular sight marching purposefully around the perimeter path of the Maple Manor Retirement Village between nine and ten o'clock in the morning. Paul had renamed his new surroundings 'The Barracks' and found much to his liking there. He was dressed like a country squire, having jettisoned his old camel hair coat in favour of a green Barbour jacket and a tweed flat cap.

The grounds were extensive and well-cared for with mature trees, lawns and great rhododendron bushes. Even in December, thanks to all the evergreens, the garden was lush and beautiful and full of promise for the coming spring. His life felt good.

There had been three major, almost miraculous, revelations in the last few weeks. The first was the art of podiatry. For years, Paul had suffered from afflictions of the feet, with corns and hard skin. Neither had rendered him immobile but had spoiled his pleasure in walking and it had never occurred to him that anything could be done about it.

On seeing a card on the notice board in the reception area, he rang a telephone number and soon after was established in an extraordinary chair with a footrest that divided into two. He was in a bright, fresh-smelling room and the young man in attendance wore a spotless white tunic. After thirty minutes of skilful manipulation with a scalpel, accompanied by delightful conversation, Paul's feet felt like a child's; soft, smooth and pain-free. He felt as if he was walking on a pair of small goose down pillows.

The second revelation was his entry into the world of computing. It was magical. The class for beginners didn't start until the New Year but Matthew had given him some basic instruction and he had a user manual. Paul was intelligent and absorbed new techniques quickly. He could already touch type but the astonishing range of functions on the word processor relegated his old Olivetti to a state of pitiful obsolescence. The facility for looking up any information he wanted was thrilling beyond belief.

Paul had a good army pension. He had also inherited money and took very seriously the task of investing it wisely. Much time each week had been spent poring over the *Financial Times* and drawing up complicated graphs. Now, at the touch of a few buttons, all the information he needed came straight up on the screen. He felt a moral duty to nurture his capital, also Laura's, in order to pass it on, intact and ideally increased, to the next generation. However, judging by the manner in which Matthew and Connie threw money around, it would appear that they didn't really need any more. You'd think they'd never heard of words like saving, frugality or economy.

Perhaps, he should leave all his money to the Battersea Dogs Home. That would give them a shock. The only reassuring aspect of the situation was the hope that they weren't yet anticipating his demise too eagerly. He felt an enormous pride in his family but he certainly wasn't going to inform them of this.

The third revelation, possibly the most important, was the availability of prepared meals from Marks & Spencer. Paul was a simple man in some ways, with no interest in matters involving philosophy or psychology. All his life he'd been supplied with regular meals and other basics like clean clothes and surroundings. Laura had told him that she hated cooking and food shopping but the implications of this had little effect until their second day in the apartment. Connie had stocked the freezer and filled the fridge with enough food to tide them over for a few days. Paul, feeling a little peckish in the middle of the day, opened the fridge door and said, "Right. What shall we have for lunch?"

"I don't know and I don't care." Laura's response startled him into the realisation that, if they weren't to starve to death, he would have to take measures of the pro-active sort. Connie told him about M&S and he would drive off twice a week and load up with all manner of luxury foods; fish and chicken in delicious sauces, moussakas, lasagnes, pies, smoked salmon, prawns, prepared vegetables, salads and wonderful fruit. There were raspberries, strawberries and blueberries all year round as well as the usual apples, oranges and pears. There were also trifles, crumbles, pastries and cream cakes. The list went on and on. It was expensive but cheaper than eating in the Maple Restaurant every day.

Laura had settled in pretty well and, as long as she wasn't called upon to exert herself, she was good-tempered. She had a flattering way of deferring to his judgement on various matters; she relied on him and would mind if he died. He would mind if she died; the loneliness would be terrible. She had joined the Ladies' Bridge Club and spent three afternoons a week with congenial companions. Paul loved having the apartment to himself on these occasions, concentrating without interruption on his computer.

Twice a week, the housekeeping team would arrive to clean everything. Bright and chatty in pretty uniforms, they would swoop into the apartment, render it sparkling and sweet-smelling and then swoop out. Laura looked forward to their coming. Paul made himself scarce.

Military life had been full of camaraderie and good fellowship. It was hard to keep friendships going in the long term but there were occasional reunions on neutral territory. It took energy to sustain the 'heartiness'. Also, people had a habit of growing old, becoming ill, losing their marbles, even being careless enough to die. Dying wasn't on the agenda for himself or Laura. Paul had read countless articles in newspapers and magazines advising on how to avoid it. They were all the same and it was easy. You didn't drink, you didn't smoke, you had a good night's sleep, you took exercise, ate good food and socialised.

He had never fully understood what constituted good food as opposed to bad but Connie told him to buy lots of vegetables and fruit and to lay off cakes and biscuits. He absolutely refused, however, to buy another cucumber. He had twice discovered a polythene sausage full of disgusting sludge lurking at the back of the fridge.

As for socialising, he would leave that to Laura. These days, he didn't welcome the opinions of others unless they were closely aligned with his own. He did admit, though, that the cheery greetings and brief exchanges of pleasantries while on his morning walks could lift his spirits.

The old manor house was the social hub of the village. There were communal rooms, the restaurant, a helpful receptionist, a library and a hairdresser. Outside, there was a heated swimming pool, a bowling green, a tennis court and a small supermarket. Everything was clean and modern and someone else's responsibility.

Paul had never fully appreciated the sheer beauty, wonderful culture and fascinating history of England. Laura missed the heat and sunshine of Africa but he didn't. The temperate weather suited him and he was full of optimism as he and Laura drove out on exploratory expeditions. There were attractive buildings, ancient churches and pubs, and always hostelries serving tea and toasted teacakes. He was looking forward to visiting Hughenden and Bletchley Park, both places with wartime associations, when they opened in the spring.

He hadn't wanted to move. Connie's household ran like clockwork and he'd been very comfortable there. It never occurred to him to wonder how she single-handedly and, apparently, effortlessly managed to achieve what he'd paid six African employees to do in his previous existence. One wasn't allowed to call them 'boys' any longer. If asked, he would have put it down to all the machines, called appliances, that everyone had in England. He didn't properly understand why the arrangement couldn't have continued indefinitely. The financial savings would have been enormous and he liked to think that the presence of grandparents had a generally stabilising effect with all the wisdom accrued over the decades available just for the asking.

Paul generally regarded Connie with much favour but she'd been very high-handed in persuading Laura to chuck out all their belongings. Very high-handed indeed. At least, he'd managed to persuade her to keep the refectory table with its matching chairs and the Welsh dresser. These had belonged to his grandfather and, as well as being fine pieces of furniture, had a strong emotional attachment for him. They'd be perfect for the new extension which was going to serve as the dining end of the new kitchen. He looked forward to many meals in it.

Occasionally, Paul wondered if he and Laura would have been better off in one of the neat little bungalows Matthew had taken them to view. He was, however, sufficiently pragmatic to admit that it wouldn't have worked. The joy of having their own garden would have worn off quite quickly; it was a bit late in the day to develop a passion for growing potatoes or tomatoes. He never felt confined in their apartment because of his freedom to roam and oversee the heavenly grounds outside it. Being lord of the manor was a pleasing fantasy.

Nineteen

It took Connie quite a long time to recover her normal feeling of well-being. Fully expecting to be delirious with joy over the recaptured freedom of that first weekend, she was dismayed to find herself overwhelmed with lassitude and an oppressive sense of failure. Laura had known what she was doing with her parting shot.

Nonetheless, there was work to be done and preparations to be made. She wrote 'Multivitamins' on her shopping list and asked Matthew if he and the boys would empty the kitchen cupboards and set up makeshift arrangements in the utility room. She anticipated grumbling, muddle and chaos but couldn't face the task herself and went upstairs to clean the guest bedroom and bathroom. She worked thoroughly but slowly and without enthusiasm. On coming down some time later, she was astonished to find that Jamie and Ned had taken charge with military efficiency. Enough crockery, cutlery and cooking equipment had been set aside for everyday use and the rest stored in packing cases left behind by Paul and Laura.

Matthew had been dispatched to Comet to buy a small electric oven which now sat on the worktop in the utility room. He'd also bought a plug-in hotplate with two rings, having been advised by his sons that the camping stove with its great gas container and flimsy legs would not be practical. The fridge and freezer had been manhandled into the garage, which was easily accessed through a side door. Mats had been put down to avoid floor contamination while passing back and forth. With the kettle, toaster and microwave in place, they had everything they needed. Connie felt her spirits rising.

Punctually at eight o'clock on Monday, the vans rolled up. An enormous skip and a portaloo were deposited on the drive. The work area was screened off with sheets of hardboard; demolition of the outer kitchen wall began. Connie welcomed the activity and purpose after months of stasis. The men were highly professional and self-sufficient. They would sit around a small incinerator at the far end of the garage to have their breaks, having been invited to help themselves to logs from Matthew's ample store. The foreman was relaxed and genial but his perfectionism soon became apparent and Connie trusted him completely.

Her spirits remained stubbornly low. She entered a state of self-imposed purdah, avoiding social contact. She couldn't be bothered with the business of trying to please people, feign interest in their opinions and massage their egos. She would lie awake at night, listening to Matthew gently snoring beside her, brooding over negative thoughts. She was awestruck by the exquisite politeness with which people could exploit and then crucify others. It wasn't just Laura; it was human nature.

Her father, who had been a deeply moral man despite his fun-loving disposition, had always impressed upon her that the act of giving was more conducive to happiness than that of taking. It hadn't done him a lot of good and Connie couldn't help wondering if the joy of giving to the ungrateful was overrated.

She turned her attention to the neglected garden. There were dead leaves everywhere; windblown heaps of russety beech, birch leaves which had fluttered down like snowflakes almost disintegrating before reaching the ground, the bright red circular carpet that had lain beneath the maple, now dark and sodden. There were orange and yellow leaves from the sumac, leaves from prunus, cornus, magnolia and wisteria. All were raked up and piled into a chicken wire enclosure to start the miraculous metamorphosis into nutritious leaf mould.

The lawn was cut for the last time that year and the mower sent off for a service. Connie trimmed the lawn edges, weeded the beds, pruned the roses, cut back the perennials. The boys made a bonfire at the weekend, with crackling flames and fragrant woodsmoke curling into the crisp air. A tarpaulin appeared on the lawn outside the shed. Flowerpots, watering cans, an old kitchen bin full of bamboo canes, old washing-up bowls full of string, hose fittings and rubber gloves, containers of plant food and bug killer were placed on it. Tools were put on one side to be washed and oiled. Connie reversed out with a wheelbarrow full of sacks of compost. They were heavy. The shed was swept, divested of cobwebs and spiders, and then everything was put back.

Finally, a coat of cedar woodstain was applied. The fresh air coupled with the satisfaction induced by the whole operation were therapeutic. The former generosity of spirit and optimism, which had withered inside her, seeped back. She was sleeping well and taking an enthusiastic interest in the building development. Then Charlie came home for the vacation and it was as if he had never left.

~

The boys were in their rooms; Matthew and Connie were on the sofa in front of the log stove. There was nothing on television that they wanted to watch. Dinner had been salmon fillets with vegetables and parsley sauce followed by yogurt and rich purée made from July's crop of blackcurrants. Cooking was easy in the utility room; it was the dishwasher that they all missed.

The sitting room was warm with cream silk lampshades giving out a lustrous brilliance. Connie sat with her feet tucked up, a pale pink angora jumper lending her an aura of gentle softness. An open copy of Henry James' *The Portrait of a Lady* was by her side. Matthew was reading the newspaper. Outside, it was stormy with gusts of wind hurling raindrops against the windows.

"I'm worried about Christmas," she said.

"There's nothing to worry about. We'll get a tree and put up all the usual paraphernalia. You'll say it looks tacky and tasteless but it can't be helped. We're booked in at Maple Manor for lunch with Mum and Dad. Dad will then frog-march everyone around the estate and Mum will complain about the weather. Then, we'll all come back here for tea and play Monopoly, or watch something on television."

"Yes, all that will be fine but the morning will feel a bit sterile with no tasty turkey aromas wafting around. Perhaps, I'll cook some crispy sausages to have with our coffee."

"That sounds like a good idea. The boys aren't babies anymore. Jamie told me that all his friends hate Christmas but he really likes it. So, don't worry."

"I wrote to the headmistress of the local school today to say that if there were any vacancies going for next September, I'd like to apply."

Matthew briefly wondered how this might impact on his own comfort but said, "That's great. Good for you. Incidentally, I forgot to mention that Tim has asked if we'd like a trip to Prague next May. He's very excited about a new European research project which includes scientists from the old eastern bloc. Since 1989, everything has been opening up and a lot of collaboration is going on with Poles, Czechs, East Germans, Hungarians, Ukrainians, Romanians and Russians. It's all very exhilarating and a major conference is being organised in

Prague. Tim will be giving a keynote talk and he has invited me to go along. Bella will be going, not to the conference, but for the sightseeing and wonders if you would like to keep her company."

Connie was silent. She'd had over two years to recover from nearly drowning in Corsica. She didn't want to believe that Bella had wanted her to die and tried to convince herself that she alone had been responsible for what had happened. Nevertheless, a sense of distrust remained. Bella was still officially a friend but not someone to go to for reassurance, kindness or help of any kind. Tim and Matthew still met regularly for a beer in the same old pub and, occasionally, would have a weekend of climbing in North Wales. Apart from Shotover Hill and Wytham Hill, the land around Oxford was flat. The Chiltern countryside, although charming, lacked the majesty of the mountains. In Wales, they could recapture the thrill of their student days.

They still had evenings out as a foursome. There was safety in numbers and the pleasure Connie felt in Tim's company outweighed the lesser pleasure of Bella's. Their last get-together had been a performance of *Nabucco* at The Royal Opera in April. They met by the bar in the main concourse. The theatre had seating for over two thousand people and there was something magical and uplifting about seeing familiar faces among a great mass of strangers. The men were formally dressed in dark suits. Bella wore a bright green dress, which set off her blonde hair; she looked magnificent and stood out in the crowd. She cast a knowing eye over her friend's outfit.

Gone were the days of homemade simplicity. Connie was the epitome of refinement and allure with a shapely black skirt, velvety high-heeled boots and a fitted jacket of purple and black, edged with fine black piping. In her ears were gold double-hooped rings. There was something graceful about the set of her head on the slender neck and she moved like a ballerina.

The omens for the evening weren't particularly good. While Tim radiated pleasure and warmth, Bella's eyes had the usual look of crushed ice and her smile seemed nothing more than a constriction of the muscles on either side of her mouth. The dulcet tones were the same. "Hi, Connie. You're looking thin. Are you alright? Have you lost weight?"

"I don't think so but I never weigh myself. We do have some scales but only use them to check suitcases before we fly anywhere. You are looking wonderful."

"Thank you." Bella could not be described as portly but she had solidified over the last couple of years. She had also developed a flirtatious way of rotating from side to side in front of Tim and fluttering her eyelashes. A bit like a child showing off a party dress. Tim smilingly indulged her but Connie felt that his heart wasn't in it. She was glad that the greater part of the evening would be spent listening to Verdi rather than talking.

They bought drinks and pre-ordered some for the interval. Their seats were in the Grand Tier. Opera, especially the Italian variety, was more than entertainment for Connie. It was therapy, a sort of spiritual workout. All the emotions were invoked, heightened and stretched to breaking point. Fear of failure, shame of inadequacy, pathos of loneliness, savagery of jealously, agony of loss, intensity of love, madness of lust, pain of betrayal, grandeur of courage, nobility of self-sacrifice, horror of vengeance, hatred of cruelty, redeeming purity of kindness; all could be acknowledged and vicariously experienced before being hidden away again beneath a veneer of outward calm.

She felt a thrill of anticipation looking out at the beautiful theatre; there was always the same electricity in the air, the hum of conversation, the deep silence when the lights went down, the applause as the first violinist followed by the conductor entered the orchestra pit and bowed. Then, the overture and the raising of the curtain.

Connie moved to a higher plane of consciousness and she forgot about everything except the drama. Even during the interval, she didn't want too much conversation because it impinged on the euphoria. She preferred to sip her wine in the luxury of silence and it was with some difficulty that she managed to respond to Bella's chatter.

Tim and Bella had recently moved into a brand-new house on a large development. Bella was thrilled with it and Connie half-listened admiringly to details about the kitchen, bathrooms, fitted wardrobes, Upvc windows, curtains, carpets and, finally, the neighbours.

"They're all such lovely people. We had such a warm welcome. They couldn't have done more to help us settle in. Was it like that for you, Connie, when you moved house?"

Connie thought back. Her neighbours had been kind and friendly in an understated way but she couldn't, at the moment, face the tedium of competition.

"I don't recall any throngs flocking to the door, bearing gifts," she replied.

"Oh, what a shame. But do you get on really well with any of them?"

Connie appeared to think hard. "Well, apart from the miserable swine who reported us to the Parish Council for having too many bonfires and, apart from Mr Fatso next door who made a big fuss when we had a potentially dangerous tree cut down, we are on civilised terms with most people in the community."

"Is Fatso a Hungarian name?"

"No, purely descriptive."

"I find everyone so fascinating. Don't you, Connie?"

"No, I don't."

Tim's expression was inscrutable but a faint look of alarm appeared in Matthew's. Connie wasn't obeying the social rules and he didn't know what to do about it.

Tim diffused the tension with some perceptive remarks about the staging of the production and instigated a spirited debate about the relative merits of the performers playing Nabucco, king of Babylon, his daughter, Fenena, Zaccaria, high priest of Jerusalem, Ismaele, Fenena's Israelite lover, and Abigaille, Fenena's half-sister.

Driving home afterwards, Matthew expressed tactful surprise about Connie's earlier hints at a less than perfect relationship with their neighbours. She was amused. Tim would have understood but there was an innocent and simplistic quality to Matthew. She knew herself to be on generally good terms with everyone. She avoided cliques but often managed a trusted rapport with those who were not universally popular. There was no disharmony.

"I was only joking," she said, "but the thing is, I just can't stand too much sanctimonious twaddle about the perfection of human nature and I hate having virtue rammed down my throat."

"I see," he replied.

But he hadn't seen. Sitting beside Matthew on the sofa that December evening, she reflected on how lucky she was to have married him. His open, kind, intelligent face looked at her enquiringly as he offered the chance of a lovely holiday. The insecurity and self-doubt, which had plagued him when they first met, had gone but he was still incapable of understanding why anyone should ever want to put anyone else at a disadvantage in any way.

"Where does your good nature come from?" she asked.

"I've no idea. From you, probably."

"Quite impossible but I'd love to go to Prague. I've always wanted to see it."

Twenty

There was a light tap on the door and Tim's head appeared around it.

"Can I do anything to help?"

"Yes, you can. Please come in and shut the door behind you. Things are not altogether under control in here but I don't want anyone to know about it."

He came in and looked around at the new kitchen and its huge extension.

"This looks like a cross between a baronial hall and the Ritz Hotel."

Connie nodded. She was looking a little flushed. "We were persuaded to have the ancestral furniture in here. I wasn't keen to start with but I like it now."

It was April and the building work had finished in March. The good-humoured band of craftsmen had packed up and left. For four months, Connie had observed, fascinated, the progression from foundations, damp-proof course, floor, walls, windows, doors, ceiling and roof. She had learned about wiring, heating pipes, cavity walls, insulation, soffits, fascias, gutters, joists and rafters. They had done a magnificent job.

The old kitchen units had been replaced with oak; the worktops and floor were cream. The new dining area was flooded with light; the west-facing side was made up entirely of glass sliding doors opening onto the terrace. The south end, facing the lawn, was mostly window reaching down to a low wall with a generous sill. The eastern wall had been left blank, to take the Welsh dresser, on either side of which were antique brass wall lights and pictures. Morning sunshine would filter through from the window over the sink.

A pretty Victorian brass ceiling light was suspended over the refectory table. It had three delicately curved brackets around an ornamental central column. Connie had found it lurking in the corner of a junk shop and it had been completely blackened from neglect. Matthew polished it to a golden lustre and they bought cut-glass shades for it from an antique lighting shop. When newly-installed, there had been a terrifying bang and half the house had short-circuited.

Shaken, the electrician had removed it. Mortified and grateful not to be sued, Connie had taken it to a specialist shop to have the wiring replaced.

Venetian blinds screened out the occasionally excessive sunlight and Connie had made curtains out of a vast acreage of rich William Morris fabric to keep the winter cold and gloom at bay. Paul's heavy chairs had been stripped, waxed and reupholstered in a soft green. A vase of spring flowers graced the centre of the table.

A celebration lunch was underway. Paul and Laura and the Melrose family had been invited. A large, free-range turkey had been ordered to compensate for their Christmas deprivation.

"Tell me what to do," said Tim.

"First of all, pour us both a glass of that wine over there. I need to get a little bit drunk to cope with the social stress."

"Well, you won't have to worry about keeping the conversation going. There's a hell of a racket in the sitting room. Matthew is dishing out champagne, sherry and Pimm's and everyone is talking at once; that's why I've come in search of a bit of peace. I left Laura telling Bella that the retirement village is very pleasant except for the fact that it's full of old people and the only reason they're still there is because they know they can leave whenever they want to."

"I know. They're ten years too young to be there and the maintenance charges are astronomical. They spend much of their spare time, and they have quite a lot of that, trawling round local estate agents to see what is available. At his computer class, Paul has learned how to do diagrams, so he gets hold of the floor plan of any property he likes the look of and redesigns the interior. It fascinates him. He should have been an architect instead of a soldier."

"Oh, I think being in the army suited him. He's been telling me all about the 'land manoeuvres' he carried out while sailing in the Mediterranean, including on Corsica."

Connie laughed. "Now, would you like to stir this bread sauce, please, while I attend to the gravy?"

Tim took charge of the pan with its fragrant aroma of cloves, onions and peppercorns. "This looks rather special. We make ours out of a packet."

"I often do as well but, today, everything is being done properly, including the stuffing."

The table had been laid beautifully with all the best knives and forks, china, mats and glasses.

"You see those napkin rings?"

Tim looked and saw that they were exquisitely pretty, each composed of three flowers, crafted with multiple, delicate, brass petals.

"When we went to visit my mother a couple of weeks ago, I saw them in an arty shop. I wanted them but was crippled by the brainwashing constraints of my childhood which dictated that you should only buy things for yourself if you really need them. I certainly didn't need them, so I devised a cunning ruse. I would buy them as a birthday present for my sister-in-law. Then, when we got home, I regretfully decided that she was far too sensible to appreciate them and I'd have to keep them for myself. You would never be devious like that, would you?"

"If I want something, I go for it. If it is available." He looked at her and she smiled.

"You're looking very well, Connie. Domesticity suits you."

"It does but it's not going to last much longer. I start work at the local school in September."

"So, you're going to develop a loud voice and a bossy manner?"

"I very much hope so."

"Well, I'm sure you'll be brilliant and be made a headmistress in no time at all."

"I'm more likely to be sacked after a few weeks."

"Why?"

"Something they call an 'attitude problem'. My 'conforming' skills aren't very good. I've grown used to having my own way. We'll see. I think it might work out."

"I've managed to get opera tickets for our last evening in Prague."

"That makes me very happy indeed."

"I thought it would." Tim looked pleased.

"Which opera?"

"Traviata."

"Perfect. Thank you."

The turkey was done and resting under a tent of tinfoil. The vegetables were cooked, decanted into serving bowls and smothered in butter. They were keeping warm in the oven. The sausages were crisp and brown and the potatoes roasted to perfection. The succulent residue and juices from the turkey had been scraped out of the pan and added to the herby stock made with giblets boiled with herbs, onion, celery and carrot. Connie couldn't bear thick gravy but added a small amount of cornflour dissolved in water and a couple of stock cubes for extra flavour. Making enough for ten people was a challenge.

It was a fine day. The garden was bright with late daffodils; terracotta tubs filled with newly-opened pink and purple tulips contrasted with the pale, natural stone of the terrace; fresh green leaves had appeared on the magnolias and the lawn had an air of unusual robustness of health. Squirrels were chasing each other around the trees and there was a chorus of birdsong.

Tim and Connie stood side by side in front of the hob; he in charge of the bread sauce and she stirring the gravy. There was a companionable sense of ease and pleasure. One of the many qualities Tim had in common with Matthew was a complete disregard for clothes. They had all the right togs for work and formal events but, otherwise, any old shirt would suffice and any old trousers, as long as they weren't too frayed around the hems. Today, Tim had made an effort and was looking very attractive. Everyone had turned up looking smart.

Paul was in a Harris tweed jacket and regimental tie; Laura looked glamorous in a suede skirt and silk blouse; Bella was in a pinstripe trouser suit and Marina wore a long dress. The boys were in jeans. Their hair was a bit long but that was how they liked it. Under Connie's flowery apron was a white blouse, multi-panelled denim skirt and a wide, tan, Italian leather belt. Her earrings were striking, consisting of cascades of tiny green wooden discs. They'd been found in the same shop as the napkin rings.

"I'm glad you're coming to Prague," said Tim. "Bella claims to have dozens of friends but you are the only one she really trusts."

"What makes you think that?"

"She's natural with you. Not always polite but natural. When some of these other friends ring her, she doesn't just say 'hello' but 'oh hi' on a long-drawn out rising crescendo, like someone out of an American soap opera." His mimicry was so funny that Connie couldn't help laughing and she knew exactly what he meant because Bella had done it to her once, thinking she was someone else.

"It's important to adopt the right mannerisms if you want to be accepted. It's all part of the social game. Nothing to worry about."

"Trouble is, the game is something to worry about for Bella. She aspires to happiness, as we all do, but it seems to elude her. She decides in advance of an event what level of joyous euphoria should be experienced, not just by her but by anyone else who might be there. It's as if emotion must be manufactured and then appropriately displayed. If there is a shortfall, and there often is, she becomes grumpy.

"She wouldn't admit it but she is permanently in acting mode with her counselling work. She knows in her heart that talking about problems doesn't necessarily solve them. It can make them worse. She pretends to feel sympathy and interest; she tries to supply what her client craves and she genuinely wants to help. But she's often frustrated by the lack of tangible results and, also, by a perceived lack of gratitude. The client, on the other hand, knows in her heart, that however kind, conscientious and professional the counsellor is, ultimately, it's just a job for her and on a profound level, she doesn't have the emotional resources to care all that much.

"Bella knows that one thing you're incapable of, Connie, is pretence. Your refusal to be goaded into stereotypical attitudes annoys her but she believes in you."

Apart from an indeterminate murmur of assent, Connie was silent.

Tim glanced over at the oven. "This food looks and smells absolutely delicious. What have you got lined up for pud?"

"Fruit salad, chocolate mousse and pavlova. Matthew suggested an apple pie but I don't have a light touch with pastry. There was going to be a fourth pudding. Yesterday, I made a cake with a large bar of dark chocolate, butter, soft brown sugar, ground almonds and six eggs. I was going to smother it in whipped cream and raspberries. Sadly, there was a catastrophic event."

"Sounds scrumptious. What happened?"

"I took it out of the oven at the appointed time and tested it for gooiness by sticking a knife in. I decided it needed another five minutes but on the way back to the oven, it slipped out of my hands and crashed to the floor, breaking into several pieces. It was a bad moment, I can tell you."

"It must have been awful."

"Yes, I was aghast but Bella would have suggested positive thinking, so after a few moments hesitation, I said 'damn, bugger and bollocks', scraped it up and we had it for supper. There was full disclosure about the circumstances and nobody minded."

Tim's face had creased into a wide smile. "You never fail to cheer me up, Connie."

"I think everything is ready now. Let's call people through and get started."

Twenty-One

The Berlin Wall came down not because the East German Government suddenly decided that it was unpleasant to imprison their citizens behind two walls, each four metres high and a hundred and fifty-five kilometres long, separated by a space full of mines and called the 'death strip', or that it was inhuman to authorise the guards in any of the three hundred and two watchtowers to shoot anyone trying to escape into West Berlin. Nor was it a moment of kindly enlightenment on behalf of the regime, which employed a vast army of informers to spy on others, including their own family members, and have them arrested, tortured and often executed for inappropriate attitudes.

The reason for this dramatic political upheaval had been a simple bureaucratic error. On the evening of the 9 November 1989, a premature announcement of a new regulation had encouraged vast numbers of East Berliners to head for checkpoints where the border guards hadn't been told what to do. To relieve the pressure of the crowds, but without official orders, a few people were allowed to pass through the Bornholmer Strasse checkpoint and were followed during the next few hours by an unstoppable twenty thousand more.

Like millions of people around the world, Matthew and Connie had watched, transfixed, the television footage of events unfolding. It had been intensely moving and, if it hadn't happened, Connie wouldn't now be on a flight to Prague and about to have some lunch. Many people were impolite about plane food but she loved the compact little tray with its pots and packages so neatly arranged. Food that she hadn't had to prepare herself was always gratefully received and eaten with relish.

This was her first holiday without children and without responsibility. Charlie was back in college, Jamie and Ned were staying with school friends. Her suitcase bulged with all her favourite things, including a long, silk, violet skirt for the opera and some glamorous black trousers with floating panels on the front and back for an evening reception. She ate the potted shrimps and then removed the foil lid from the chicken and rice. There was a bread roll with butter, a fruit jelly, crackers and cheese, fruit juice and water. She enjoyed it all.

She liked to think of the Wall coming down as a timely intervention by the Almighty on behalf of an oppressed people. It reminded her of God parting the water of the Red Sea to allow the Israelites to escape from Pharaoh's armies and then letting it flow back over the vengeful pursuers. The Old Testament story had always fascinated her. She'd once read a speculative account of how it could have been caused by a tsunami relating to the eruption of Santorini around 1600 BC; the same event possibly being implicated in the earlier Plagues of Egypt. All very unlikely, according to Matthew for whom science capped romanticism.

There were eight members in their group. Apart from Tim and Matthew, there were two lecturers, a post-graduate student called Rachel and an immensely tall Nigerian post-doctoral fellow called Emeka. He was extremely handsome. He'd been to Eton and had a regal air and a plummy voice. Rachel was clearly smitten but, beyond normal courtesy, he showed no interest in her. She was pretty enough but very thin and rather nervous.

There was a sense of heady exhilaration among the group. They were entering formerly forbidden territory and embarking on pioneering research. Connie didn't pretend to understand it, except in a superficial way, but it involved correlating 'basement' rocks in Central Europe.

Having arrived, gone through the formalities and collected their luggage, they clambered into a large taxi outside the airport. The driver had started the engine and was on the point of pulling out when there was a low moan followed by a suppressed scream and a series of semi-hysterical instructions.

"Stop! Everyone get out. Quickly, quickly. Get out, get out. Now this minute!"

They all stood, bewildered, back on the pavement.

"What the bloody hell was that all about?" Emeka asked in his rich voice.

Rachel looked abashed. "Sorry. There's a spider in the car. I have a phobia." She pointed her finger at a tiny creature, about a centimetre wide, on the ceiling of the taxi.

Bella was sensible and sympathetic. She carefully removed the minuscule offender with a tissue and deposited it at a safe distance. Her manner was kindly, reassuring and totally non-judgmental. The driver, standing to one side, was clearly annoyed. Duncan, the red-haired and bearded palaeontologist, looked as if he was suppressing impatience with some difficulty, while John, a petrologist specialising in age dating using isotopic chemistry, looked on quietly and benignly.

Connie happened to catch Tim's eye and his expression of suppressed humour and complicit warmth took her straight back to County Mayo and his glance in the rear-view mirror when she was sitting on a crate of rock samples in the back of the van on the way to Bangor, having given up her seat to the lady with the chickens.

The drive from the airport was uneventful but as they approached the city, Connie had glimpses of the famed spires and domes. The taxi rumbled through a series of cobbled streets bordered with white-painted houses, charmingly ornate lamps fixed to their walls. All was clean and beautiful.

The hotel was on Kampa Island, next to the Charles Bridge, on the western side of a lovely concourse. The road, made of square granite cobbles laid out in swirling patterns, circled around an inner area with benches and newly-leafed maple trees. The pavements were a mosaic of basalt and marble. Opposite the hotel were gracious four-storey houses in soft colours; eau de nil, apricot, peach, yellow, cream, pale cinnamon and gold. They had ornamental dormer windows and red pantiles on the roofs. Wood pigeons fluttered around in the evening sun and the Vltava River could be seen beyond. To one side, a handsome double set of stone steps with pretty handrails led up to the bridge.

The party of eight dined together on the first evening, although it was understood that people were free to do their own thing on the following days. There was general satisfaction with the rooms, which were newly-renovated and had modern bathrooms. The conversation was erudite but not pretentiously so. These scientists were too conscious of what they didn't know to be complacent about what they did know. There were bursts of humour and a feeling of good fellowship. Also, a shared and palpable excitement at the prospect of great swathes of hitherto forbidden parts of Europe to research and analyse.

Connie and Bella made a vague plan to visit the castle the next day and the Old Town on the day after. An outing to a glass factory had been arranged for the third day and on the fourth day, Friday, they were going to split up and go their separate ways with Tim and Matthew because the conference would be effectively over. Bella asked to borrow a guidebook and Connie agreed to pass it over later on.

Connie was feeling well. The problems of the past year had been resolved and the boys were fine. She hoped that, without families and homes to compete over, she and Bella could recapture some of the fun and ease of their student days. She was full of optimism. It was short-lived.

After dinner, they both went upstairs to finish unpacking while the others headed for the bar. Their rooms were on the same corridor. Having located the guidebook, Connie walked along the passage and tapped gently on Bella's door. The door opened; Connie handed over the book with a smile and turned to leave.

"Thank you," said Bella. "I must make it clear, though, that I don't want you coming along and knocking on my door whenever it suits you."

"Certainly not." Connie was shocked. She walked back to her own room muttering some fairly ripe profanities under her breath. What a cheek! She sat on a chair by the window and tried to calm down. The best tactic was to convert her rage into amusement. Bella's remark was an outward manifestation of inner animosity. These things just slipped out; they were sometimes beyond one's control. Savagery was part of the human condition and Connie wasn't immune to it herself. It was an emotion that couldn't be cured, only managed. In order to manage it, you had to pretend it wasn't there; the whole basis of good manners.

She and Bella were part of the group as a courtesy. They were hangers-on, camp followers, expendable, supernumerary. In other words, they had to behave themselves. It was tacitly understood that there would be no complaints and no whingeing and whining. She would just have to have to muster reserves of self-control and tiptoe around, taking care not to invoke trouble. There was no escape; she didn't want to wander around Prague on her own. She would have to exercise forbearance. Within certain limits.

Bella had instructed her to meet for breakfast at eight-thirty. Connie arrived at nine. The others had left for Charles University before eight. The usual offerings were on display with the addition of bowls of halved stewed plums. They were in a light syrupy juice and must have come out of a tin but they were delicious. She had slept well and recovered her good spirits. The sun was shining.

They climbed the steps to the Charles Bridge, turned left and walked under the arch connecting two gothic towers into the Little Quarter, Mala Strana. They followed the road leading towards the castle, which was the official residence of the Czech President. There were a great many cultural and architectural treats on the way.

According to the guidebook, Charles IV, the Holy Roman Emperor, had been the main inspiration behind the construction of Prague in the forested valley of the Vltava River in the fourteenth century. He built the famous bridge named after him and, for five hundred years, it was the only road across the river. Connie remarked to Bella that he must have been a man of extraordinary artistic refinement and, also, one with a joyous disposition because every detail of every feature demonstrated beauty and perfection.

They strolled along a cobbled shopping street lined with gracious, baroque houses and came to St Nicholas' Church with its stunningly beautiful dome and clocktower. In Connie's opinion, it stood out as the loveliest landmark in the cityscape. They went inside and gazed, awestruck, at the magnificent fresco on the ceiling, the great marble columns, the white, gold and pink, the carvings and statues, the black and white chequerboard floor. It was overwhelming.

It was saddening to think that, during the Communist era, the clocktower had been sickeningly polluted by being used as an observation and spying station.

Connie was braced for some sort of negativity from Bella but didn't know straight away what form it would take. There was no chilliness of manner. On the contrary, Bella was cloyingly attentive. They stopped at a gift shop because Connie wanted to buy postcards. There was a fine display. She wanted several and would have enjoyed choosing them but Bella wouldn't leave her alone to do it. She was by her side the whole time, commenting and advising and even muscling in on buying the stamps. It left Connie feeling flustered and a little upset.

Halfway up the hill, a sharp bend in the road curved around a flat paved area on which was a display of water colours. They were arranged on easels and absolutely heavenly. They included paintings of all the popular Prague locations; the castle, Charles Bridge, Loreta, St Vitus, the Old Town bridge tower, the Astronomical Clock and several churches, including St Nicholas. Presiding over them was the artist; a slim, blonde girl, a Czech art student who spoke perfect English.

Connie stared at these works of art, enthralled and humbled in front of the youthful genius. She couldn't have them all but she had to have one. She needed time to decide. Bella was hovering and making pronouncements but she appeared to have no intention of buying anything.

"Bella," said Connie in slight desperation. "Why don't you go to that café over the road and ask for some coffee? I'll join you in five minutes or so."

"No," she replied. "I prefer to stay with you. I like helping people."

Connie gave up. She checked that the artist would be there on Friday and resolved to come back with Matthew. She had, in fact, made her choice. It was the painting of St Nicholas with the soft but brilliant blue-green of the dome with its lantern and the ornamented top of the clock tower, star-like sculptures rising above them both, the walls a honey-gold, red pantiles, pillars, classical carving, the leafless branches of a tree to one side. It was all so incredibly lovely. She wanted Matthew to see it and want it in the same way as she did.

They went together to the café. It was the second coffee stop that morning because it was pleasant just to sit and process the surroundings and think about what they'd seen. In each place, Bella approached a waiter and, in a discreet manner, would ask, "Where is the toilet, please?"

When she came back, Connie looked up from the guidebook. "Bella, why do you keep asking where the loo is? There are clear signs up all over the place."

"I like to connect with people. Toilets are a universal requirement. It's a way of establishing some meaningful contact."

Connie found it embarrassing but she said no more on the subject. They carried on up the wide approach to the castle and stood with hundreds of others on the cobbled square looking at the magnificent white building behind gilded railings. Supporting the railings were massive stone pediments topped with great sculptures depicting victors doing unpleasant things to the vanquished. To one side was the panoramic view of the city in all its red-roofed glory.

It was time for lunch. Following a sign to one side of the main square, they found a restaurant tucked away in a garden at the end of a little passage. They didn't want much because they were scheduled to have an early dinner followed by a performance of Vivaldi's Four Seasons that evening. They ordered soup and, while Bella was on the customary escorted tour to the facilities, Connie glanced through the guidebook.

"We can't possibly see everything today," she said when they were both sitting down. "There's just too much. Perhaps, we should come back tomorrow. There's a funicular at the western end of the complex and a lovely walk along the top, through some gardens, which takes in the Strahov Monastery. It's imperative to see that. Also, Loreta, another beautiful church."

"I thought we'd planned to do the Old Town tomorrow," replied Bella. "This soup is delicious."

"Yes," murmured Connie. "Perhaps, we could come back independently on Friday with Tim and Matthew. Apparently, in the fifteenth century, if they wanted to bump people off, they would throw them out of a window. There is a paragraph here about the Prague defenestrations. Protestants and Catholics didn't like each other very much. In the seventeenth century, two Catholic governors and their secretary were chucked out of a window but survived because they fell into a heap of manure. No laughing matter," she said sternly, looking up from her soup. Bella giggled.

"Shall we wander through the castle and various palaces and gardens and see inside St Vitus Cathedral after lunch?" Connie asked. "By that stage, we'll be so exhausted from cultural overload that we'll be ready to stagger down the steps to the river. We'll have to pass through Golden Lane which has pretty old houses, all painted in different colours. Franz Kafka lived at No 22 for a spell between 1916 and 1917. It wasn't his house, though; he rented it from his sister."

"Have you read any Kafka?" Bella asked. "You seem to have read just about everything else."

"Not yet, but I've brought one of his novels, *The Castle*, with me to read while we're here. I don't expect it to be uplifting. I think he was fairly 'screwed-up', as we all are to some degree or another."

The nature of the tactics dawned rather slowly on Connie. Bella's chatter had all along been peppered with allusions to her social life with Tim. Apart from the glamorous evenings in the Senior Common Room, there had been a wonderful weekend in Istanbul with a Turkish couple. They had been entertained by the well-heeled, royalty-connected parents of one of Marina's school friends in a Cotswold manor house and they had been invited to join a couple of very dear friends for a weekend on a canal boat. With all these people, a deep and meaningful rapport had been established and they had really, really enjoyed every minute.

Connie had listened good-naturedly but gradually became aware that Bella's brightness of manner concealed a less than benign attempt to undermine her own social confidence and, unfortunately, it was succeeding. Connie didn't resent the good aspects of Bella's life but there was something a little callous about her determination to establish superiority. It was hurtful. She had always thought of herself as being possessed of emotional equilibrium. When growing up, feelings of worthlessness induced by her mother were counterbalanced by the unconditional approval and love from her father.

She was neither vain nor lacking in self-esteem. She liked to be on good terms with others. She could fight when necessary but, if faced with hostility, she generally chose to withdraw rather than confront. Just at present, it wasn't practical to do either.

It was a long walk back to the leafy enclave of their hotel. Connie felt drained and low in spirits. Back in her room, she made tea and sat on the bed, her pillows and Matthew's stacked up comfortably behind her. She picked up her paperback, skipped the introduction and started chapter one, *'Arrival'*.

It was late evening when K. arrived. The village lay deep in snow. Nothing could be seen of Castle Hill, it was wrapped in mist and darkness, not a glimmer of light hinted at the presence of the great castle. K. stood for a long while on the wooden bridge that led from the main road to the village, gazing up into the seeming emptiness.

The door opened and Matthew walked in.

"Had a good day?" she asked.

"Brilliant. How about you?"

"Very interesting. However, if Bella mentions one more instance of how she and Tim have 'just clicked' with people they like better than us, I might do something desperate."

Matthew found that very funny.

~

It should have been a pleasant evening. The four of them had an excellent dinner at a charming restaurant and this was followed by the concert which was performed in an exquisitely gracious room of a palace. They sat in rows on gilded chairs, looking rather smart and very civilised. They clapped as the perfectly dressed chamber orchestra entered and bowed.

A form of nervous tension had gripped Connie. She didn't know how the others were feeling and didn't really care because she was suffering from a sort of smouldering irritation. She hadn't enjoyed the meal and was having trouble thinking of agreeable things to say. She kept brooding on how Bella had spoiled her pleasure in choosing postcards. She couldn't be bothered to write them now. She knew she was being petulant and childish and this compounded her misery.

She couldn't concentrate on the music and what completely tipped her into a state of abject wretchedness was committing the unforgivable crime of clapping between movements. It wasn't entirely her fault; someone else had clapped and she had automatically followed.

She wasn't sitting next to Tim. Bella always managed to ensure that she didn't. On this occasion, she was glad. Perhaps, he hadn't noticed. She wished she was back at home; safe and happy in her own sitting room, with nothing to worry about.

That night, she took two aspirin, had a wonderful sleep, woke up feeling refreshed and restored and looking forward to some stewed plums for breakfast.

Twenty-Two

Tim had asked Bella to buy flowers for him to give Eva, the conference organiser, that evening at the reception. She and Connie decided to attend to this pleasant task before doing anything else and duly returned to Mala Strana where they'd seen a street flower stall the day before.

A palette of brilliant colour was laid out on the wide pavement and a fresh sweet smell filled the air. The woman in charge smiled encouragingly.

"Are any of your roses and peonies scented?" Connie asked.

"Yes, certainly, and these carnations have a strong perfume."

"I'm not madly keen on carnations," said Bella.

"I'm not either."

"The roses and tulips are beautiful but they fade and droop rather quickly."

"Yes." Connie spied a container of long-stemmed freesias. "How about a mixture of delphiniums and peonies with some freesias for scent?"

"Yes, that's a good idea. Some of those violet irises would be lovely as well, mixed in with gypsophila and eucalyptus."

A glorious bouquet was made up and they walked back to the hotel with a sense of mutual achievement. The receptionist supplied a bucket of water and offered to put the flowers somewhere cool.

The Charles Bridge was already filling up with tourists as they walked across to the Old Town, Staré Město, and through the tower called the Powder Gate because it had been used as a gunpowder store in the seventeenth century. There was a great deal to see. They walked around the Old Town Square with its gracious buildings and looked inside another very beautiful church dedicated to St Nicholas. This one was called a cathedral. They joined the crowd in front of the Old Town Hall and stared up at the Astronomical Clock as the hour approached. Connie was scanning her guidebook.

"That clock doesn't just tell the time," she read out, "but also displays the movement of the sun and moon through the signs of the zodiac and the movement of the planets around the earth. The calendar plate below the clock shows the months in paintings by a nineteenth century Czech artist called Josef Mánes. Every hour, that skeleton consults his hourglass and yanks a bell cord to remind us of our mortality. Then those two little windows open and puppets of Christ and his Apostles appear and do a circuit. Finally, that golden rooster in the alcove above the clock will crow. It's about to start."

"Well, that was all very nice." Bella was underwhelmed. "Let's find somewhere to relax. That looks a good place over there." She pointed to a restaurant on the far side of the square. They sat under an awning, overlooked by the gothic spires of the Church of Our Lady before Týn, and asked for cold drinks. The sun was very hot. Connie was wearing the same filmy palazzo pants and cool blouse that she'd worn at Filitosa but she'd forgotten to pack her sunhat. She took the guidebook out of her bag. There was so much to see that it was almost overwhelming. "Do you fancy a boat trip up the river?" she asked. "It would be a restful way of enjoying the sights while sitting down in a gentle breeze."

"Yes, good idea. I'd like that. I'd also like to go back to the Charles Bridge and have a proper look at the statues."

Connie was turning the pages. "There's a beautiful building somewhere called Clementinum. It was a Jesuit college but is now a library. There's Wenceslas Square which looks enormous. We can't do everything."

"No, we can't and I wouldn't mind doing some shopping. I've seen some lovely boutiques."

"There is the Old Jewish Cemetery but I don't fancy that."

"Nor do I."

They sat in companionable silence for a while, enjoying their drinks. Suddenly, Bella asked, "Did you mind turning forty, Connie?"

"I think I did mind but I quite like it now."

"What's there to like?"

"Um," Connie thought back. "Well, forty was a bit of a turning point for me. I changed. I lost my sense of chronic inferiority, stopped needing approval, stopped grovelling and appeasing."

"So, now you have a sense of superiority instead?"

"Unfortunately not. More a sense of having no importance at all."

"You must be important to your boys?"

"Yes, but they're growing up."

"And important to Matthew?"

"I believe so, yes." Connie smiled and shrugged. "I agonise about the mistakes I've made and how I could have done things better but I have things more in perspective now. I feel liberated. I've always felt that the opinions of others are more valid than my own but I'm not so sure now."

"I find that talking to people is very helpful. It is my job, after all."

"Yes, and I'm sure you are very good at it but I don't like talking all that much. I prefer reading. Conversation can become repetitive and unproductive. Also, if you don't follow the prevailing fashion and express the 'right' ideas, people can go off you very quickly."

"Well, obviously, there are ways of being diplomatic. Shall we have some coffee now? There's no hurry to go anywhere."

"I'd love some coffee and why not something to eat as well? Something fattening." Connie paused. "I've read so many books about how to stay healthy and live forever; some of them quite scientific and heavy, all about physiology, stem cells, DNA, metabolic markers, telomeres etc. The funny thing is, I've come to the conclusion that nobody really knows because the advice coming from all these thousands of words is invariably the same and totally unimaginative. For instance, it assumes that the company of other people is pleasurable but having to be with someone who doesn't like you very much is quite the opposite.

"Of course, smoking is bad for you but this morning, after breakfast, I observed one of the guests in the garden as he lit up a cigarette. I could feel his physical ecstasy as he inhaled that deadly vapour. On some level, for him, it was beneficial. It's the same as watching someone savour a fine wine or tuck into a slice of chocolate cake. I find the puritanical disapproval of self-indulgence rather depressing.

"Depending on others for well-being doesn't work. Self-sufficiency is the thing because even the kindest of people have a 'cut-off' point and even the most generous know when they're being exploited."

"That's why people like me can be useful." Bella looked a little smug.

"I've heard it said," continued Connie, "and I don't know if it was by a famous philosopher or just someone with a bit of common sense, that there are three basic components necessary for happiness; somewhere to live, something to do and someone to love."

"Well, then, you and I have absolutely no reason to be anything other than gloriously happy. How are you getting on with Kafka?"

Coffee and some little cheese tarts arrived.

"I haven't had time to read much yet but I certainly wouldn't recommend it to any of your clients. If anyone was teetering on the brink, this book would definitely tip them over the edge."

"Why?"

"Well, the chief character, referred to as K., is a land surveyor employed to do some work at the castle. Everywhere he goes, he's met with hostility, rudeness and obstruction. Nothing can proceed and everything seems hopeless. Mind you, K. is quite impolite himself. He describes some peasants as having tortured faces, their skulls looking as if they'd been smashed flat on top and their features having taken shape in the agony of being struck, as well as having thick lips and open mouths."

"Dear me," said Bella, laughing and brushing pastry crumbs off her designer shorts.

"Did you mind about being forty?"

"No, not really. I don't think so." Bella had to think rather carefully. She was reluctant to admit to any dissatisfaction let alone to analyse it. However, all was not perfect. Her blonde hair received regular attention from a skilled coiffeuse but was losing its natural lustre. She had two deep frown lines between her eyebrows. She tried to eat sensibly but the weight would creep on mercilessly. Tim was kind and loyal but obsessed with his work. He was away a lot and never appeared to crave her company. He seemed somehow disengaged. Marina was fine but there was no real closeness between them. Connie had mentioned that Charlie and Marina kept in touch but she, herself, hadn't known this, although she pretended she did.

There was something about Connie which invoked a churlishness within her. Bella was ashamed of this but couldn't control it. It wasn't a complacency but a transparency which was irksome. She appeared to have nothing to hide and nothing to fear. Bella wanted to unsettle her, to invoke anxiety, to ruffle the calm. Not all the time; she didn't want to lose the only friend she could completely rely on, but just occasionally, to balance things out a bit.

The day passed pleasantly and that afternoon, Bella and Connie were to be found walking along the Charles Bridge admiring the famous statues, all thirty of them. There were portrait artists offering their expertise on the sidewalks.

Bella, for some reason, chose a cartoonist. Connie's artist was a young, serious, Taiwanese, who wielded his charcoal with great thoroughness and dispassion. He took a long time to complete the work and Bella grew impatient. Eventually, appraising the finished article, she said, "I think he has flattered you."

"Yes, of course, he has," replied Connie. "I said I'd pay him double to do that." But he hadn't flattered her. He had faithfully copied exactly what he'd seen, including the inexpertly applied eyeliner. Connie was happy with it.

~

The venue for the reception was an ancient inn next to the river and within easy walking distance of the hotel. It had been taken over for the sole use of the fifty or so conference delegates plus any partners. It had the magic acquired by many old buildings, difficult to define, but as soon as Connie passed beneath the massive stone lintel of the front door, she knew that the evening ahead was going to be good. There was something in the atmosphere which dissolved any tension, made you feel beautiful even if you weren't, loved and admired even if you weren't, valued even if you weren't.

There was a subtlety of lighting, the smell of wood smoke and haunting Bohemian music which entered the soul and lifted it. The walls were thick, the windows small, the floor stone-flagged and the ceiling supported by great oak beams. Tables with white cloths were arranged on three sides of one room, all prepared for the feast. The other room had a bar and a dance floor.

Connie sensed that there would be no stilted conversation, no anxiety, no need to appear interesting and amusing. There would be pleasure, simple hedonistic pleasure of the sort that only East Europeans seemed to know how to invoke.

Bella was in red tonight. It was something she'd bought in the Old Town that morning and she looked ravishing. Connie was in her Gina Bacconi trousers and a top she'd found in a Dress Agency. It had a high black satin bodice and long sleeves made of a fine transparent fabric, which also swirled beneath the bodice around her hips, allowing a few inches of slender midriff to be glimpsed beneath.

Glasses of wine and beer materialised from seemingly nowhere and sizzling dishes of delicious food were served as soon as they were seated. The room was filled with contented chatter interspersed with bellows of laughter. Connie found that she wasn't required to talk and there were no awkward silences to be filled.

She felt totally relaxed and spiritually nourished. She didn't know the people sitting next to her and it didn't matter.

Tim gave a brief but gracious speech of thanks and handed over the flowers to Eva. There was thunderous applause. It had grown dark outside. There were stars and a crescent moon. The Vltava turned black and reflected the lights from the inn, the bridges and from the Old Town. Inside, the alcohol still flowed and the music still played; there was no sign of the party winding down. It might go on all night. Connie found her way to the ladies room at the far end of the building beyond the dance floor.

On coming out, there was an encounter with a tall Belgian called Jacques who grabbed her and was disinclined to let her go. He wasn't unattractive and Connie wasn't in the least disconcerted. The evening had a Bacchanalian feel to it which she was enjoying. However, he was clearly drunk and she was having a problem disentangling herself. She heard a gruff voice say, "Get off her." It was ignored. A hand appeared on his shoulder and he was yanked back quite roughly. "Get off her, I say, or I'll throw you in the river."

Tim wasn't tall but he was of powerful build. Jacques decided to concede defeat. He gave an unsteady little bow of apology and retreated.

Tim took Connie's hand and steered her into the middle of the dancing crowd. He held her, very close; she could feel the beating of his heart. It wasn't a correct way to behave but no power on earth could have persuaded her to withdraw voluntarily from that embrace. There was a diffusion of such sensual purity and trust, such gentleness and strength, such worship and longing, such simple goodness.

There was a pause in the music. "Right, that's all we're allowed. You can go back to your husband now." He released her.

Walking back to her seat, Connie was troubled. She wasn't a natural cheat but nor was she a natural liar and she couldn't pretend to regret what had just happened. She was profoundly relieved to observe Bella flirting shamelessly with Emeka and happy to see that Rachel was receiving pleasing attention from a fair-haired geologist called František. Matthew was in deep conversation with Duncan and John.

~

"There was one awkward moment this evening," said Connie as she and Matthew were in bed and dropping off to sleep.

"What was that?"

"I found myself standing next to a dark, short-haired, pretty woman and asked her name. She looked at me and said 'You stinker'. I thought I must have offended her in some way and should make myself scarce but then I realised."

Matthew gave a grunt of mirth. "Justynka. That's Justine from Wrocław University. She's very bright."

Twenty-Three

There is a certain human quality that is not highly valued because it is not well-defined. It involves no words or gestures but is instinctively recognised by others, including children, animals and even enemies. It is the ability to recognise pain, physical and mental, however well-concealed, and a corresponding wish to alleviate it. Connie had this quality and also an understanding that misery was not conducive to graciousness. Recipients of her unobtrusive ministrations felt no tiresome obligation to be grateful.

Thursday was the designated date for the escorted trip to the Bohemian glass factory at Nizbor, about forty kilometres north of Prague. Various partners of conference delegates climbed into a minibus. Bella was feeling very unwell. She had overindulged the evening before and now had a crashing headache. She metaphorically cowered under the umbrella of emotional protection and sympathy provided by Connie, not leaving her side except to sit at a table and wait for tea to be brought when they had a halfway stop at a restaurant in a pretty park. Connie supplied aspirin and a glass of water and sat in gentle silence.

"The doctors in my practice don't approve of aspirin," Bella said in a feeble voice as she gulped down the tablets.

"I know," replied Connie. "It's out of fashion these days but aspirin is the only thing that works for me and there is evidence suggesting that it helps prevent heart disease and cancer. The danger of a fatal haemorrhage is very small."

"I couldn't be bothered to wash my hair this morning and that's almost making me feel worse than the headache."

"Your hair looks as beautiful as always. You don't have to worry about that."

"It's funny how important these rituals are."

"I know. I often think that life wouldn't be worth living without hot water, moisturiser and clean underwear. Would you like some more tea because I think I would?"

"Yes, please."

Connie returned to the service counter, nodding and smiling at other members of the party sitting at separate tables. All looked pleasant but, apart from conveying goodwill, there wouldn't be an opportunity to get to know them. It was hopeless trying to start a conversation in the minibus, except in the blandest way. Everyone could hear if a private remark was ventured, so nobody spoke. It was like travelling on the London Underground where people had mastered the art of avoiding eye contact and pretending that fellow passengers didn't exist. There was something dystopian about it.

Returning with a tray holding a plate of cookies and some more life-giving brew, Connie noticed that Bella was beginning to perk up. She would not wish a hangover on anyone but it had the effect of lowering Bella's levels of latent antagonism almost to extinction. It was restful. There was no need to be braced in anticipation of the next smoothly-voiced barb. It was almost like very old times before either of them was married.

It didn't last. As the minibus turned into the car park of the glass factory, it became clear that Bella was suffering something of a relapse. "I'm feeling dreadful," she said. "Your useless aspirins haven't helped. They've made it worse."

They entered the showroom; a dazzling fairy tale wonderland full of twinkling diamonds. Glittering teardrop crystals cascaded from the many chandeliers; illuminated translucent shelves held a magnificent display of lead crystal glassware, bowls, vases and decanters; their exquisitely cut surfaces scintillating and shimmering with lustrous radiance. Table lamps blazed through incandescent pendants; everywhere was brilliance, purity and beauty.

Desperate to linger but conscious of duty, Connie steered Bella towards the café and ushered her into a comfortably padded seat in the corner, by a window. She brought her a tray with soup, more tea, a roll with butter and a scrumptious-looking piece of confectionery, sensing that Bella might not have too much trouble demolishing it all. She then sped off to join the rest of the group who were waiting patiently with a guide outside the workroom door. She hoped that her diminishing levels of compassion and sweetness of temper weren't too obvious.

Any sort of craft thrilled Connie. She felt an almost spiritual reverence for the skill of creativity. An ecstasy filled her soul at the thought of turning a humble lump of clay into a graceful pot, a piece of wood or stone into a glorious sculpture, a length of thread into exquisite lace, various pigments into magnificent paintings and now, something as simple as sand being turned into glass.

There could be no greater contrast between the elysian beauty of the showroom and the fantastical, satanic atmosphere of the factory floor. As the guide opened the door, they were met with a low rumbling, like distant thunder, from the many furnaces, their white-hot contents bathed in halos of red. It seemed dark but this might have been because of the bright sunshine outside. It was like a scene from an imaginary depiction of hell; infernos surrounded with sorcerers, wizards and alchemists, their faces shining in the heat, wielding long poles, dipping them in and out of the flames, rotating constantly and blowing through the hollow tubes. The figures moved with balletic grace and total concentration, oblivious of their audience. It was magical.

The guide, who spoke excellent English, explained that knowledge of glass-making had been around for thousands of years but the technique of glass-blowing was much more recent and had been developed by the Syrians shortly before the Christian era.

The basic ingredients for lead crystal were fine silica sand, lead oxide, potash and barium carbonate; the lead component making it softer than regular glass and easier to cut. This mix, with the addition of a few other chemical compounds, was compressed into pellets called 'batch' and heated in a furnace for eighteen hours at a temperature of 1,200°C to form a syrupy liquid called the 'melt'. Excess broken or rejected crystal called 'cullet' was added to smooth out the 'melt' and this ensured that there was no waste.

Connie and the group watched as a glassblower called a 'gaffer' dipped the metal blowing pipe into the furnace, twisting it to coat the end with 'melt'. Once out of the furnace, the molten glass was called 'gather'. Constantly rotating the pipe, the 'gaffer' rolled and shaped the glass on a special table and then blew down the tube to form a bubble called a 'ball'. After a short cooling period of ninety seconds, this was dipped again into the furnace for a second fortifying coat of 'melt'. The 'gaffer' rested this on a support and shaped it on a hollowed-out block of wood with a handle. He then lowered the 'ball' into an iron mould, rotating and blowing down the tube to form the bowl of a glass.

After a minute of cooling, another craftsman called a 'stemmer' took over. He held the glass while an assistant put a dollop of 'gather' onto the base of the bowl, which he then shaped into the stem of the glass. This was followed by another dollop of 'gather' which was shaped into the foot of the glass. The process wasn't mechanical and depended entirely on the extraordinary skill and instinct of the 'stemmer'. Because of this, the guide explained, no two items were precisely the same. Connie was intrigued to see that pads of wet newspaper were used as part of the shaping process.

At this stage, the glass would be put into an 'annealing oven' and allowed to cool down slowly overnight, whereupon it would be cut to shape with an oxy-acetylene torch and the rim smoothed and bevelled on a diamond-coated steel grinder. The whole process was painstaking and perfectionist.

Finally, the group was taken to the studio where artists created beautiful designs on the glass, cutting it with diamond-tipped wheels. The delicacy and precision of the artistry were inspirational. With a satisfying feeling of cultural enrichment, Connie returned to the café.

Bella was still sitting in the corner and looking furious.

"Where have you been all this time? I'm fed up with sitting here all on my own for hours. The trouble with you, Connie, is that you only think of yourself. As long as you're okay, you don't give a damn about anyone else."

"If I may say so, that is an impressively accurate analysis of my horrible character. I'm going to get a coffee and something to eat. Would you like anything?"

"I think I could manage a coffee. Also, I wouldn't mind another of those fruit and custard pastries, please."

"Okay. Then, we'll go and do a bit of shopping before the minibus takes us back to the hotel. I think there are some wonderful bargains to be had."

Twenty-Four

It was their last day. After a quick glance at the street map, Matthew led the way to the funicular, bought tickets and stood back, smiling and courteous, as Connie stepped aboard. He was full of energy and boyish enthusiasm and Connie felt a lightness of spirit as the carriage rose through the lush parkland, dotted with trees and intertwined with walkways.

At the top was the Petrin Tower, a metallic and modernistic structure; an excellent viewpoint but teeming with people. They didn't linger but carried on along the path weaving its way through sun-dappled, beautiful gardens with soft grass and newly-leafed trees. There was the lightest caress of a breeze and a morning freshness in the air. Strolling through a series of formal rose gardens, they felt rapture at the sight of new, delicate buds opening to form a display of fragrant loveliness.

It was soothing being with Matthew with his unfeigned pleasure in her company, his ungrudging wish that she should be happy, his uncritical approval of her appearance, even when unmerited. He was clever about many things but found it easy to admit when he hadn't a clue. He was calm when things didn't go to plan, and so, when they arrived at their destination, the Strahov Monastery, and found the front door to the famous libraries firmly shut, he laughed.

There was a notice with information about opening times. They had about forty-five minutes to fill; easily done with a look inside the next-door basilica. As with all the Prague churches, the beauty was overwhelming; a magnificent altar, frescos, much gold and white, pillars and arches, an exquisite criss-cross pattern on the floor and sunlight pouring in through high windows. This was followed by a visit to the ticket office and a short stroll across a pretty cobbled square surrounded by grass, mature trees and low stone walls to a rustic hostelry on the far side.

There was a peace and joyousness in the air, difficult to define but something that Connie associated with monastic establishments, both functioning and ruined. The monastery was a long white building with the usual red pantiles on the roof and a couple of graceful towers topped with green copper ornamental cupolas.

There were two rows of long wooden tables and benches in the café. A smiling waitress walked down the aisle in between and placed a large tankard of cold beer and a glass of iced apple juice on their table. Matthew had picked up a leaflet in the ticket office. Looking across at the tall, thin, unassuming man opposite her, frowning slightly as he began to read, Connie felt a surge of love and gratitude. Without asking for anything in return, he had supplied the emotional and practical wherewithal to make her own life good; with projects completed, problems resolved, mistakes rectified. Not too many loose ends, not too many people feeling let down, opportunities taken advantage of. It was largely his doing.

"Right," he said, "to cut a long and quite complicated story short, this is a Premonstratensian Monastery established in the twelfth century, with the first monks arriving from Steinfeld in what is now Germany.

There were various episodes of damage from fire or being attacked and plundered but an abbot called Jan Lohelius took over in the sixteenth century and oversaw a lot of new building.

In 1670, Jeroným Hirnheim became Abbot and he built the library called the Theological Hall.

In 1779, Václav Mayer became Abbot and he built the second library called the Philosophical Hall.

In 1950, after the Communist regime took over, the monks were interned. After the fall of communism, eight years ago, the monastery was returned to the original order and all was restored to how we see it now."

Connie nodded, rather dreamily. She had already forgotten the names and dates.

"About this evening," Matthew continued. "Tim suggested that we have an early supper in the hotel and take a taxi to the Opera House. We could go on the Underground but you and Bella will be all togged up and it wouldn't seem right. Rather than take a taxi after the performance, we thought we might walk back to the hotel down Wenceslas Square. It would be a good way of seeing it and there are lots of bars and restaurants if we feel like a drink and a snack. Are you okay with that?"

"Sounds fine to me."

Matthew checked his watch and they wandered back to a massive door which now stood open. They climbed a stone staircase which led to a long, dimly-lit antechamber lined with glass cabinets. To one side was a desk and sitting behind it was a glum-looking woman. The gloom was a perfect foil to the startling beauty of the libraries. The tiny pictures in the guidebook hadn't prepared them for such stunning opulence.

They stood silently in the doorway of the Philosophical Hall. It was utterly, astoundingly magnificent. An illuminated fresco covered the whole of the barrel-vaulted ceiling, the soft but vivid colours depicting a heavenly setting. The walls consisted of thousands of books encased in richly polished wood which formed shelves, ornamented pilasters and richly curved embrasures around tall windows. There was a gallery with a delicate balustrade encircling the whole chamber; above this were more gleaming casements full of books rising up to the ceiling. There were busts, urns and a very lovely parquet floor.

Connie and Matthew walked along the antechamber to the doorway of the Theological Hall. This was different but equally majestic. The curved ceiling was covered in individual frescos, each framed with ornamental white stucco, like a voluptuous froth of white lace; enchantingly pretty. All was rich and curvaceous. The walls were lined with graceful casements containing thousands more books. According to the information leaflet, there were over two hundred thousand books in the Strahov libraries. There were huge globes, supported by sturdy wooden frames.

"I wish we could go in and look at those globes properly," said Connie. "It's a bit frustrating being stuck in the doorway behind a little barrier."

"It would be interesting," Matthew agreed and then mimicked his mother, "but they can't have people traipsing in and out, morning, noon and night, leaving dust all over the place."

"I don't see why not."

"The globes are presumably seventeenth century. I've seen a 1635 map of the world made by a Dutchman, Willem Blaeu. It was rather good on the northern hemisphere but very vague about the south. It was assumed that there was a 'Great Southern Continent' but only the northwest coast of Australia was featured speculatively as extending further to the west and south of Africa and South America. The shape of Australia and Antarctica wasn't known at the time and nor was the existence of New Zealand. Interestingly, the Bering Strait between Siberia and Alaska was known."

They stood, mesmerised, but eventually had to make way for other people. They went back out into the sunshine.

"There wasn't much monastic austerity and simplicity in there," remarked Matthew.

"Perhaps not, but definitely a sacred aura and it has had a strange effect on me. I feel full of religious fervour even though I'm not religious. I'm floating on a higher plane and feel capable of all sorts of noble and generous deeds. I have a vision of a soprano in a white dress singing Mozart's *Exultate Jubilate*, and I'm pretty sure the singer is meant to be me."

"That must involve a considerable stretch of the imagination," replied Matthew with a judicial air. Connie laughed. They both knew she was a rotten singer. "However, I have also been affected by the general spirituality, although I am too modest to imagine myself performing acts of great nobility. There was a harmony, an erudition and creativity in those rooms which entered the soul. My choice of music to express this unusual sensation would be the *Sanctus* from Gounod's 'St Cecilia Mass'."

"We'd better make the most of this euphoria because such things can evaporate rather quickly." They passed through an impressive gateway and were immediately and unexpectedly plunged into the noisy traffic of a busy main road. The spell was broken.

~

They were back in Hradčany Square, leaning on a wall and looking out over the city, having spent an hour or two exploring the castle complex with its palaces and gardens. Earlier on, walking down the hill and across the road from Strahov, they'd come to Loreta, described in the guidebook as a 'sparkling seventeenth century baroque pilgrimage site'. It was shut due to internal restoration work being carried out. Connie hadn't admitted it but felt relief. She needed time to process the glories of the libraries before ingesting the next cultural feast.

She and Matthew admired the outside of the incredibly lovely white and gold building with its graceful, green-capped central tower and then moved on towards the castle where they had lunch in the garden restaurant off the square.

"I'm beginning to wish," said Matthew, "that I'd spent less time in the conference room and more time looking around. Some of the talks were more interesting than others, as is always the case. Tim's was excellent. He's quite a big shot internationally these days. His work is cited all over the place."

"Do you envy him?" Connie asked.

Matthew looked surprised. "No. As far as I'm concerned, Tim is just a good mate." He paused. "At this precise moment, I'm having difficulty thinking up anyone to envy. It's quite worrying." He took her hand. "Let's go and find your art student and buy one of her water colours."

Twenty-Five

There is nothing square about St Wenceslas Square. It is a hugely long and wide thoroughfare lined with great buildings which are filled with shops, offices, hotels, restaurants and bars. The top is dominated by the national museum but to the left of this and on the far side of a busy main road, but out of sight from the square, is the State Opera House, an imposing neo-classical building with steps leading up to a pillared portico. Above the portico is a great balcony with more pillars leading up to a Romanesque pediment full of sculptures.

The four were in high spirits, laughing and joking as they climbed into the taxi. The driver observed that they were a handsome bunch; the men confident and sleek in evening dress, a beautiful blond woman in a long, black velvet gown and a slender, dark-haired women wearing a cream, raw silk top over a violet skirt which seemed to kick out at the back below the knees.

Passing through the doors into the main entrance hall was like walking into a magical world of white and gold, full of sparkling chandeliers and glittering people. Up the stately staircase to a wide corridor curving around the second of four tiers of boxes. Then into the bar, a lovely room with luxuriously draped windows opening onto the balcony. The white marble floor was stamped at intervals with gold fleurs de lis and the rounded white ceiling was delicately ornamented with what looked like gold threads. Lights sparkled from crystal globes and pendants.

The walls were panels of soft red divided by graceful white pilasters. There were great mirrors encased in more white and gold. Above the glass and nestling within the opulent frames were charming paintings of classical scenes.

Almost silenced with awe, the four sipped glasses of chilled wine before seeking out their box. This was a narrow, wedge-shaped room with red plush walls, a large gilt mirror and red velvet curtains with a heavy pelmet. At the front was just enough space for three armless chairs with padded seats but behind were stools for the less fortunate.

"I believe the French would refer to this as a 'loge'," said Matthew. "It has a more attractive ring to it than 'box'." Because he was the tallest, he insisted on taking one of the stools.

The auditorium was another dazzlingly pretty feast of loveliness. The ceiling was made of huge frescos surrounded by white and gold stucco. The vast central light resembled a mass of pearls set in filigree gold. There were sculptures of angels and cherubs holding golden musical instruments. Even the fire screen in front of the stage depicted a charmingly classical sylvan setting with frolicking nymphs.

Verdi's *La Traviata* is about love and not much else. After a poignant overture, the first act opens onto a lavish party scene, redolent with glamour, seduction and the intoxicating magnetism between men and women, so perfectly expressed by the contrast and harmony of the tenors and baritones with the sopranos and contraltos. Alfredo declares his passionate love for the beautiful but consumptive courtesan, Violetta, and she responds with joy.

The second act is about a different sort of love, that of a parent for his children. Alfredo's father, Germont, fears that his family's reputation will suffer as a result of his son's liaison. He asks Violetta to give up Alfredo but then comes to realise that she is by far the nobler and more generous-spirited of the pair. In a deeply moving scene, she agrees to Germont's request and asks him to embrace her as a daughter. Anything to do with loving fathers had a resonance with Connie.

Then came the interval and the four trooped off to the bar with Connie diverting briefly to a scented powder room. As soon as she located them, standing around a high, circular table with their pre-ordered drinks, she became aware that the ambience had changed. She braced herself. All the signs were there and she thought she knew the reason. Bella hadn't been able to organise the seating and was feeling cross.

Connie smiled in response to a hard, appraising look.

"I was just telling Matthew all about our day out with Franz and Sophie," said Bella. "We went to the Troja Chateau and had a really lovely time. Didn't we, Tim? I suggested it this morning when the conference was being wound up and we were having coffee together. Sophie looked so pleased; her face lit up with a huge smile. They were such good company. Sophie said she was on the minibus with us the other day, going to the glass factory, and she'd noticed that

I was ill and felt really sorry for me. Unfortunately, I was feeling too rotten to notice her.

"It was so nice talking to some different people and they were so interesting. It was 'a laugh a minute'. We just 'clicked', didn't we, Tim?"

Tim raised his eyebrows in a sort of polite assent and Bella continued.

"Troja is a beautiful place. There's a magnificent house with lovely gardens and orangeries. You enjoyed it, didn't you, Tim?"

"I'm glad to have seen it," Tim replied, "but I wouldn't necessarily want to go back there. There was a heaviness about the place and a lot of weird arty stuff which didn't appeal."

"Well, I thought it was marvellous. What have you and Matthew done today?"

Connie felt reluctant to describe the libraries or even the other simple pleasures of the day. She shrugged. "We wandered around in the sunshine, looking at this and that and enjoying the peace."

"Of course, you don't like talking to people, do you, Connie?"

"Yes, I do."

"No, you don't. You said so the other day. Don't deny it. You said you found conversation was often repetitive and unproductive and you'd rather be reading."

"I didn't quite mean it like that."

"Well, if you didn't mean it, you shouldn't have said it."

~

Returning to their box, Connie felt upset. It wasn't just Bella's hostility but the knowledge that there was justification for it. She'd found it deeply pleasurable sitting next to Tim. There had been a hidden intimacy and enrichment from the shared enjoyment of the music. On countless occasions, she had sat in a theatre next to a total stranger. After an initial smile or nod of courtesy, an impenetrable wall of indifference would go up; a complete blank-out of any rapport. It was normal; people weren't there for chattiness. Outwardly, it was like that with Tim, except for the fact that the chairs were positioned very close to each other. Inwardly, it was quite different.

There was an irony in Bella's intimidating coldness in that it had the reverse of the intended effect on Connie. A spirit of rebellion rose up inside her and, far from dampening her own feelings, it exacerbated them.

The third act was highly dramatic and full of provocative sensuality. The setting was another outrageously opulent party with a group of gypsy dancers swirling around, heating the blood and arousing the passions. There were gorgeously dressed women and swaggering men, lots of drinking and gambling and glorious, heavenly music. It might have been the wine but Connie found herself physically responding. She felt luscious and beautiful and acutely aware of Tim, only inches away from her. His hands with their long, artistic fingers rested on his knees.

She was aware of his breathing, his pristine warmth, his stillness. On the stage, a heartbroken Violetta was being insulted by a furiously jealous Alfredo who doesn't know of her reasons for leaving him. He hurls his gambling winnings at her. The music is beyond impassioned and totally heavenly.

It was then that Matthew tapped Tim on the shoulder. Tim turned, inadvertently pressing into Connie. A bolt of lightning shot through her and she gasped, shocked as her disbelief was belied by the involuntary convulsions deep within her innermost body. Germont enters the stage and berates his disgraced son, who is then challenged to a duel. Violetta collapses and the curtain comes down. There was a profound silence before the last act.

Months have passed and Violetta is dying, abandoned by everyone except her faithful maid. She has very little money but asks the maid to give it to the poor. The doctor comes and says the end is imminent. Alfredo and Germont arrive and there is a deeply emotional scene of love, forgiveness and unbearable sadness, with the beautiful voices rising and falling in despair. With one last exquisite crescendo, Violetta breathes her last. Connie could take no more.

While the audience clapped, cheered and roared their approval, Connie pressed a thick pad of tissues over her face and tried to stem the tears. She didn't want to be an embarrassment but her distress ran deep; a combination of Bella's coldness, her own flagrant reaction to Tim's accidental touch and the tragic end to the opera unhinged her. As soon as appropriate, she stood and led the way out of the box, along the corridor, down the stairs and out into the starlit evening. The tears were streaming down her face and she wanted to get ahead of the others. Half-blinded, she stepped off the kerb to cross the road to Wenceslas Square. She was pulled back.

"In God's name, Connie, what the hell are you playing at? You were two seconds from death just then." It was Tim. He steered her over the busy road while Bella and Matthew were held up by traffic lights. They walked in silence past the great statue of St Wenceslas on his horse. The buildings blazed with lights and activity. Connie had run out of tissues. Tim passed her his handkerchief. The air was cool and he helped to drape a pashmina over her shoulders.

"That was powerful stuff," he said, although he knew her tears weren't just a reaction to Violetta's death.

She nodded and there was a pause.

"I'm sorry about Bella. Today wasn't at all marvellous. Franz is an interesting guy but Sophie hardly said a word. They're from Potsdam and her English isn't very good. Bella has a smattering of O-Level German and did her best but it was heavy-going. To describe it as 'a laugh a minute' was a pathetic travesty of the truth."

Connie was silent and Tim knew she didn't care about Franz and Sophie.

He tried again. "I don't know why Bella talks such rubbish." He paused. "Actually, that's not entirely true. I do know why she tries to make you uncomfortable." He was thoughtful for a few moments. "She thinks you and Matthew have something in your marriage that we don't have in ours."

"And what might that be?" Connie's voice sounded muffled but she was regaining her composure.

"I don't know and she doesn't know but it maddens her. It's nothing material. I'm not a rich man but Bella has plenty of money of her own."

"Does it ever occur to her that you might have something in your marriage that we don't have in ours?"

"No, that never occurs to her. It never occurs to me, either. You and Matthew seem to have some sort of emotional symbiosis. I can't explain it. Wherever Bella and I go, she is on the lookout for other people. It was other families to begin with and I thought she was just concerned about Marina having enough companionship. Marina has grown out of that stage and now Bella tries to recruit other couples to keep us company. When we're on our own, there's a sense of flatness, a sense that something is missing. We both feel it although we don't like to admit it. Some things are best left unspoken. I let her down in some way. She says that I don't cherish her. I do try but you can't manufacture these things to order."

Matthew and Bella had almost caught up and Connie was relieved to hear them laughing.

"Connie, I want you to promise me something." There was a note of urgency in Tim's voice. "Whatever Bella does to try and undermine our friendship, I want you to promise never to abandon it. I couldn't bear it. I depend on it. Will you promise?"

"Yes, I promise. Of course, I promise."

Twenty-Six
2019

Bella had chosen a nearby hotel for an elegant reception after the funeral service at the crematorium. Connie was exhausted from suppressing emotion and didn't want to talk to anyone. She had made her usual effort to look good and was wearing a soft Italian jacket in black and white teamed up with a black midi-skirt and high-heeled boots.

Marina was on the far side of the room. She was slim and graceful in a black suit but the tension around her jaw suggested that she was feeling the strain. There was a tall, distinguished-looking man standing protectively by her side. It was Charlie.

Tim's brother, Mike, approached. In appearance, he was completely different but when he spoke, his voice and Geordie accent were exactly the same as Tim's. Hearing him caused Connie's sadness to rise up again. He handed her an envelope with what she considered to be an entirely inappropriate wink. He had his back to Bella but Connie could feel her watching them. She managed to slip the envelope into her pocket while appearing to be extracting a tissue and smiled at him.

She decided to go outside for some fresh air and to sit in the car for a while to regain her equilibrium. She opened the envelope and took out the handwritten letter.

Deathbed
February 2019
Dearest Connie

I don't know what sort of sentimental pantomime Bella will have organised to impress our unfortunate family and friends but I'm relieved that I won't be around to find out. All I have asked is that I should not be put into an elongated laundry basket and that there shouldn't be any hymns. My brother, Mike, has promised to keep his eulogy short and business-like. He is allowed one joke as long as it is a good one. His jokes have a tendency to be extremely weak. He has also agreed to hand this letter over to you with maximum discretion.

I'm resigned to what is happening but, at the same time, absolutely furious about it. I have so much work still to do. I try to express gratitude to all who have looked after me but I don't feel any at all. Having endured eight months of treatment with unpleasant side-effects, I was pronounced clear of the disease. I was then informed that things had taken an unexpected turn for the worse, which meant that I was going to die quite soon. Could anything be more inept and inconsiderate? I feel nothing but rage.

Connie, I have always valued your friendship and I believe you have valued mine. We both know that there is a correct way to behave and have conformed accordingly. As a result, I have never been able to tell you how much I love you. I first realised this at Erris Head. It wasn't a respectful or sympathetic way for you to behave towards someone in my piteous state, but your laughter penetrated my soul with a profound intensity of joy. I have never forgotten it.

There is something else I want you to know. In the Prague Opera House, I was sitting between you and Bella with Matthew behind. Something caught his attention and he tapped me on the shoulder. When I turned to respond, I inadvertently pressed against you. It was during Act Three with that exotic gypsy dance and a heartbroken Violetta trying to deflect Alfredo's passionate rage. There was something so glorious in that music; it intensified every emotion and that momentary physical contact induced such a powerful longing for you that I swear that, if it hadn't been for the presence of your husband and my wife, I would have had you there and then.

There would have been no mercy for you in that sweet, soft, velvet-lined 'loge'. You wouldn't even have been able to heave me onto the floor because we'd already have been there.

This is shocking stuff, Connie; enough to put me behind bars in this age of sexual paranoia. There is worse to come. During my chemo sessions, I allowed myself to muse upon this unlikely but delicious scenario, with various embellishments. As a result, instead of feeling dread, I found myself anticipating them with a certain pleasure.

A few years ago, I landed at Gatwick after a night flight from Ottawa. I'd been working with geologists from the Canadian Survey at that time. Feeling *jaded and a bit grubby, I went to the Hilton outlet. After a shave and a freshen-up, I went through to the restaurant and asked for a full English breakfast and a large pot of tea.*

The place was full of businessmen in smart suits, all with laptops open. The place was humming with bonhomie and prosperous commercial activity. I sat next to a man whose trading partner had just left; he was finishing his coffee and staring into space. We exchanged a few pleasantries and then he launched into a tirade about the awfulness of his life.

He told me that he lived in a big house with a beautiful garden. He earned lots of money but found his job soul-destroying. His teenage daughter was expecting a baby and the repulsive, unemployed oaf who'd impregnated her was living under his roof, contributing nothing and expecting to be treated with courtesy. His wife, who was a brainless idiot, went round telling her friends that she was 'over the moon' about the forthcoming child and couldn't understand why he wasn't. His son, who'd had the most expensive education that money could buy, was making a nuisance of himself with Greenpeace. His mother-in-law was a cow and he'd like to kill her.

He then stood up to leave. He shook my hand and said that it had been the most enormous pleasure talking to me. He explained that he suffered from bi-polar disorder which was very well controlled with medication. However, if he said anything at home which his family considered inappropriate, his psychiatrist would be alerted. This person had the power to 'section' him, so if he didn't want to be carted off to a mental hospital, he had to behave with tedious circumspection. As a total stranger, I was a safe recipient for his real thoughts and he was very grateful.

This is rather how I've always thought about you, Connie; you have been a safe recipient of my most unmentionable thoughts and have never responded with anything other than humour and understanding. It has been my greatest delight to talk to you and be with you.

I can't bear to say goodbye and have decided not to. I know you'll understand.

Tim

The letter made Connie laugh and she knew that it had been Tim's intention. She returned to the reception room with her feelings of loss mixed with the old enrichment. Bella approached. Her eyes were glittering but not with tears. The tight smile was there and the silken voice.

"Oh, there you are. Matthew has been looking for you; I think he is ready to go. Thank you so much for coming. I know you had a very soft spot for Tim. We used to laugh about it. I always thought he felt a bit sorry for you. I hope you don't mind me telling you."

"No, Bella, I don't mind at all because I already knew it. Tim was a man of exceptional sensitivity and his compassion for me has always been a source of the greatest happiness."